NO HEROES

To Chris,

3 stories for the scar:

1) Your girl has a mean left hook.

2) What made me think I could beat Mike Tyson?

3) The other guy is a permanent resident at the grace.

NO HEROES

KILL & BE KILLED

JAMIE HALL

NO HEROES
KILL & BE KILLED

Editor: Christine Lachance
Savannah Gilbo
Cover Image Design: Sync Digital Solutions

This is a work of fiction. All of the characters, names, incidents, organizations, and dialogue in this novel are either the products of the author's imagination or are used fictitiously.

iUniverse books may be ordered through booksellers or by contacting:

iUniverse
1663 Liberty Drive
Bloomington, IN 47403
www.iuniverse.com
1-800-Authors (1-800-288-4677)

ISBN: 978-1-5320-3560-9 (sc)
ISBN: 978-1-5320-3561-6 (e)

Print information available on the last page.

iUniverse rev. date: 12/14/2017

"In the search for answers we are challenged to do what we feel is right, but before you judge someone based on their actions, understand that you will never know the full story behind them."

This book is dedicated to anyone who's put up with my shit; including, but not limited to, my complaints about writer's block, and the many nights I cancelled plans to "just write". Thank you for being patient with me.

Jamie Hall
On Facebook: https://www.facebook.com/jaywritesonhere/
On Instagram: https://www.instagram.com/jaywrites.ca/
http://noheroesbook.com

Please sign up for updates on the website. Jamie will be releasing short stories from the various different perspectives of characters throughout *No Heroes*, to members only.

Table of Contents

I

The Funeral

HOW LONG DO I HAVE TO STAND HERE? Is there a set time? Is three-minutes enough, five? How about thirty-seconds? Has anyone gone out of their way to decide what proper funeral etiquette is? Maybe I should have Googled it before I left the house. I don't know why I do that. I always think of Googling something only when there is no chance of being able to do it. If no one's done it yet, that would be a pretty good idea for a website, or an app. You could pull out your iPhone and find out how long you have to stand looking at an open and eerie casket, or how many drinks are too many. Then again, it's not like people go to funerals everyday. The app would only be useful to a person twice a decade tops (at least one would hope). A website—it needs to be a website; as if I'm going to make it with my vast Tripod and Geocities experience. I didn't even get past the first step in making a WordPress site; that was needlessly complicated.

I think these things as I stand beside my father's body in a coffin. Somewhere between being a cop and a shut-in, the old man got old and clearly didn't groom the way he did when mom was by his side.

The box itself is nice enough. A deep, dark brown wood—almost black—and white silver highlights make up his final bed. I don't have a problem with it, nor do I really have a problem with the flowers, or the room. The coffin actually looks comfortable, like the old man is just getting the best sleep of his life. No, I have no problem with this funeral. My problem is with what's inside the coffin.

There's this odd tradition in my community where, if a cop did not have a spouse at the time of their death, the force takes care of the funeral. It dates back over a hundred years. I guess it started as a noble gesture, but now it's just another aspect of his existence that makes me feel wholly disconnected from the man the city would know as *Martial*; a man destined—at one time—for greatness. A man that took on the criminal underworld with fierce vigour. A man that feared not, wanted not, and ruled the streets. A man's man, and a very long shadow.

I had no idea Martial died until just a couple of days ago. No one bothered to tell me. Then again, I guess I wasn't much of a son, so perhaps the boys in blue thought there wasn't much of a reason to disrupt my daily life with a funeral. Sure, it was Martial's fault that we were disconnected, but now that I'm sorta-kinda-maybe an adult, I probably should have made more of an effort to rekindle the relationship. My aunt eventually told me about the funeral after realizing she had yet to hear from me. Martial had been shot in the chest, and bled out on a sidewalk about three blocks away from his old precinct. I'm still not sure whether dying on that sidewalk—a place he'd walked the beat so many times, and had so much history—would be considered a fitting departure from this world for him. He either saw it as a nice nod to his former life, or was embarrassed about the fact that everyone on the force would know, and see that he was gone. There lies a prime example of falling from grace.

I should, and will, digress. I had no hand in planning this funeral, which is why I take such issue with what's in this coffin. Why did the police decide to put him in this uniform? He looks like a member of the Village People. That's not how I remember him at all. Who puts shorts on a corpse? This makes no sense to me. Having an open casket makes no sense either. I didn't think anyone still did this. It's a bit creepy; Hell, it's a lot creepy.

There was hesitation inside of me regarding the simple idea of approaching Martial in his coffin. When I first entered the room and saw him laying there, still, perfectly so, I was sick to my stomach. It's not natural. The outfit (more like a stage costume) isn't my only issue either. Whoever put makeup on Martial deserves a cock or box punch, depending on gender. Our family has a naturally dark complexion. The makeup on Martial's face makes him look as white as a ghost. It would seem that either the makeup artist was attempting to be funny, or was just really bad at their job. Either way, this darker skinned man, who wore jeans and a t- shirt with a leather jacket to all outings (including weddings) was now an albino in shorts and a uniform two sizes too small. What a discount store funeral this is.

What am I doing here? Why are any of us here? The man was locked away in a cupboard for ten years and none of these people helped him. My father would have been much happier being cremated and having his ashes spread over a Burger King parking lot where he busted cookers and crooks, not laying here, having people talk about how "good" he was. That very goodness ultimately led to his downfall, and no one did anything about it. Shorts ... on a corpse. Unbelievable.

While examining the harebrained nature of this funeral, I do as I suspect many have done in the presence of a dead body; I put myself in the old man's shoes—or coffin, as it were.

One day this will be me. I'll be laying here. I wonder how long people will look at my dead body. I'm just as handsome as Martial is, or ... was. I think I deserve some serious face time when I kick it, decades from now.

I really don't want to die, which is why I think I've convinced myself that I'll be the one to live forever. Something will happen that will make it possible.

If only there were some proof of an afterlife, then sure, bring it on! Who doesn't want to live on a cloud somewhere, relaxing with family and friends? The thought of nothingness though—it all being over suddenly with no control—is about the scariest thought one can imagine. Many a night, I've stared at the ceiling with thoughts of death racing through my mind—the ceiling creeping away into space. I get anxiety in those moments, just imagining nothing.

One of my biggest peeves in life is when people say that they're not afraid of dying. Everyone's scared of it; everyone but the God fearing folk, the real religious types (not the fakers). These are the people that have completely deluded themselves as to the scary nature of death. It's not that they're wrong, or at least I don't know if they are. But the fact that they truly believe they know ... it seems delusional to me.

I wish I had faith, but my mind can't seem to get over some very simple facts that have been discovered in the last couple thousand years. One, obviously people thought Heaven was high above, because they couldn't reach high above. Then there were planes. Two, science was basically witch craft, and thus dismissed. Now it solves some of our most challenging problems. Three, the Bible says the earth is 6,000 years old, but we now know it is likely a few billion years old. I just don't see the religious path making much sense in this day and age. If the Bible and religion could be wrong about all of those things, who's to say it's not wrong about it all?

That's why I'm scared to death of dying. There are just no answers, at all. Yeah, I'd say most people are scared of death the way I am. Just take a moment, close your eyes and imagine it all being over. The world slips away as you gasp for air. How fucking freaky is that? Ray Kurzweil—who is one of the smartest men to think, look him up—better hurry up with those life extension drugs.

I stand there for a few more moments, staring at my father in those shorts. I'm solemn but oddly calm, likely due to my father's absence in my life over the last decade. At the age of 26, I've gotten over the psychological impact of Martial running out on me. He went from hero to ze ... no, I won't rhyme two words together, simply to sound intellectual. I picked up that habit from my mom, and I'm trying like Hell to break it.

I feel as if there's a slightly comical element to this gathering of cops, robbers and people he barely knew. Cops, because he was one. Robbers, because he helped some. All the others; probably old high school friends, and those people in their latter years that live to attend funerals. The older some people get, the more they seem to have replaced school with house parties, then with nightclubs, followed by dinner parties, and now with these sad social gatherings. You know the type. They check the obits right after the headlines, and they're the first to fire off a Facebook status when they find out that someone they kinda knew once has died. "So sad to hear that my old basketball coach from grade 9 has died. He was a great man." That's how the status goes. What it should really read is, "So sad to hear that my old basketball coach, a guy whom I haven't thought of for decades and really had no valid impact on my existence in any way, has died. I'll be attending his funeral because I like free food, and a feeling of belonging. #death #mourning #isad." Yep, some people are just living to die. It seems like an inevitability that I'm not excited to experience. Have you ever given birthdays some serious thought? No one wants to die, but everyone celebrates getting closer to death. It's an odd ritual in our world.

As an employee of the funeral home passes me on my right with yet another vase of flowers, I rack my brain trying to figure out if I have these types of thoughts regularly, or if this funeral is just tripping me out. I think I do, but my mind isn't clicking the way it does on a normal day without dear old Ghost Dad laid out in front of me.

Few knew Martial enough to understand that he didn't want people fussing over him, but the cops should know better. He hated big social gatherings celebrating a person in any way, whether it be an accomplishment or a birthday. I can only guess, but I believe he felt like an accomplishment is only so if you're humble about it, and being born isn't much of an accomplishment since billions of people have done it. Now, as I glance behind me at this room of seventy-five people or so, everyone's playing a role and making a fuss over him—ceremony for the sake of ceremony.

Maybe it's a blessing that we didn't talk. I gave the old man no reason to fuss over anything I have done. Really, if I were in his place today, the world would not remember me at all, and seventy-five people would not be in attendance.

Yeah, this feels like long enough. If I were to turn around right now, I don't think anyone would hold it against me, but I should probably cry. I've done a lot of that lately, and I don't think I have any tears left. My life is, some might say, in a downward spiral. Nevertheless, I've stood here for long enough, and no tears have come.

I stand still for a moment more, trying to cry—nothing. I scrunch my face intensely, while thinking of the good times with Martial—still nothing. Then, a thought occurs to me. Eye drops! I have my eye drops. In the summer months my eyes dry out, even though I live in a city with nearly 100% humidity most days. Sneak one into each eye. Slip the bottle back in my pocket. Turn around. No one thinks less of me.

That should be a part of the website! A funeral survival pack; Kleenex, shoe shine, hand sanitizer, and eye drops. Yours for only $19.95! Don't take that, I may be looking to get a start-up going, and a funeral survival pack is as good an idea as any.

I take my seat, which cues the start of the ceremony. This really depressing elevator music plays as a hush comes over the crowded room. Sniffles and coughs break the silence enough to not make it awkward.

The minister, or pastor ... or whatever, does a decent job of speaking at an agnostic person's funeral. Martial believed in neither God nor the descent into nothingness. He simply came from Bill Maher's church of *I Don't Know*. I guess it's easier for this man of God to officiate this funeral, given Martial left the "I don't know" loophole, and he wasn't a full blown Atheist. It makes me wonder though, what kind of ceremony do Atheists have when they die? I'll have to Google that, too.

The whole service takes about twenty-minutes, which I feel is pretty good time. At one point this messenger of the Heavens recites a prayer, which for some reason made the entire congregation say in unison, "Lord, have mercy". I attempt to contain my snicker as I picture Will Smith reciting these very same words before chasing after a hot girl on the Fresh Prince. Luckily, only the woman sitting beside me takes notice of my odd disrespect; boy, the old bat has a nasty sneer.

Just two family members actually show up; my Aunty Joy and I, so there isn't the usual reserved pew. We sit amongst the people like common mourners, not even together. My mom is a no-show, and likewise are the rest of our nuclear—I mean that in the destructive sense—family. Mom is probably eight ounces deep in some liquor and too busy suntanning on a cruise ship to even listen to my voicemail. She had won the lottery, and coincidentally found herself a man half her age, equal to mine. After she won, I was hoping for a payout in response to my odd upbringing after Martial left, but she decided to not be so generous. She disguised her greed as tough love. The only time I hear from her is through the occasional email. She, living the high life ... me, not. In fact, the emails stopped about a year ago. My aunt and I are the sole family representatives.

Not being a person of faith, and having never attended a funeral before, I'm not familiar with the ways of the Lord. The entire process from opening to close is uncomfortable at best. The hard wooden pews are clearly a throwback to a time before cushions, when people filled churches to find redemption for stealing their neighbour's goat. People don't put enough in those offering plates to get some padding? There's another thing that I don't know: Do they toss around that plate at funerals? I hope not. One, it's kinda rude. Two, I'm broke off my ass right now. Come to think of it, how did everyone know to say, "Lord, have mercy"? All of these people can't possibly belong to the same religion. Am I that out of the loop?

I kinda want to go to church on Sundays, just to be a part of the whole *Lord Have Mercy Club*. The communal elements of religion seem attractive enough, until you think about it for ten-seconds and realize you then have to believe in talking snakes, a man living in a big fish, that big boat built by a guy who never built boats, and an invisible God that is both vengeful and kind. No, I think I'll stick to my slightly social-introvert ways, and let them have their club to themselves. Oh, and before you call me a cynic, let's talk Noah. If God gave him the power to build the ark, animals the ability to travel continents at basically the same pace, and his family, the patience to not check him into a loony bin ... why then, did he not just give them the power to float, and then gracefully fall back to Earth when the flood was over? Seems just as easy, if not more-so. Fairytales; and we think kids are stupid for believing in a big bunny that hides chocolate.

Once the awkward ceremony is over, everyone just kinda stands around in a small room off the main hall, sharing stories about a man that none of them had seen in a long, long time. At least, that's my assumption. If Martial didn't want to see me, I'm going to go out on the limb and say he didn't want to see anyone.

As I walk over to get some dry sandwiches, my father's partner from back in the day, Andrew, comes shuffling up to me with his cane made of oak (for reasons more *House*-like than old age related). Andrew is Martial's age and a bullet to the leg meant he would walk with a cane from 38 on. "You're taking it hard Michael," he says as he puts a hand on my tricep and squeezes. "You stood there for a long time looking at your pop. If there's anything I can do, anything at all, just ask."

A lot of people have been saying that to me today. "If you need anything, just ask". I don't even know three quarters of the people here, however for this moment of quid pro quo platitudes, they're here for me.

"If you need anything, just ask," professed some woman in an ugly purple wool dress—wool, in summer.

The Police commissioner: "If you need anything, just ask."

Some of my father's former cop buddies: "If you need anything, just ask."

After more of the same, Kyle Davis spots me from across the room. Kyle was the cop that got Martial fired from the force, although somehow everyone managed to forget that today. Martial never forgave him and by association, neither did I. Being unceremoniously dismissed led to my father's depression. That depression led to the decline of his marriage and locking himself away. Locking himself away cost me my relationship with Martial, whom I considered a great man at one point—the greatest.

Kyle saunters on over, in his well pressed uniform with pants—not looking like a member of the Village People. I wonder if he's the one that picked our Martial's outfit. I really don't like this guy. The way he walks makes me sick. His face makes me sick. He's all about the show—he's one of those guys that smiles while he walks. You know the type. Before he enters a room, he needs to look in the mirror. His hair has more gel than actual hair—a Ken doll would be jealous. To top off this loser's persona, no one told him there's a point where that many white strips are too many white strips. I remind myself that I only have to be on my best behaviour for a little while longer now.

He talks for a moment. I don't really hear anything he says until the end, "If you need anything, just ask."

I stare at him, playing out the different scenarios in my head. I could punch him. I could choke him. I could cuss him out. I look down at the table next to me. There's a butter knife, a nail file, and a pretty solid looking vase. If I grabbed any of these things and knocked his head off of his shoulders, or got a little stabby, I could probably plead out—temporary insanity brought on by grief. I bet it would make Martial proud. Oh, the vengeance would be sweet, horrible but sweet. However after day dreaming for a moment, on this day, there is no bloodshed.

"Well Kyle, how would I ask? What's your email, cell number, Facebook, Twitter? You got LinkedIn? How do I ask?" I'm making him uncomfortable, and nothing could make me happier. My tone is sarcastic and clear to everyone—designed to put him in his place. "I probably will need something at some point, and since you've been so helpful towards my family in the past, I think it would be a good idea if I had all of your contact information so if I need anything, I ... can ... just ... ASK."

He doesn't quite know what to say. He even stammers a bit. "I was just trying to help, Michael," he says while straightening his posture.

"Just like you helped Martial? Everyone else might be pretending you did the right thing, or whatever, but his son, his blood, and the one left behind knows better," I shoot back. The look on his face is priceless. On one hand he is stunned, taken aback, and unprepared like a deer in headlights. On the other hand, he's trying so hard not to look embarrassed, portraying an air of confidence that only my gaze can rip through. The two mix to make him flush in the face.

Seeing that hostility was about to break out, the Police Commissioner and my Aunty Joy step in to ask about the current events in my life (a short conversation, since my life is basically eventless). Kyle takes the interruption as an opportunity to duck out of the conversation—insincere prick. Five-minutes later, I can't see him around the room anymore. I'll consider it a victory that his discomfort caused him to leave early.

I did the whole kissing hands, shaking babies thing for a while until it was just the funeral director and I standing in a room. Me, tired and just wanting to go home. Him, with his practiced sense of understanding and a bill for $8,297.

"May the Lord be with you, Michael," he says.

Damn. This was the first time I had seen the bill. "May his insurance company be with me instead." That was probably rude, but at this point, who gives a shit? "Well, it's a good thing it's thirty-days payable," I say as I take the piece of paper from his veiny hands. Yep, the police plan the funeral and the family foots the bill. Cool, right?

It must take a special kind of human being to work in the funeral business. If I had to confront death everyday, I might be a little less fearful of it—though not entirely, because even a funeral director is scared of death, I'm sure. But really, when you think of it, a guy that works in a funeral home fills his days with tears, dead bodies, dark clothes, depressing music, and broken lives. What morbid son of a bitch wants to make a living this way?

"How do you do this job?" I ask.

"I'm sorry?" He replies, probably shocked that I have any interest in conversation.

"I mean c'mon. There's so much death around you everyday. Isn't it depressing?"

"Death is just a chapter in our lives."

"I wish I believed that."

"You don't believe in God?"

"I don't know what to believe, just like Martial. I can't say one way or the other."

"Well then, let me ask you this. Do you believe in some version—any version— of the soul?"

I think for a moment. "Yeah. I'd say some version of it makes sense to me."

"Well then, if there's even a chance that anything continues on after you die, don't you want to make sure you protect and nurture that piece of you?"

"I guess, but I wouldn't even know where to begin," I retort while exhaling. This conversation is endlessly exhausting when you just want to go to bed, but somehow interesting enough to continue. "Any advice?"

"I nurture my soul by being there for others when they need it. I help families put matters to rest. You just have to find that which makes your soul vibrant. No one but you might understand it, but that's not what matters. I feel a sense of worth and accomplishment as a Funeral Director. Someone like you thinks I'm morbid, but I sleep well at night, and live a perfectly happy life. Out of the darkness of my job comes a light through the rest of my day."

"Now that is an interesting way of looking at it."

"Find your light, sir."

All I can think about when someone says something like that is how far away from any kind of light I am—but an eclipse. Seeing that I have no interest in any further conversation, the Funeral Director says goodbye, and leaves the room. I take one last look at the cherry wood and staged pictures of happy families before exiting into the bright, burning hot sun. In the first few seconds, the light stabs me in both of my eyes. I can't see. It's just too bright. When my eyes finally adjust, I see a calm city laid out in front of me to enjoy, so I start my peaceful walk, and examination of life.

Earlier in the day, Martial's lawyer gave me a box, which I have yet to open. It has a bit of weight to it as I hold it under my arm walking down Main Street. I'm not sure if I'm even interested in the contents. I mean, I want to remember the guy that would watch Superman cartoons with me on Saturday mornings. I want to hold onto the memories of us out at the range, shooting impossible targets to the amazement of those looking on. Martial taught me to survive, hone my instincts, and be ready for anything. I could drop most in a fight, and in all likelihood I could hit a target hundreds of yards away. It's been a bit, but my survival instincts are still in there somewhere. This was all because of Martial; the black belt in Jiu Jitsu, amateur wrestler, and sharp shooter.

Yep, he was hardcore to the max. He won Provincial championships in high school for any kind of sport or combat you could think of. He did two tours overseas, putting bullets in bad guys. To top off his life, the old man spent his nights dropping bad guys with the police on the regular. He asked to be put in the worst neighbourhoods on the beat, and never backed down from a biker. When the UFC came to town, Martial was GSP's bodyguard. The living legend himself named Martial *a tough son of a bitch*. His nickname was Martial because of his fighting skills, and Martial kicked ass.

The last thing I want is to open this box and find

something that makes me realize how truly depressed a man he had become. My mother had always said that Martial lost a step, and now preferred darkness over the light that the Funeral Director was speaking of. Nonetheless, I carry the box with me on the journey home.

My place is only about fifteen minutes from the funeral home, so I decide to walk the entire way, instead of taking a bus. Even though it's extremely hot outside, the walk is meant to do me some good—clear my mind. It does the trick in the moment. Sometimes the hot sun can make the world beautiful, just when its at it's ugliest. As I walk down the street, I see a couple making out. My mind manages to conjure up images of the hot receptionist, Monica, at my doctor's office—probably as a coping mechanism. I have yet to see her naked, but I have an active imagination. For years, I've wanted to ask her out, but Martial helped me hone my survival instincts in every area except that of women. Every time I open my mouth, I sound like a sarcastic prick; zero game.

As I enter the hallway of my apartment block, the air conditioning makes the hair on my arms stick straight up. The old door slams behind me, and echoes down the damp hallway just barely eclipsing the sound of the loud ass air conditioner. It may be old, and loud, but it's also refreshing after the walk. Less refreshing however, is the notice on my door.

EVICTION: Due to a prolonged period of overdue rent, the management company, Sage Realty has chosen to evict resident. If you are the former occupant of this unit please contact us to arrange a date and time to pick up your belongings.

Not even naked Monica can comfort me now. All I can really do at this point is laugh. This is just another in a series of unfortunate circumstances. First, I lost my job because some bitch with an acne problem in the cubicle next to mine framed me for stealing office supplies. I fought tooth and nail, but I guess she was banging the boss in the copy room after hours, so by default she wins. I wasn't going down on him for job security.

Then, while looking for a job, I came to the conclusion that the recession was real and the job market sucks. Until the hunt, I was unconvinced that the world had fallen on hard times to the magnitude that CNN suggested. Turns out, it's a blood bath out there. Getting a job as anything short of a waiter at a dive or pumping gas is next to impossible. On my way home from a day of pushing resumes, my tranny went on my truck—that's a $3,500 fix, and it might as well be a million dollars at this point. When the mechanic comically asked me how I'd like to pay, I just walked out and left the piece of shit there. Now, Martial dies and I'm evicted. The last two months have been a cosmic bitch slap.

"Evicted. Evicted. Evicted. Not good. Not good at all," I hear from behind me. It's my crazy old neighbour that sounds like a parrot, standing in the hall with his basket of laundry.

"Hey Earl," I reply.

"Dem guys came by just an hour ago and posted that there paper on your door. It's all kinda fascist if you ask me."

"The hits just keep on coming, Earl."

The old guy mutters more nonsense before prancing into his apartment. A war vet, Earl had seen the ugly side of life, and had no interest in therapy. He just let his mind go where it needed to go, and now he's bat shit crazy. I can't even count the number of times the Police have escorted him back home in nothing but his tighty whities, and a muscle shirt. Regardless, he has been a good neighbour; he watches out for the building.

After a futile attempt to have my key and the shiny new lock connect, I sit on the floor and examine my options. I could stay at a friend's place, but that's simply a short-term solution. I don't really have any close friends to speak of, anyway. Maybe Derek, but even then, we're not bff's close. Then there's the Wii Universe, but that doesn't exactly lend itself to lasting, meaningful relationships. Maybe I can ask all of those people from the funeral that said they would help me out in my time of need. Problem is, those were empty words, and they've already forgotten all about that while they eat their lunch or watch some mind-numbing reality TV. There's my aunt's place, but she's more religious than Jesus. I mean there is a good chance that if she swam in the Pacific, the whole damn thing would turn into Holy Water. I don't know that I could handle all that praying. These are my options and they all suck.

Sitting next to me in the dimly lit, moist hallway, is that box Martial left for me. Since, at the moment, this is my only worldly possession, I decide to open it. I get a bit of a chill as I do. What could be in this box of mystery left behind by a man that very well could have been in a darker place than most people will ever experience? Inside there are various pieces of paper, some keys, and a few sealed envelopes. The first piece of paper addresses me.

Dear son,

I'm sorry that I couldn't be the father you needed in the last few years. Your mother probably told you I was depressed, but she had it all wrong, and at that point there was no explaining anything to her. I was obsessed rather. There was a job to do, and no one but me to do it. Either way if I had fought her on custody of you nobody would have won. Frankly, you were better off. I'm sorry to say that, but it's true. I'm writing this letter to you because I have a feeling my time is nearly up. If that's the case I just want you to know that I love you, and never stopped. You're my only child, my legacy. I've left the keys to my place, the deed to my house, and the keys to my car. They're all paid off, and yours to keep. Sell them, use them. Whatever. Do what you need to do, but you're walking in on a shit storm of research. Take some time to learn about your pop a bit.

Alive, all of this might have made you think I was crazy. Now, maybe you will see the world for what it really is. Keep these secrets safe. I miss you, my boy.

Dad.

I place the note back in that box, sitting there for awhile, just staring into the abyss. He also left some insurance certificates, and a bunch of other trinkets that I didn't really see as important, but clearly he did. This whole situation is fate, it would seem. My father giving me his house in lieu of an eviction, his car in lieu of mine being inexplicably broken, and naming me his beneficiary, providing me the money to pay for the funeral and get me back on my feet.

I will not look a gift horse in the mouth. I write down Martial's address on a small piece of paper and slide it under Earl's door—just in case someone comes looking for me—because if anyone knocks, he'll surely jump out of his chair and *investigate*. That done, I leave on my journey to learn more about what Martial meant by obsessed.

I feel better about my finances now, so I take a $31.82 cab ride across the city to his place. I had tried to see him here once after the divorce, but he wasn't having it. Martial didn't even come to the door. I'm ninety-percent sure he was inside, too. After about twenty-minutes it started to rain, so I left and never returned.

As the cab darts in and out of traffic, I ponder what's next. What kind of answers would I find in his little shack of a home? How could my mother have gotten it so wrong? How do I reconcile the old man, with the great father he once was? In the letter he says that he felt his time was up. Martial was shot. Why would he walk into that situation knowing death was a possibility? What secrets would I learn? So many questions float around in my head.

The cab drops me off on the curb and I jump out, happy to be alive. The driver was a fucking maniac. I drive pretty fast, but that was teetering on death-wish style driving. Outside, the weeds peek through hundreds of cracks in the sidewalk. Martial clearly didn't keep the place up just before he died. The grass is longer than he ever let the family lawn get. The windows haven't been washed and the mail is piling up at the front door. This house resembles a shack more than a place to call home.

As I swing the front door open and step over the newspapers, dust attacks me through the light. It's amazing how—when sunlight hits—you can see all the dust that is around, but it never bothers you in the dark. All of the sudden, I feel the need to cough and sneeze. Oh, our weak little brains.

The house is what some might call a character home. It's old, but still in good shape on the inside. I don't know why people buy these types of homes. They're just as expensive as something new, but with aging issues. It's paid off though, according to Martial's letter, so I can't complain too much.

As my eyes adjust to another change of light, I immediately understand what Martial meant by obsessed. The sight is disturbing and actually kind of creepy. Every inch of every wall is covered with paper; some newspaper, some paper he wrote on. From many of those papers hang red string, tied to a tack, which leads to another paper. There have to be thousands of sheets on the walls. Some feature faces, and others, words. The hallway, the living room, the kitchen—papers are everywhere. With every step, the floor creaks and my eyes focus on something new.

I try to make sense of this mess but alas, I'm far too tired. My brain isn't processing the information. Exhaustion makes it impossible to remember what it is that I read just five-seconds before. It's been a long day, and I have a doctor's appointment tomorrow morning, so sleep is probably best.

The main bedroom has more of the same—papers and string. By the time I get the room cleaned up, the sun has almost completely disappeared from the horizon. Martial always had a few odd habits, but here's a new one; his bed still has the plastic on it, despite clearly being slept in. I tear off the plastic, change the sheets, and lay down. Tomorrow, I am sure to learn some things about Martial that I didn't know. Maybe all of this might lead to peace with the man he had become. Tomorrow.

Tonight, I sleep.

2

Heroes

SATURDAY MORNINGS in my house as a kid were as ritualistic as Sundays for many churchgoers. My dad would shout from the kitchen, "This food won't eat itself, son!", waking me up to the smell of bacon and warm syrup. Most mornings I would wake up earlier, but I'd always wait for the same line bellowed from our oak kitchen. I'd race down the stairs, and jump enthusiastically into my chair. My mom always gave me hell for that. You could see the impression and scrape marks on the cheap kitchen flooring from the many Saturdays over the years. Still, every morning, I would scrape the floor just a little more.

We'd set up TV tables in the living room and wait anxiously for the Superman cartoon to start. My mom would roll her eyes every time my dad compared himself to Supes, (that's what the cool kids called him) which, when I think about it was every episode. During commercials, we would wrestle, build a fortress of solitude out of pillows, and assemble lavish castles with my lego. That's the kind of dad I had growing up. Every other day, he was busy being a badass, but with some seniority on the force, he had weekends off. Saturdays were our day. Sundays, he took time out for mom.

Our home wasn't fancy, not by any stretch of even the wildest imagination. Two storeys, small rooms, brown carpet to hide the crumbs of daily life. It was very middle of the road, just like us. Somehow between wars, medals, and all that comes with being a hero, Martial decided to settle into a life of ordinary. I say *decided* because I truly believe that in those days my dad did only what he wanted to do. He was bigger than life, and filled a room, but somehow despite this regular existence, he made me feel like we lived in a mansion. To him, the world was our playground.

Now, I know what you're thinking. No one has such a perfect childhood; I must be sugar coating the story. I'm not, really. This was my life and every Saturday was perfect; we were The Brady Bunch. It was important to my dad that he take time out to raise me with a strong male role model and give me a real chance in the world. Of course, that wouldn't last forever. I did say we were estranged back at the funeral. Maybe that's how life is; perfection can only last so long before the curveball comes. I'm not sure that I would have traded the short time I had with my father for a typical family experience that lasted longer. I only say that because when I sleep, my mind escapes to the past and I dream of a better time. I guess holding on tightly to these memories was always my way of coping with losing my dad to unknown forces. Now, he's actually gone forever, and I kinda wish I could just sleep.

I will never forget one sunny Saturday morning when I was about eight years old. After Superman was over, my dad said he had a surprise for me. "Go get your cape, son," he said, smiling ear to ear.

I ran upstairs, snatched my red silky cape and

jumped off the final three steps, trying so desperately to fly. My excitement about the surprise allowed me to ignore that once again, my feet had touched the ground.

"Okay, close your eyes," my dad said, opening the door to the back yard.

I closed my eyes tight. As a kid I loved surprises. "What is it Dad?"

"Keep those eyes closed for just a little longer, son," he replied.

I was busting with anticipation as I felt my dad lift me off of the ground and place me chest down on what felt like ropes.

"Okay Michael, open up."

I opened my eyes to see the grass of our yard below. As I looked around I saw a large fan blowing on me. My dad had harnessed me into a bunch of clear plastic belts.

"Dad, what is this?"

"I put this together so we could take some really cool pictures of you flying, my boy." The setup was actually very well done. I don't know how I didn't notice my dad taking time to build it. "Now put your hands out like Superman and I'll snap some shots."

We had a great deal of fun that morning. The pictures turned out—for lack of a better term—super. When he pulled on a rope, I went flying through the air on the harnesses around the tree. It was, and always will be, a sort of magical feeling. Who doesn't want to fly? I think besides living forever, it will be an aspiration of man until the day we can achieve it.

After, my dad and I sat at the picnic table in the backyard playing checkers. As awesome as he was, Dad wasn't the type to let me win. He was teaching me how to get the upper hand. I would get mad sometimes, but later in life would appreciate his tough love approach. His challenges prepared me to be a straight-A student in school, championship volleyball player, and for a time, excellent fighter. There was a lesson in everything, and little did I know this would be one of my first in a long curriculum.

"Son, I know you really like Superman, but I want you to understand that it's not that easy to be a hero in this world," he said with a serious tone.

"What do you mean, Dad?"

"Well, you know I'm a police officer. Me and my friends go out everyday trying to stop bad people from doing bad things, and bullets don't bounce off of us."

"Have you been shot?"

"A long time ago. Right here," he said, as he pointed to his lower abdomen. "It hurt. A lot of guys have been hurt keeping this city safe. It's kinda dangerous and I just want you to know that it's the cops, firefighters, doctors, and paramedics that you should really look up to. One day, they will probably save you. Heck, maybe one day, you'll be one of them and save someone yourself."

"I want to be a cop and catch bad guys like you, Dad."

"That would be great, Michael, but it's not easy. Sometimes we have to do things that leave a little piece of us behind. Sometimes to stop the real bad, we have to do some bad of our own. It's just the way of the world."

At the time I didn't understand what it was that my dad was talking about. I just shrugged my shoulders and played my turn on the checkerboard. Now, of course I know exactly what my dad meant. It's a cold harsh world out there, and I guarantee my dad did some things that left him up at night—all in the name of safety. It's probably why, in this age of the Internet, so many cops are getting in trouble. There was a way of doing things that had undeniable results, but those things don't play well on camera for people sitting in the comfort of their homes.

People rag on cops all the time, but their job is nearly impossible, and tough choices need to be made. Recently, I've seen a lot of activity on my Facebook bashing cops. People just don't get the job. Yes, there are bad cops out there, but they're not actually bad cops; they're bad people, or they feel trapped. When a cop nightsticks someone for the hell of it, either he's frustrated with the job, or he enjoys hurting people. Either way, that person needs help, the same as a banger that goes around ruling the neighbourhood just because he can. There's also situations where you would have to take a guy down, and that's someone's son or husband. People will give cops shit about it, but at the end of the day, it's likely that outcome came about out of that person's own making. There is an exception to every rule, but the rules are so for a reason. If you want a perfect cop, you would need to take the human out of it. We'd need cyborgs or something. The job is just too hard for a person with complex emotions and access to copious amounts of alcohol to handle. At the end of the day, though, if your house gets broken into, or your wife is killed, you're going to call the cops. We need them. I can't imagine the stress.

As I reflect on that day, and many days like it, I've come to realize that Saturdays were therapy for my dad. He could tell me anything and he knew that a lot of what he was saying would likely be too complex for me to ever repeat. He probably thought I wouldn't remember, either. Aside from therapy, I think he was taking the ugliness of the world and preparing me for it. He would always say to my mom, "The world isn't getting prettier. We prepare for the ugliest, so we can find delight in our daily lives."

That night when dad tucked me in, I asked him a question that I know he had been dreading. "Dad, have you ever killed someone?"

He took a breath and then sat next to me. Placing his hand on my forehead to brush the hair from my face, he replied, "Yes, son." A moment passed, and then he continued. "Once a man was doing some very bad things to women. When we caught him, he pulled a gun on me and Andrew. It was either him or us. I had to do what I had to do."

"You saved the women?"

"Yes son, we did."

"That's good, Dad. You're a hero just like Superman," I said as I faded away and my eyes began to close; the light from the glow in the dark stars on my ceiling fading to black.

Looking back, I'm sure that was a moment my dad held onto for years. He was Superman, and not just in his eyes, or the eyes of strangers. His son believed in him, and I think that was pretty important to someone that believed in legacy. If we had more time, I feel like in adulthood we would have been the best of friends. He was a great man and a great dad—a hero, as I said. I only wish I could make the world a better place, just like Martial.

I think we all want to leave our stamp on this world; some sort of a legacy, but few ever do. Martial was a bad ass while maintaining good, and I have appreciated that about him, even when he was a shut-in. I still have time though. There is a chance that I'm just a bit of a late bloomer in the areas of success and impact. Ten years from now, if I could just catch a break, maybe I'll be viewed by many in a positive light. It's possible ... if I could just get out from under this mountain of debt and indecisiveness to find something I can be passionate about.

3

Death Follows Me

THE ALARM ON MY IPHONE goes off at 6:30am; then again at 6:50am; once more at 7:20. My doctor's appointment is at 7:30 and of course, with ten-minutes to spare, I jump up and make haste for the door. The whole way there I'm wondering why that snooze button was so appealing with such a good night's sleep. In my rush as I'm getting ready, I constantly bang into things, still not familiar with my surroundings. Most nights in the last few months, I've been getting less than four hours of shut eye. It was probably a combination of bad diet and stress. I'm pretty sure I've seen every movie that's ever been released on Netflix. Last night; eight hours sleep on the money, but still, I'm groggy. There's no time for a shower, I don't have a change of clothes, or even a toothbrush—not exactly my finest look.

Luckily for me, my dad left his Durango in the will. It's a couple of years old, but looks brand new, as it should with just over 4,800 kilometers on it; definitely better than the truck I was driving before. At one point last year on my way to work, the gas tank on my dilapidated piece of shit decided to spring a leak. I was, of course, in the middle lane of traffic during rush hour. No one got out to help. They honked and swore at me, but no help at all. It was embarrassing and renewed my faith in a philosophy I was adopting, Anti-Socialism.

This new life of mine still seems a bit on the surreal side. It's almost like William Shakespeare is writing my life script; the perfect timed poetry of my old life issues, and my new life solutions, mixed with the horrible tragedy of losing my father. I wake up to my first full day of my new life with wanderlust. I haven't really gone anywhere outside of this polarizing city, and with the stresses of yesterday, had little desire to jump on a plane (not that I could afford it). My mom has a ton of cash, but certainly doesn't share. Now, I don't need to make anymore awkward phone calls to her when I'm actually in trouble. Sometimes she answers, sometimes not. Lately, not. I will make something out of myself, and do Martial proud. Opportunity will not slip through my fingers this time. I've woken up with energy and goals, now that the grogginess is gone—a new feeling for me in recent years.

Martial's truck has great pickup, so I'm able to hit the right lane at nearly every light and beat slow drivers off the line. Why do people line up in two lanes as far the eye can see, but leave one of the lanes wide open? That's a mystery of life I will never understand. You're fucking up the flow. I end up arriving at the doctor's office a minute late—7:31am. Who knew a Durango could be driven like a *NASCAR*? I had the perfect bob and weave strategy, without the insanity of that cab driver from yesterday. He must need new brake pads monthly. As I walk in, Doc Scorpio's hot receptionist, Monica, gives me this look of disapproval. She's the girl I fantasized about while walking home from Martial's funeral ... and pretty much any other time I need an escape from the every day.

"You're late," Monica says.

"Well technically I was in the parking lot by 7:30, so I'd say I'm right on time," I retort.

"Whatever. If he decides to bill you a bit more, it's on you. You're never on time," she argues as she picks up my file and walks around her desk. Monica gives me a once over. "Did you sleep in those clothes?"

I look down at my wrinkled shirt, and pat it with my hands like that's going to do anything. "One minute? That's crazy, and besides, the Doc probably won't even see me for another half hour." Doctors always book you for a time, and then make you wait. I don't really get how that system came about and everyone just became okay with it. You'd figure that at some point people would have banded together and done something about what can only be seen as disrespect. Think about it. A doctor says come for a given time, and then you end up waiting, so now you might get even sicker, sitting with all of these other sick people coughing and sneezing germs into the air, and because you never know how long anything will take, you can't plan around it. As far as customer service goes, doctors need to step up their game.

"Actually, he's waiting for you in his office."

My heart immediately sinks into my stomach. Doctors don't meet with you in their office unless they have bad news. That has to be the way of things. I've never met a doctor in their office, and I've always been healthy. *Shit*, I think to myself as the door opens and a drab Doctor Scorpio looks me dead in the eyes.

I can hear the sound of my heart thumping and every footstep I take echoes through the silent room.

Just like when I saw that eviction notice, not even the sight of Monica can help me now.

The doc looks up from his papers. "How are you today, Michael?"

"Well I'm standing in your office. That can't be a good thing, right?"

"How about you have a seat, and we discuss some things?"

As I sit, I take in the décor of his impeccably clean office. His desk is marble. I feel that's pretty pretentious for a doctor, but the guy's wife is always dressed in fur so it's not all that surprising. The paintings on the walls are an ode to South America, which is odd, since my doctor is clearly and unmistakably African. Usually when someone decorates, they do it in the style of their culture, or display no culture at all.

He has a lot of plants and everything sparkles like Mr. Clean is his personal butler. I'm thinking that this can't be a bad thing. Who doesn't want a doctor that pays attention to detail, and has a respect for life—even it if is the life of vegetation?

"So what's up? You find a tumour or something?" I inquire with a bit of a chuckle. He just stares at me, unsure of what to say. I try to read him. "Oh shit. You found a tumour."

The doc lets out a reserved sigh, "You have Cancer, yes."

"C'mon. How is that possible? I come in for a physical, I feel great, outside of some itching and a stomach ache, and all of a sudden I have Cancer? I have an okay diet, I work out almost every day. That's not real. This isn't real."

"I'm sorry, Michael. I wish I had better news, but you have pancreatic Cancer; stage four of four, which means if we have any hope of getting ahead of this, we need to start treatment immediately. You working out and having a good diet is a positive first step. You're in great shape. But, I need you to please pay attention to everything I'm saying. It's all important, and if at any point you don't understand something, ask about it. I'll take as much time as you need."

And there it is; the reason why some wait longer than others to get in with a doctor. I've only ever been here for a physical, or an easily diagnosed condition like the flu or something like that. We wait because the doc is taking time to help those that are really sick understand what's next. All of those hours spent reading crusty magazines so old that the celebrities are no longer celebrities seem so poignant now. Someone is losing patience by the second out there, while I get the bad news.

"I'm going to die?" I ask with tears welling up on top of my bottom eye lids, waiting to pour down my face like an overflowing bucket. "I mean, I know I'm dying someday, but I'm gonna die soon?"

"How about I run through some things, and then we get to questions like that at the end? Fair?"

I nod as if I believe any of this is actually fair. All I can think of is my dad's body in that coffin—those fucking shorts. I'd surely be a good looking corpse now, all of twenty-six and dead. My heart is beating so fast and hard that I can't concentrate on much else. It would be *just hilarious* if, while I get a Cancer diagnosis, I die of a heart attack. The joke would be, *What do you get when you cross no job, Cancer and a heart attack with a guy that can't talk to girls?* Punch line: *Me, Michael Burton*. Okay, so it's a bad joke ... but that's a kinda the point.

The doc is speaking but it's tinny. There's an echo in this small office, and I can't really make out his words.

I try to concentrate but a headache is setting in. My heartbeat can be felt throughout my entire body. I feel sweat from under my clothes as if my body exploded, and I'm not really a sweater. My stomach; oh God, I think I'm going to puke. My heart beat is actually drowning out any other sound. His words have faded away. *Fuck, what is this?*

The panic button has officially been pressed in my brain. Looking down at my hand, I get the sense that it's not real. Nothing feels real. I'm itchy, but numb, cold but hot. Phased out of the world, but trying so hard to stay intensely focused on everything.

I spring up from the chair, knocking it to the ground. The doc stands, putting his hand out, as if asking me to stay calm with a gesture. A ringing in my ears takes over the sound of my heartbeat. *AW!* It's so fucking loud. I frantically attempt to open the door but the handle doesn't seem so simple. I know that all I have to do is turn and pull, but the room is closing in and such a task seems nearly impossible.

Focus.

Finally, I manage to nearly tear the door off of its hinges and stumble down the hallway to the waiting room. I run square into another patient about my size, but ugly, and mean looking. *Who wears plaid anymore? You look like a dish cloth*, I think to myself. The contact feels staticky.

"Hey buddy. Watch where you're going," he shouts at me.

My adrenaline is pumping, and the room is spinning. I throw my full weight into a push that takes the man down to the ground and causes the handful of patients to gasp. The men in the room get up, but hesitate to get involved. The man I pushed is angry, but I get lucky; Doctor Scorpio jogs briskly out of his office and takes control of the situation. "Calm down," he yells at me.

For whatever reason, his yelling snaps me out of it, but the panic is still inside of me, needing to burst out. My heartbeat returns with a vengeance. "Calm down? I just buried my father and now you're handing me my death sentence, and you want me to calm down? Oh, okay. Why didn't you say something sooner? I'm more than happy to oblige." I flail about, grab a magazine rack off of the wall and throw it across the room. "How's this for calm?" The male side of the species are a different kind of dumb in moments of stress. A woman would likely sit quietly and take it all in. Guys rip through adrenaline and testosterone in such a reckless way. I know I'm being an asshole, but I can't help myself.

"You're scaring the other patients," he replies.

"Fuck you, and fuck these other patients. Everyone's here for runny noses and sore throats. I'M GOING TO DIE! You couldn't catch this sooner? I've been coming here religiously for twelve years, and there was nothing before this. All those times you barely even looked at me, even though I had obvious symptoms ... maybe that was Cancer. Maybe you could have saved me if you were better at what you do." My words cut through the doc like a knife, of course. I'm calling into question his life's work. In one breath, I've managed to make all those years of missed social events, hours studying, sacrificing relationships for rotations; everything he's done to be a doctor, seem like a waste of time. I can see the hurt in his eyes, and the sting in his body language.

The patients cower away from my blind rage. It's like a scene out of a movie. They run away and take cover anywhere they can. Admittedly, this is not my finest moment. I stop when I see an old lady in her wheelchair in front of me. I'm frozen in place, just staring at her. She's in rough shape. All sound vanishes as we stare at each other. I'm never going to get old. Every wrinkle surrounding her eyes is a wrinkle I'll never get. I always said I'd be that cool older guy that everyone says got better with age. Tears stream down my face as I feel nothingness with a profound sense of reality like never before. As I stand there, and the immensity of my situation wafts over me, the doc places his hand on my shoulder.

Crunch. That's the best way I know to describe the sound of my fist connecting with his cheek. I feel my ring rip at the flesh by his lip, causing an instant stream of blood as he falls to the floor. Martial's training to release the rage so that panic can vanish is still instinctually built into my DNA, although I don't think this is what he had in mind. As soon as my fist connects, I feel my mind snap out of the haze. I stand there motionless with a few small drips of blood hanging off of my ring, waiting to drop.

"Aw shit Doc. I'm sor ..." I don't get to finish my sentence. Two cops happened to be visiting the pharmacy connected to my doctor's office. Lucky me, right? They haul me to the ground with authority, and cuff me behind my back, one with his knee to my spine, the other pressing on the side of head with his left hand. They have me on lock down; I can't move. Those words I never thought I would hear directed towards me start, "You have the right to remain silent ..."

As they pull me up and escort me outside, I try my best to apologize to everyone I pass. Panic is gone, and remorse is all I feel. No one wants to hear it, and I can't really blame them. They all just look away, down at the ground, or stare at me with anger. The last person I see before making my way outside is Monica. She wears her emotions on her sleeve; a little bit of fear and a big bit of disappointment. Who can blame her? A man is supposed to face difficulty with strength. This situation, and all my past issues, have been met with a level of *pathetic* Martial would have been ashamed to see.

As I sit in my cell later that day, I contemplate all that has happened. What an asshole I had been. Why did I throw that magazine rack at the other patients? Why did I do any of that? It's no one's fault that I'm dying. Cancer is just one of those things that hits you without warning. No amount of chocolates or cheesy Hallmark cards could fix this mess. I think for hours while sitting on the uncomfortable metal table in my ten-foot by ten-foot white brick room. At least it used to be white, now it's the beautiful colour of light grey with decorative scuff marks throughout. The door being shut would give many a feeling of claustrophobia. Not me, Martial trained that kind of weakness out of me a long time ago. I guess I was rusty earlier; weakness won out when I heard the Cancer diagnosis. No one really knows how they're going to react when they hear the worst news possible. It's a bit like hearing you won the lottery. How is someone supposed to relay their emotion? There are extremes in life we never see coming.

Despite having everything removed from our pockets, those who sat in this place before me managed to write stupid shit all over the walls. There are carvings; mostly one gang calling out another from the looks of it. I guess that's how they get at each other from in here. The next guy from the opposing gang is supposed to be pissed, I guess—truly the pinnacle of human evolution.

After the fifteen-minute drive to the station, two

hours to book me and seven hours of waiting in a holding cell, a cop opens the door and tells me I'm free to go.

"You got off easy, kid. No one at the office, including the doctor, are willing to press charges," a cop says as he opens the door. "Apparently the receptionist has a soft spot for you, and made everyone understand what you are going through. Just follow Sergeant Davis here."

I walk out of the room, and Kyle is standing there with judgement all over his face. I wonder if it's irony that put him here, or if he wants to relish in seeing me at my lowest after berating him at the funeral. Option C is that he just loves to be a part of all my family lows. He craves our misery. As we walk down a long hallway, into an elevator and out through the lobby, Kyle actually makes an attempt at being human. "Look Michael, you got dealt a pretty shitty hand from what we understand. Now the doctor couldn't tell us specifically what's wrong, but we do know you're sick. While that sucks to be sure, you can't just act like an asshole and scare everyone as a result. Think before you act. Your dad would expect at least that from you."

"You're right," I say while hanging my head in shame. This is not a time to argue. Today, Kyle is the better man.

"I took care of everything. It's the least I could do. Your dad is still an icon around here. His son being in a cell doesn't sit right with anyone."

He's waiting for a thank you, which I begrudgingly have to give him.

"There's actually something I've been meaning to speak with you about."

This guy actually wants to connect with me on some level. "There's nothing I want to hear, Kyle. Just because you're right today, does not mean you were then." He tries to get me to hear him out, but I'm not having any of it. "What's done is done, and I hate you for it. I always will. So thanks for helping me out, but next time, I'll take what I have coming to me. No amount of help for me will make up for what you did to him."

That walk out of the police station is quite poignant. You know you're leaving a place you hope to never see again. That's rare. It almost carries the same weight as the last time you walk the hallways of your high school. I guess it depends what you're in for. To some, leaving jail would be far more impactful. As the door swings shut behind me I look back into the dark hallway where Kyle stands. He didn't try to put up a fight. That's a good thing; no more fighting for today.

It's 5:25 in the afternoon, but feels like days have passed. I decide that it would be a good idea to take a cab, pick up my dad's truck and head over to his place to start learning a bit more about this disease. For a moment, while I stand in that parking lot, I contemplate going inside the doctor's office to apologize. Saner heads prevail. I already acted poorly. Now it's time to act as if I'm my father's son, and draw strength from fear.

Another two-hours go by before I walk through the door with a loaf of bread, back into the dust. I make myself some peanut butter and jam sandwiches, then sit down to learn everything I can about pancreatic Cancer. Turns out, I have gotten a really raw deal. When the doc said I am in stage four, he was speaking about the Ann Arbor staging system. Simply put, the Cancer is basically everywhere. It's spread from my pancreas to other organs, and a transplant at this stage is not in the cards. I'm staring at a screen with the worst information possible. Getting shot at this point would be a mercy kill.

I make two trips to the copy store on the corner—one to buy more printer paper, and the other to buy more ink. When it's all said and done, I have about 800 pages of paper detailing the fight in front of me. My dad covered the walls with his paper, now it's my turn.

Two days pass until the printing and hanging of papers is done. I absorb about as much information as one man can regarding Cancer and all things *pancreas*. I basically have two options—treatment with the likelihood of death and no treatment with certain death. Both meant I would likely not see the end of the year, but depending on which road I take, one would be considerably more painful than the other. The real question is, how do I tackle this thing? Do I go the Western medicine route, or holistic? I've thought a lot about this debate in the past, as Cancer has always been a looming threat in my family. Sure, all families have a ton of Cancer in their tree, but my family has lost nearly everyone to this disease. While holistic carries a lot of weight, there's no question that modern medicine has benefited us. However, it's such a corrupt system, so it's hard to come up with a clear answer. Anytime you get a bunch of old men in a room, making decisions that could impact their greedy nature, they win; we lose. It's that simple. Again, you may think I'm a cynic, but consider this: You're at a bank requesting a loan. The bank manager says, *I'll give you $100,000 if you develop your product using the cheaper method, because you're likely to make more, or $50,000 to develop your product the more expensive way, thus minimizing our risk.* What do you choose? Now amplify that by billions, multiple it by unlimited quantities, factor in everything you've ever dreamed of having in this life, and you tell me if the rich old men can be trusted to make the decisions that are best for you and I?

Cancer is industry. It's a computer, a car, massages, hockey cards, clothing; Cancer is a product to be enhanced and packaged. Luckily for the rich old men, we are given Cancer, and then need to spend money to deal with it. Just like a computer is upgraded, a car has options, massages are timed, hockey cards are traded, and wardrobe is added to—Cancer is just the beginning, and there's a lot of money in helping people deal with it. Nature makes the product, man benefits.

I've seen videos on Facebook with new tech and procedures. There's even one that tricks Cancer cells into eating other cells that kill them. It's really cool stuff, but while I may have some money after Martial left everything to me, I don't have enough to get on those trials, and even if I did, I have no idea where I would start. This is where the Internet comes in really handy. I can't begin to imagine what it must have been like just two decades ago when someone got a Cancer diagnosis. The only information available to them would have been that of a brochure, and whatever the doctor chooses to tell them. Now, we have all the information we could possibly need, and then some. Once you learn how to filter out the crap, you're golden.

800 pages of paper is a lot of info. Have you ever tried to read a book that big? Most of us haven't. It's a daunting task, but I've done it. I need time to think about all of this; absorb, digest, process. Now that I have all of the details organized my brain knows it's time for some sleep. Over 48-hours is a long time to go without some shut eye, but that's what I've done.

It's for a good cause, as they say. Exhaustion sets in again, and I can't even bring myself to get up from the computer chair. My eyes get heavy, and my mind's eye conjures up images of my youth. My dreams will take me to a place without Cancer. As I slip into that dream state my arms fall, my body relaxes, and my head slips back.

You know you're tired when.

4

Fight Club

FIGHT! FIGHT! FIGHT! FIGHT! The sounds of kids screaming and yelling at a prepubescent pitch sounded more like hungry puppies than blood thirsty emperors cheering on their Gladiators. Here I was, all of ten, and embroiled in my first fight. I stood there in that field behind my school with my fists up, pretending like I knew what I was doing. I didn't know how to fight. I'd never even tried. Dad had taught me some wrestling moves, but I guess he felt I was too young for fisticuffs. Of course, I knew about as much as I'd seen on TV, or in movies. Right foot and fist forward, left side back, pick your spot and hit. That's about as far as my knowledge of combat went. Still, there I was, standing in a circle of of my classmates about to fight the class bully on a warm spring day. The sun was shining, the birds were chirping, and the grass was freshly green. Even the air smelt good. The beauty of nature sharply clashed with the ugliness of kids screaming and hoping to see some blood.

My opponent's name was Kirk Jennings, and as far alpha males in grade school go, he was the chosen one. With about three or four inches on the tallest kids in our school—giving him five inches on me—Kirk was feared every time he walked down the halls. There were stories about his father abusing him, but nothing was ever really proven that I knew about—not that anyone would tell a ten year old if something went down. He picked on everyone, and today just happened to be my day in the spotlight.

One of three things was going to happen.

a. I was going to die at the hands of Kirk.

b. I would discover that I had a warrior with powers in me the entire time, but I needed an event such as this to bring them out, just like in the comics.

c. I would be so bad at fighting that I would become a laughing stock amongst my classmates, and I wouldn't die. No. Not right away. My soul would be broken by the cruel kids of the fifth grade, forcing me to transfer to a new school, only for the camera phone footage to end up haunting me there, too.

My first fight was over a locker that was assigned to me, and I couldn't trade even if I wanted to. Let's just say my school was no Excelsior, and we were not the gifted children of this world, so the subtlety of the situation was lost on the bully. Kirk would taunt me by calling me *Mikey*, over and over again. He knew it drove me nuts. The thing about bullies is, they're generally smarter than the rest of the kids on the playground. They can smell fear, and pick up on the factors in this world that annoy people. This gives them power. They press your buttons until someone takes them down or they're punching you in the face, which is what happened next.

Kirk hit me square in the right eye, which sent me flailing and falling to the ground at the feet my peers. I froze as soon as he came at me. Not one muscle in my body moved, except to brace for the punch. He didn't waste any time, jumping on me and continuing to throw hay makers at my body and face. All I could do is cover up and hope for the best. After about a minute, teachers broke up the fight. Kirk was unscathed. I had a bloody nose, swollen eye, and I hurt all over. Teachers yelled at the other kids to move along, but those that liked to challenge authority stuck around to laugh at me. I could hear the whispers; *wimp*, *loser*, and *dummy* were some of the popular insults. Like I said, we weren't gifted children.

The school sent us both home, and since it was a Thursday, the Principal politely requested our parents keep us there until Monday. Martial was at work, and my mom didn't have a cell phone so no one could get ahold of her. That meant I had to walk home. The school nurse had stopped any bleeding, which helped but I was still sore all over. Each step left me wincing a bit but I didn't want to give Kirk the pleasure of knowing I was in pain, so when the Principal asked if I was okay to walk home, I lied. By the time I reached the doorstep, I felt like passing out. Once inside, I immediately went to bed.

Most parents would reprimand their children for fighting at school, but not Dad. He reassured me that getting beat up was nothing to be ashamed of, that a weakness had merely been exposed which I had to turn into a strength. He felt now that I was in the position to learn, it was time to pass on his knowledge that would keep me safe, but I was in the *lick-my-wounds* stage, and had no interest in listening. The mere suggestion of Jiu-Jitsu sent me back to my room crying. I'm sure Dad would have gladly traded me in for another model in that moment, *weak little crying boy*. I ran to my room and stayed there for most of the weekend. Getting hit hurt, and I had no interest in going through that again. I also figured—like most kids—that size was all that mattered. I was small for my age, skinny—almost frail. In my mind, there was no way I could do anything about Kirk wanting to beat me up again if he wanted to.

That is, until my dad slipped a VHS tape into my room. I pulled it out of it's dusty cover, and played the tape. What I saw was my dad kicking ass. Martial law was declared in his dojo. Not one person came close to taking on my dad. The sight of him taking down guys, and manhandling the Kirk's of the world excited me to my core. He too, was not the biggest, but he was the toughest. A week later, I was standing in front of him on mats, wearing a traditional Jiu-Jitsu uniform, very eager to learn. That first day was exhilarating. Of course, I couldn't do much, but I learned a lot. When I look back at my childhood, this was the first moment I felt any sort of rush or power. I didn't want the afternoon to come to an end.

The really exciting part of the day was watching Dad and the teacher take each other on. Dad had met Carmine when they served in the war together. They were good friends and always down for some friendly competition. I learned that my dad still attended Jiu-Jitsu twice a week to keep his skills sharp. It showed when Carmine couldn't get the upper hand.

"Your dad is a tough man, Michael," Carmine said as he walked off the mat, breathing deeply. "Listen to him and bullies at your school won't have a chance."

"I can't wait to find Kirk," I replied, while making

some gestures in the air thinking I was already a black belt.

They both laughed and told me to go change.

I really connected with Dad that day, but it was important that he taught me violence is a last resort, and having the ability to fight does not make the man. *You fight when no other recourse is available*—that was his mantra. He made sure to let me know that while I wasn't in trouble for my first fight, if I go back to school and seek out Kirk, I would be.

"Learning Jiu-Jitsu is about more than just physical power. It builds character and teaches you that only through practice will you ever get good at anything in this life. While most people take the easy route, you're given a skill set that will help you react to all kinds of situations. A smart fighter will walk away from more fights than he'll be in, simply because he knows he can win; fairness and understanding being the lessons here. Life is filled with conflict, and it's how we react to that, which is the true character of a man." At least, I'm pretty sure that's how Dad's speech went.

Monday came and so did Kirk. I walked away from his attempts to fight me time-and-time again. Eventually, he moved on to his next victim, and I was left alone. I didn't win any popularity contests for what I had done, but as I learned more skills in Jiu-Jitsu, I found an inner-pride through my actions. My grades improved because Carmine and my dad taught me how to focus. Out of nowhere, C's turned to A's, and my reputation as a wimp faded. I became known as the kid you want to cheat off of. Still, I wasn't very popular, but I found a group of friends in the smarter kids of my grade.

Two years later, in grade seven, Kirk was in the hallway beating on a kid from grade five. His violence kept escalating, and this time, he was trying to slam a locker door on the kid's head. With no one around, I had no choice but to teach him a lesson that he'd never forget. It took but three hits to put him on his ass, and a fourth to put him down for good. The bully in him died that day, and in his place was left a boy too scared to step out of line. For this public service, I received no punishment. The kid in grade five was so grateful for my help, as were his parents, that I was given a pass.

Throughout the years, Jiu-Jitsu would be just one of the many classes I took with Dad; firearms training, boxing, parkour before there was such a thing. Many nights after classes, Dad and I would sit and talk, like friends. That's what really tore me up when he left—I lost a father, but more importantly, I lost a friend.

5

Queen Elizabeth

I WAKE FROM MY SLEEP stiff from the chair. How one even falls asleep like this I don't know. My neck is all kinds of cricked, but nothing a really satisfying crack can't cure. The stiffness in my back tries to keep me down as I get up. After two attempts to stand, I'm up on my feet, slightly dizzy, but no worse for wear. I'll never fall asleep like that again. My research stares back at me as I focus my eyes on the room around me. When I fell asleep it was 5pm. Unbelievably enough, it was now early morning—2:15am. I slept for over nine-hours in an office chair. My body doesn't let me forget how angry it is with me throughout the day.

As I walk down the hall to the living room, I decide it is now time to make this place look like a home. One can't live amongst dust and dirty dishes forever. Two-floors of dirt await. The bedrooms and bathroom are upstairs, kitchen, dining room, living room, and office; on the main floor. Even though the place is under 900 square feet, it will take forever to clean. When you can simply wipe any surface with your finger to reveal black smudge, you know there's some cleaning needed.

Once I start, it feels like the mess starts to multiply. I clean like a madman, starting in the kitchen, washing dishes that had sat for over a week. The bedrooms and bathroom are next. It's so gross that I fill the vacuum twice. In the living room, where it is clear Dad spent most of his time, I wash everything including the little wall space without papers hanging. I open up two closets to find them stacked and stuffed full of crap. I'll leave those for another time. Martial let this place become a pigsty. A small castle for a king without it's servants to keep it fit for the royalty. I guess I'm just looking to think about something besides Martial's death and mine. As the hours wear on, it feels like this place will never be as spick and span as my doctor's office.

Eventually though, the smell of *clean* enters my nose to my sense's delight. I get a real feeling of accomplishment out of the task. It's been almost six hours since I started cleaning, and it looks like a new home, short of the papers on the walls throughout, and a bunch of books and magazines strewn around the living room. I make an attempt to stack them neatly but the entire pile falls over ... twice. Frustrated and over it, I decide to leave the pile in a collapsed heap. As I go to turn away, the light from my dad's gigantic TV catches the title of a binder that was tucked away in the middle. The title *Obsession Roadmap* is written on the cover in blue marker across two pieces of masking tape. I guess Martial had never heard of the label aisle at Staples; keeping it old school.

Obsessed was the word that my dad used in his note to me, so I'm intrigued. I grab the book and head over to the only chair in the living room, pointed at that giant TV. I guess he wasn't planning on entertaining anyone, and given my limited circle of friends and family, I don't see parties in this home anytime soon.

From the moment I open the front cover, I'm hooked. Inside I find a road map for the walls written in a shorthand language Dad taught me years before. It was kinda our way to communicate with no one knowing what we were talking about; maybe consider it English 2.0. Whenever my mom did something to piss me off I'd writes notes to Dad in this shorthand. He would write back, and my mom was none the wiser.

Turns out the chaos on the walls isn't actually chaotic at all. There is a purpose behind this mess. It would appear that my dad was keeping a diary that contained the illicit affairs of many of the city's worst criminals. The papers on the walls were like reference material. Think of a paper published on the Internet, with the links to each source. Once again, Martial keeping it old school meant the "paper on the Internet" would be this diary of sorts, and the pages on the walls are those links. The information is so detailed, from drug dealing to child molestation, and even murder. My dad literally wrote the book on crime in our city.

Hours go by as I connect the passages in the book with the crimes on the walls. Dad created the ugliest, most sadistic piece of art he could muster up. You'd have to be obsessed, and frankly dark, to be surrounded by this much horrific imagery every waking day. The stories that Martial wrote about really got to me. Dane Cook once told a joke about checking the child molester map online. He talked about all the dots that popped up, and how disturbing it was. This took that concept to a whole new level. Everything's documented from the crimes themselves, to the half-baked reasons that criminals were released from prison, to their whereabouts, haunts, and there are bios on almost everyone. John Grisham would consider my dad's work the Holy Grail of research. I can't imagine how long this must have taken him. The earliest passage I can find dates back about ten years ago; right around the time Dad left us behind.

As I make my way into the bedrooms following the book's order, I find that Dad has a small section dedicated to Kyle. Various news clippings about busts that Kyle was involved in cover about three feet of wall space. I guess Martial's side project was to try and find something that could get Kyle fired, just as Kyle did to him. Oh, I wish for a chance to bring that fucker down. It would be sweet irony, and such a rewarding task before I die.

You walk through life under the assumption that generally speaking, everything is going to be alright. You don't commit crimes, or hang out with the wrong people, so you're safe. This book contests such assumptions. Martial wrote of his frustrations with crime stats, calling them lies and political bullshit. There are some really messed up people out there, just looking for their next victim the way we would look for the right kind of cheese at a grocery store. No wonder Mom and Dad couldn't see eye to eye; they existed in two different worlds, and I was quickly packing my bags to move into my dad's.

He was right. This wasn't depression. I mean, yes, I could see how Mom thought that, but knowing now what he knew then ... everything would be dark. Depression, though? Based on my limited knowledge, depressed people don't function very well. Martial was highly functioning. His notes are meticulous; his reference material, spotless. No, Martial wasn't depressed. He was more realistic than anything, I think. Real on a level that many of us can't possibly comprehend. He wrote stories about encountering criminals in the mall or at a restaurant, just living their lives like they hadn't killed or harmed anyone. He wondered if their families and friends knew what they had done, and occasionally would drop a post card in the mail to enlighten certain people who were clearly oblivious.

Martial would write about stakeouts, even though he wasn't a cop anymore. He'd study criminals, and build a case against them. Every five or ten pages he would re-write his goal: *The largest apprehension of the city's criminals*. It would appear that he was building up this evidence to really deal a blow to the heart of the city's criminality. Martial wrote about what needs to happen in the city for it to survive.

> Taking them down one at a time won't do. No matter how it's done, they need to go down all at once to win!

I guess most cops just deal with the hits as they come; Martial was studying the ugly side of the city, welcoming the hits. That had to take a toll. I read, and research. Hours go by this way, and I'm not too much of a man to admit that some of the stories really freak me out.

> Jason White
> Drug Dealer & Pedophile
>
> Jason's whole M.O. is getting mother's hooked on his product long enough, so that when

they run out of money, those addicted moms will offer up their kids to him in exchange for their next fix. He has spent years in-and-out of jail, constantly beating the system with shifty lawyers, and convoluted alibis. Currently he's in jail awaiting trial, but that won't stick for long. The arresting officer was close with one of the mothers and really laid into Jason, leaving him with a couple broken ribs. All the lawyers have to do is prove the cop beat him, and the charges will be dismissed.

Carey Greening
Burglar & Pyromaniac

There are few women in my book, but Carey makes up for the sexual inequality by being a bad bitch. She always breaks into homes with animals. After stealing she leaves a calling card similar to the burglars in Home Alone. Only, her calling card wasn't for the faint at heart. Before leaving, Carey lights the family pet on fire. Amazingly enough she's never been caught because she has never been placed at the scene of the crime. As if she isn't a big enough scumbag, she picks low income families as victims, knowing they can't afford security systems or cameras. She was once brought in for questioning, and actually admitted to her crimes off the record, and then accused the officer of sexual assault when he turned off the camera. This is one sick bitch.

Ryan Tyler
Rapist

I can't count the number of times I arrested Ryan. He made the news plenty of times, which couldn't have made him happier. He's currently serving life in prison, and was sentenced recently. It's been said that he's raped over 30 women, but could only be prosecuted for five. I'm glad he's off the streets—fucking animal.

Allister Becket

White Collar Scum Bag

Allister's story is well known because he's just one of many to rip off middle class families with a stock market scam. Allister is currently on house arrest awaiting trial. It's not much of a punishment considering his house is an eight bedroom, 3 bathroom castle, complete with a movie theatre. The chances of him seeing any jail time are slim. White collar crime is hard to prosecute even with clear cut evidence. It's more likely one of his victims goes ape shit and kills Allister. Then the victim will go to jail for life, which is the perfect example of the system not working.

These are just some of the humans Martial surrounded himself with. Many of these class acts had case files on them from when Dad worked on the force. He really did know them better than they likely knew themselves. As I read through these stories, I can't help but tear up at times. The emotion just overcomes me. From the papers on the walls to the diary, I connect the worlds of some truly disgusting people.

WE ONLY KNOW WHAT WE KNOW, AND THAT IS LIKELY NOT EVEN HALF OF IT!

Martial wrote this on page 171 in big bold lettering. He etched the words in to the page, nearly tearing the paper. In that moment, Martial was mad!

Then I get to page 172, and reference to a section of the house I had yet to check out—the basement. It didn't even occur to me that I should go down there. Most of the houses in this area have pretty shanty basements, full of cobwebs, and mould. Martial's is no exception. There is little more than some crappy old furniture, and a bunch of building supplies. It's really quite ugly and gross. I hate the moisture in the air of old basements.

It doesn't quite have that serial killer vibe, but I would easily believe that a new breed of spider was taking over a basement like this; so creepy. Given his system for locating parts of the house referenced in his book, I figure this particular set of articles should be in a closet on the North wall. It's easy to de-code the encryption in the book with the locations; Martial used superhero references as a key. It's like he wrote this all out for me.

When I open the door to the closet I find nothing but a stack of floor tiles, leaving me to wonder why he referenced this location. There's a chance that he moved whatever was here, and it's now located elsewhere. The book is so detailed though. I have an uneasy feeling—instinct maybe, that I'm not supposed to walk away from this dirty, dusty closet. The light isn't very good, so I have to feel around inside. Nothing but more cobwebs now attached to my hand. Getting it off is never an easy task, but eventually I shed my Spider-Man traits.

I look down at those floor tiles. None of them seem to match any floor I've seen in the house. All that is left to do is dig. I start tossing tiles out across the basement. It's already a disaster so why not fuck it up even more? Its kinda fun, in a destructive way—therapeutic even. My dad had jars of nails and different little bolts across the room, hanging from a crappy work bench. The tiles become bullets for target practice; I love the sound of smashing glass, and nothing is safe. After about two-minutes I've made a huge mess and discover two big green garbage bags basically buried in a hole under the tiles. The papers referenced in the diary must be in these bags. It's not the best filing system in the world, but who am I to question the old man at this point?

I tear into one of the bags to verify that my instinct was right, and it kinda was. There's plenty of paper inside. I stand back for a moment, staring at the contents of the bags, then through them. I snap out of it and pull the bags out of the closet. The first, I place on a shelf behind me. The second one snags on some of the tiles and rips. Thousands of little Queen Elizabeth's stare me down. As I tug harder, I slip and fall on my ass. The bag on the shelf tips over and bathes me in thousands of tiny little Robert Bordens.

For whatever reason my dad had two big garbage bags full of money stashed in the basement of a shitty little house, in a shitty little neighbourhood. Well actually, I guess *I* have two big garbage bags full of money stashed in *my* basement. *What was he doing with all of this cash?* The little kid in me comes out. I throw bills into the air, and watch as they float down over me. The holograms catch light from a small basement window in such a way that for seconds at a time as I toss that money in the air, it appears I have a mirror ball in this dilapidated basement.

After I'm done playing in the money, I run upstairs to crank some Kanye. I feel so alive, which is a huge feat in the face of death. Ripping through the cupboards, I find a bottle of vodka. Off comes the cap, and down it goes. I order up some Chinese, because, well, why the hell not? It's the most expensive food I can think of, and when you live your life on McDonalds and Subway, only to find a ton of money, you splurge. I dance up and down the stairs as I collect the money and pile it in one of the bedrooms. When it's all said and done, I have just over four-million dollars stacked in front of me on the bed. Four-million! From head board to the foot of the bed, piles of money stack up to form a beautiful sight. Sure, I'm dying, but I'm a rich man dying. There are worse ways to go.

The Chinese arrives—$160 plus a $40 tip. The delivery guy leaves happy, even if he is a bit of a let down. I want that authentic, *you get wice and chicken baw* experience; not some vanilla, pimple faced, teenager. It's not racial, it's cultural. Not one to hold a grudge, I feast on chicken fried rice and barbecue lean pork in front of the TV while watching that really bad Brandon Routh take on Superman. Why did they think it would be a good idea to introduce Superboy? I'm just happy they finally figured out how to tell the Supes story properly with Henry Cavill.

Full and drunk, you'd think I feel pretty good. I mean, who can complain when they have more money than they could possibly spend? Oh right, me, the Cancer patient. I hadn't even thought about the disease for hours, but of course just as I'm finishing my food—as I turn off the movie—a commercial for Cancer medication comes on. *Fuck you*, whoever it is that programs this shit! I was doing so well, just thinking about being rich. Then the thought of symptoms creep back into my head. I'll lose weight, my stomach and back will ache more, I'll have trouble going to the washroom ... there's quite the list of wonderful issues to look forward to. That's just the disease. You add in chemo or radiation and now I'm puking all the time, and too weak to stand. I know I have to make a decision regarding treatment, but I just can't bring myself to make that choice tonight.

Here's the thing about all of it; I have no one to take care of me. Even if miraculously some woman knocks on my door and instantly falls in love with me, it wouldn't be fair to make her a part of this mess of a disease. These facts alone are swaying me to the *live fast and die quick* mindset. Hell, I have the money to do it now. Why not go out sky diving, drinking, partying, and traveling? It sounds like as good a plan as any. It sure as fuck sounds like a better plan than getting treatment, only to learn it has failed, and I'm left dying in a bed I haven't moved from in weeks. BUT, of course, the thought of dying is scary, and my instinct is to hold on as long as possible. I also don't want to die without doing something truly awesome that people will talk about after I'm gone. Man, how does anyone decide what to do in these cases?

No decisions will be made tonight. Instead, I polish off the vodka and drag my ass to bed. Tomorrow, I'll start on option A—living fast.

6

Shot Down

THE HOSPITAL can be a scary place to visit. I remember the day dad was shot clearly.

I was cozy in my slumber, dreaming of whatever it is that kids who have hit puberty dream about. My mom came bursting into my room like a bullet out of gun. The sound of the door hitting the wall woke me sharply. As my haze gave way to clarity, I could see her frantically pushing clothes in my closet across the pole used to hang my shirts. The scraping noise of the hangers against the worn painted metal was not a welcome sound at ... 5:24am! *Why is my mom in my room looking for clothes at 5:24am?*

She found what she was looking for and tossed a shirt I'd never wear otherwise, sweats that didn't go with the shirt, and boxers, nearly missing my head and hitting the wall behind my bed. "We're going to the hospital," she says, as she power walks out of my bedroom.

Hospital? Oh no, the hospital! I don't know why I didn't see it sooner. This is *the drill*. My parents prepared me for the day my dad was seriously injured at work. Knowing how grumpy children can be about having to get out of bed, the drill was hammered into me young. "Don't give your mom any shit if I get hurt", Dad would say regularly.

I jumped out of bed, and frantically put on the mismatched outfit mom picked out for me. Within two-minutes, we were out the door, and speeding towards the hospital. The street lights captured my mom's tears that streamed down her face for just a moment at a time. I'd never seen this face. I'd seen my mom happy, sad, angry and disappointed, but this face was new to me—despair. That's the only word that comes to mind to describe the absolute definition of the lines, tears, and brokenness in her eyes.

While I was taught the drill young, it was but a drill. No one actually thought that Dad could get hurt. I mean, we all knew he was human, but he'd been through so many bad situations that it just seemed like he'd always find his way out without a scratch. Bullets can come from anywhere though, so no one's immune to their effects. Great men have been shot, and Martial was just another in that long line of greats.

As we arrived at the hospital, we immediately saw the many cops lined up, trying to look strong, instead of sad. Dad was the ultimate cop, so him being in the hospital had to weigh heavily on their minds. My mom left me with the guys to talk to a doctor. The reassurance started. *Your dad is tough, he'll be fine. Nothing can stop Martial*. I'm not sure people should say such things when they have no idea what they're talking about. Cops are cops, not doctors. They meant well, as do all people in situations such as these, but in hindsight, perhaps they should have just said, *We're here for you and your mom*.

By 8:05am, Martial was out of surgery, and matter

of factly, he would be fine; it seemed that truly nothing could stop him. As we walked from the waiting area, crowded with other patients and the cops that stayed, I remember feeling scared for what awaited me in that hospital room. Not fully understanding what a gunshot could do to a person, I had images of gaping holes and veins permanently popped from Martial's neck to his forehead in my mind. The reality was much less dramatic. He looked like ... well, Dad.

The look was the same, but the feeling was not. He could barley keep his eyes open, and every movement made him grunt like a dog with a chew toy. Pain was his reality now, and that was not something I'd become accustomed to. The doctor came into the room a short time later and asked to speak to my mom and dad—I was sent to the waiting room. Before I went into the room, I heard the cops talking—telling the tale of how Martial was shot.

"The guy beat him down pretty good and then just shot him. I've never seen anything like it," said one cop. "I wish we could have gotten to him. There was just too much happening; too many people."

"He got owned. I guess it's time that Martial maybe take a step back," said another.

"There's no training to prepare you for a guy like that," echoed another boy in blue. "Martial is the man, but a guy like that is a genetic freak."

It's in that moment that I decided to give up on the Jiu-Jitsu classes, shooting ... violence as a whole. Martial had all that training, and then some, but still ended up in a bed with a small hole in his body. Violence would have no place in my life. In fact, from that moment on, I avoided fights like the plague, although I did maintain some of the mental conditioning. That never goes away. Fighting though? That wasn't an option.

Exhibit A: Bar Fight. One night, I'm out at a bar with my friend Derek, when this guy decides that I'm standing too close to him. He pushed me, called me a pussy, told me he's going to fuck my mom, throws a drink on me, continues to call me a bunch of other names—some sensical, some not; none of it matters. I backed down, and went home.

Exhibit B: The Cut Off. I accidentally cut some guy off, and he followed me until I parked. This guy spent the next ten-minutes giving me shit while I sat in my locked car. He hit the windows, again I'm called a pussy, he kicked my headlight out—the works. Still, I did nothing.

Exhibit C: My Favourite. After grabbing a morning coffee before going to the last day on the job I hated, I saw that bitch that stole those office supplies chirping with her friend while watching me out of the corner of her eye. They were, no doubt talking about my eminent dismissal from that fantastic employment. I got to work, the boss called me in, fired me, and while doing so, he drank my damn coffee. Then, as I left his office, he told me he should have kicked my ass for stealing, but he won't because, and I quote, "I've taken three boxing classes, and don't want to hurt you." *Three? Bitch, I took years of training.* Still, I walked away.

I am a pussy, but a pussy that has never laid in a hospital bed due to getting my ass kicked. Yep, seeing Dad down and out like that did the trick. I would never fight again. Around this time was when my mom and dad started to argue a lot more. Once Dad was released from the hospital my mom had no respect for what everyone called Martial time. This was a few hours every couple of nights where Dad would lock himself in his office and do whatever it was he felt was important. One night, my mom showed how tough she could be and kicked in the office door. Night-after-night, they would end up screaming at each other, and all I could do was put pillows over my ears. Every weekend my mom would send me over to Derek's place to stay a couple of nights. Derek's parents were great but for the first time I was missing Saturdays with Dad, and every time I came home I could feel the tension in the air.

Then, the next blow to Martial's manhood would prove to be much worse than being shot. I was never told the full story, but from what I could piece together, the guy that shot Dad claimed self defense after being manhandled by Martial. Somehow this drug dealing piece of shit got the upper-hand and got Martial to the ground. They struggled for the gun, and Martial ended up shot on the pavement in some ratty neighbourhood. Kyle would back the guy's story, and the rest was history. What never made sense is why Kyle would back the guy's story. You always hear about the cop code, but it just didn't apply in this case. I'll always assume he is a dirty cop.

Dad came home after being let go from the force and was quiet every day after. There was no talking to him. He just sat in his office and didn't want anything to do with us. This went on for about a year, until my mom forced Dad into some counseling sessions. That didn't work, and in fact probably made things worse, because Dad didn't want to be at home much anymore, so he'd be gone at odd hours without explanation. A friend of my mom's started hanging around. I would later find out that mom was having an affair with the man. I guess if you're going to ignore your family, your wife is going to seek some sort of connection elsewhere.

One day, in fact, I came home from school and mom was sitting in the middle of the living room with a note in her hand crying.

"Mom, what happened to the living room?" I asked. The pictures were off the walls, a table was flipped over and the TV was broken.

"You never mind that," she said, clearly avoiding the fact that she trashed the place. "Here, your dad left this for you."

It was a single page, hand-written note:

> Son. Three things have hurt me. Being shot, being fired, and now being without you. This is the worst, but for the best. Take care. Dad.

That was seriously all he had to say. I went to school in the morning, and came home to a note. That was that for a great man robbed of his existence, shot down in too many ways. I was angry and confused, of course, as any kid would be ... but mostly, I just wanted to reverse my life lessons.

"What does this mean? Where's Dad going?"

"He's left and that's all there is to say."

I immediately started to cry. "Go get him!" I demanded.

"Michael, he's not coming back. You're just going to have to accept it." There was no motherly embrace, or sympathy. I think my mom had already ran out of emotion over a year ago.

We sat there in awkward silence. Tears streamed down my face, and my body language begged her for a hug, but all she could do is continue to sip on her rum and Coke. "I hate you, and I hate him!" I screamed, as I stomped off to my bedroom.

For awhile I thought Dad was a fraud, and it only further reinforced my path away from any training

I had undergone. All of sixteen years old, and I had already made a course correction in my life. Six years of training, gone, because in the end it takes a knife, or gun, or someone tougher to come along and make it all not worth the fight.

7

Buying Life

AS A NEW DAY BEGINS I wake with excitement; the kind that I felt as a kid when a birthday was on the horizon. My giddiness is unparalleled, and giddiness is not a word I take lightly. In this world, there really isn't too much four-million dollars can't buy you, especially when you're walking around with an expiry date. Especially when you come from very little. Especially when it's tax free. Especially, especially ... I could go on for days. That money is waiting to be spent, and the quickest way to do so is to start with the mall.

But before I go live a rapper lifestyle—to kick things off—today is the first day that I officially start my post-diagnosis diet and work out routine. It feels good to lace up and get outside for a jog. I also get a chance to check out the neighbourhood while I listen to some house and pound the pavement. This end of town is a weird mix of expensive homes and dilapidated dens. It feels like each block has it's own identity. You don't see that often. Usually neighbourhoods are segmented, but not here. I follow up the jog with some body weight training in the living room, before sitting down to some egg whites, toast, and ham. I usually add syrup and ketchup to the mix, but I've read enough to know that sugar is the devil at the best of times, and these are not the best of times.

I call up my buddy Derek, and tell him to meet me at the mall for noon. Derek is one of the few guys that I can actually stand, and the only friend that I've had nearly my entire life. His parents took care of me after Martial left, and Mom started drinking more. He's not overly into sports (worshiping young men in uniform), he doesn't try to "slay chicks" every night at the bar (I can't understand why any woman would want most men in this day and age. Be free, be lesbians!), and he's not needy (favour free). That last quality is important.

I feel like somewhere along the way men have lost their ability to man up. I think it happened somewhere between watching Sailor Moon instead of He-Man, collecting Yu-Gi-Oh instead of hockey cards, and when backpacks and briefcases were replaced with the murse. Derek is just like me, in that he grew up with a strong male role model, always wanted to be a super hero, and when he has a problem ... he figures it out. There are no counsellors, tears, blogging, or boring people to death—we all have our own set of problems.

Our values are pretty similar as well. We know you compliment someone when they're nice, give them shit when they're not, and under no circumstances do you ever quit (I've come close). We don't need to talk every day for him to feel a sense of self-worth, like some of the "men" I've come to know. He's not self-indulgent, just a friend. We call each other up when we feel like it, so naturally I call him up when it's time to have some fun.

As I step foot in the mall, I feel a rush. The mission is to spend like crazy, eat like a King in what will be my last unhealthy meal, and just have a good time. You're probably thinking that eating an unhealthy meal after my first healthy meal is counter-intuitive, but let's be honest—it's all about the baby steps when it comes to diet. You can eat sixteen salads and one donut, only to be filled with guilt for that one bad decision. Live a little, and do your best.

I figure spending the money will help take my mind off of this disease in me. We start at the Apple Store, where I buy myself a MacBook Air, drone, new iPhone, and some accessories. Those stores are always full of nerds in black rimmed glasses, blonds who can't understand why their iPhone contacts are gone after the latest update, and black guys stuck somewhere between the cool culture of blackness, and the acceptance of the whole for their geeky side. It's like a cultural mosaic wrapped up into one little store, and likely the reason why so many geeks can be seen with full blown hotties on their arm. Let's just say, it seems the Apple guys are less likely to be micro, and soft.

From there we hit Michael Kors where I pick up a watch that sparkles like a clear night sky. It's not the watch that I like the best, but the most expensive one in the store. I've always wanted to buy something just because I can. I guess I can strike that off of my bucket list. The saleslady is older, maybe in her early 50's. She takes good care of herself, and is just the right amount of flirtatious. I've always wanted to be with an older woman; see if they still have what it takes at their age, but alas, I just don't go for it. No ring, no filter, no reason not to—I just don't. As I walk away from the counter, I can feel her disappointment, or is that my disappointment? Who can be sure? I've actually only slept with five women—correction, girls—and they were all my age. I'll probably die never knowing the company of a real woman. In movies when a character finds out they are going to die, they grab life by the balls and do everything they've ever wanted to do. Here's hoping that instinct creeps into my life at some point.

Derek and I hop from store to store. Some of the crap I buy makes sense, some, not so much, but shopping is a good time when you have unlimited cash flow. As a kid, I wanted to be on that show, 'Supermarket Sweep'. Even though I'm male, for some reason I love to shop. I don't know if it's because it's out with the old, in with the new, or just because I'm a sad, sad consumer sheep, but it's a good time for me.

After a few hours of buying myself a new wardrobe, some of this and some of that (mostly items I'll likely use once), and doing our best to be subtle about checking out girls we'd never talk to, the decision is made that it's time to feast; I'm talking nachos, burgers, fries, beers, dessert—we go to town. The way I see it, this is probably my last meal with Derek before I need to eat completely healthy, and given our love for grease, this is just easier than answering any questions that might come from ordering a salad—I don't think I've ever ordered a salad; neither Garden or Caesar. Every time we order more the waitress looks at us like we're stealing meals directly out of a third-world kid's hands. Her judgment is actually kind of annoying. I mean, c'mon, you work at a restaurant. Why the sour face? More food, more service, more tip.

Once the plates are licked clean, the adrenaline of shopping and feasting starts to wear off and I can feel the darkness setting in. I try to convince myself that there is no deep dark corner in my life called Cancer, but no burst of energy comes to the surface. Really, I was hoping it would take longer than a couple of hours to feel like shit again. It's almost like a dullness, every time my mind snaps back to reality; there's a filter that has been put over life that is three shades of grey, and just a bit of white noise. Then comes the first real symptom. As I sit at the table, I feel my stomach turn, and the sudden urge to puke my guts out. I get to the toilet just in time, and throw up with authority. Before this, I might have thrown up two or three times; nothing like this though. It even comes out of my nose. After almost a minute with my face in the disgusting public toilet, I'm exhausted and sit on the floor. It takes everything out of me.

As I sit there, I become acutely aware that shopping won't cure what ails me. I wonder if anything will. This was a stupid idea to begin with. You can't buy life. It's not the way the world works. Man, I can be such a man child at times. I contemplate whether going back out there is a good idea or not. The nausea has passed, but the feeling of general shittiness is alive and well in my mind. Am I a bad person for trying to buy my way out of Cancer? Is it disgraceful to even try?

"You alright in there?" I hear a guy ask from the other side of the stall door.

"Yeah," I reply.

"You sure man? You're sitting on the floor. People don't generally sit next to a toilet when they feel good."

I take a beat and then open the stall door to see a hipster looking back at me. "Not feeling so hot."

"You're not looking so hot. Can I grab someone to help you out?"

"No. I'll be fine. The worst is over. Right now I'm just contemplating the mysteries of the universe while I build up enough energy to get up off of this floor."

"Well here, I'll help you out." He grabs me by the arm, and in one steady motion, picks me up off the floor.

"Nicely done."

"I'm a nurse at the hospital down the road from here. I've picked up many a person off the floor.

I splash some water on my face, and then it occurs to me that I have an opportunity to grab some info from this guy. "You're a nurse? So does that mean you take the oath doctors take?"

"Nope. They take the Hippocratic Oath. As a nurse, I had to take the Nightingale Pledge. It's fundamentally the same though."

"So if I were to ask you something about medicine in confidence you couldn't tell anyone?"

"Something on your mind?"

"I have Cancer."

We both take a moment. He wasn't ready for that, and this was the first person I told. "Sorry to hear that man. My name is Duncan."

"Michael."

"What kind of Cancer do you have, Michael?"

"Pancreatic. Stage four." Another beat. "I know I'm dying. I'm basically dead."

"There are new treatments coming out all the time."

"Well, my question isn't really about that."

"What do you want to know? I'll do my best to give you an answer."

"I'm coming to terms with my early departure from this earth, but today I just really wanted to go out, spend some money, buy some nice things, eat like a king, and enjoy myself. Then I end up in here puking my guts out, and I feel really stupid all of the sudden. I guess what I'm asking is, do you think it's wrong of me to try to buy my way out of feeling like shit?"

"Well, that's not what I was expecting. But, I'd have to say in my professional opinion, and just as a human being, the answer is no. You're not wrong for what it is you're doing. If you have the money to have a good time, have as many good times as you can. Just don't lose sight of what it is you need to do."

His answer really made me feel better about the day. Here we have a trained nurse who isn't looking down at my choice to get out and take my mind off things for a bit. Sure, it didn't work, but I can still enjoy myself. In fact, it's likely nothing will work, but I can't sit in darkness and wait to die. That's not a life at all.

"Thanks, man. I appreciate you taking the time."

"No problem. You know, I've seen miracles happen. It is possible for you to beat your Cancer." He has a look on his face immediately after he says that; almost as if he regrets it. I'll go out on the limb and say nurses aren't supposed to say such things, and instill hope in a hopeless situation. But, human-to-human, it was welcomed.

"I guess I have one more question then. If you were in my shoes, would you go for treatment, or would you just try to live life as best you can?"

"I can't actually answer that *for you*. Personally, I would do the treatment, but that's me. We're all different and we all want different things out of this life. It's really up to each patient individually. You seem like a good guy though. Find a reason to keep living and fight."

We do the guy head nod thing, and part ways. As I walk back to my table I feel better. Before I meet up with Derek again I find the manager and pay the nurse's bill. It's the least I can do for him taking the time. He really did set the stage for the rest of my day, and he deserves to be shown some appreciation. I haven't told Derek about my Cancer yet, and I know now that I won't. I'd been wrestling with the choice all day, but why bring the mood down now? I return to the table with a smile on my face. I tell Derek I ran into a friend in the washroom, and that's why it took me so long to get back to the table. He accepts the reason and continues to sip his beer. Why wouldn't he?

There's a big game on between the Blackhawks and the Ducks, and man is it intense. Every time a goal is scored or the ref makes a bad call, the lounge loses their minds. Now, the game is over, and my team won, so I buy the entire place shots. That made me feel good for about thirty-five seconds. Buy someone a $4 drink and you're a hero—pats on the back, adulation, and one table even chants, "This guy, this guy ..."

"Dude, I have to ask; where is all the money coming from?" Derek questions my spending like the child of Bill Gates.

I was rather unprepared for the question. I probably should have thought of a cover story beforehand, but perhaps I was just too damn excited to have so much money. "I actually picked up a job as a garbage man," I say with very little confidence. "Very lucrative. It's like picking up bags of money." Even though I know that Derek won't understand the clever and punny nature of my reply, I chuckle a bit in my own head. I'm not lying (not entirely).

He looks at me, confused, but even though I lack the ability to sell the story, he accepts what I'm saying as truth. Again, why wouldn't he? "I never would have thought picking up garbage would pay so well."

"Neither did I, but it's all working out pretty good."

"I'd say. Maybe I should drop out of university, and join you out on the mean streets."

"Yeah, that sounds like a solid plan for the future. Don't become a lawyer, pick up garbage!"

"You were always smarter than me. I still don't

get why you're not tryna get into something that challenges you."

"Lots of reasons that matter, a bunch that don't. Maybe one day," I say, completely avoiding the conversation.

We eat, and talk; mostly about nothing at all and nostalgic moments from years ago when we were a bit crazier and carefree, until he brings up Monica, "Have you talked to her yet? Asked her out? Does she know you even exist?"

"Well, I know that she knows I exist, but that I like her? Not one bit."

"Jesus man. You've been talking about her for what feels like decades. Just ask her out already."

"There are certain women that you need to bide your time with, and basically wait for a moment."

He balks at my explanation. "No, there are certain men that make excuses when it comes to certain women. Man, I have no idea how you go from being so confident in everything else you do, to sucking so hard with women. You could die tomorrow. Go get it!"

"That's nice. Thanks for that."

"I'm here for you brother," he says in the most condescending of tones.

"Look, I'll prove it to you. Let's hit a club tonight, and I'll talk to an endless sea of girls. I'll show you, it's the girl, not the entire side of the species."

"A hundred bucks says you don't talk to any females tonight, or any night for that matter."

After dinner, I drop my seemingly endless purchases off at the house, and then it's time to see who wins this bet. We hit up the club district, jumping from spot to spot, until we settle on our club of choice for the night. Two bottles, and four hours later, I end up owing Derek $100. It was a fool's bet, really. I'm not a ladies man. I just let my ego get in the way when I made the bet. I believe Monica to be my perfect woman ... even though I've spent no real time with her.

I can tell that she isn't like most girls I meet, just trying so hard to not let their emotional damage get in the way. She's confident but kind, except when you're late for an appointment. That I can tell by the way she talks to patients, and on the phone. Whenever the other nurse is working the front desk it's like talking to a wall. That nurse is cold, and couldn't give a shit about you. Monica speaks to the patients in such a way that they know they matter. She's genuine, unlike every girl at the club tonight. Don't get me wrong; they're fun to look at, with their extensions, push-up bras, and carefully crafted makeup. But there's little substance to a girl six shots into her night, ending things off with a hand between her sweaty thighs. Then again, on the flip side, I guess I'm that guy at the bar who drinks too much, and slurs his speech, as he self-indulgently declares himself important by way of money. Perhaps a club ho is about as good as it's going to get.

The music is awesome, and the vibe is perfect. Buying bottle service is the best way to go if you're not with any girls at the club. That's not because you'll attract bottle rats. No, it's perfect because two straight guys at the club dancing looks and feels wrong. It didn't feel that way just five-years ago, but nowadays it absolutely does. Instead, with bottles, you have a booth and you can rage out to the music without looking awkward and weird.

About half way through the night, I make my way into the bathroom. I barely know how I got there. As I take a piss at the urinal, I almost pass out. It's been a long day and someone needs to go home to bed. Two guys behind me start arguing about who's going to take home the hot girl that they've been talking to all night. *Hey guys, here's a tip, talk to two*, I think to myself. They go back and forth until I interject with some wisdom that only a drunk guy can offer. "You guys can't fight over a girl. Where's the love? You guys are bros, you need to be bros, be bros, c'moooooooooon." Pretty sure they could have done without that advice tonight, or ever.

The rest of the night is a fog. I would later learn that I ordered another bottle, tried to kiss our server, and then threw up on a security guard's pants. After the second puke in 24-hours, apparently I was an utter delight. I think it's safe to say that this time, Cancer had nothing to do with my need to spew. This was a rare night for me. I would usually drink one or two glasses, not bottles, but I guess everyone's entitled to the occasional shit show.

As I stumble into the house at around 3am, my eyes try to focus away from my dad's research and mine. This buzz feels pretty damn good, and reality can wait one more day. Getting my jeans off is a struggle. Drunk me can't seem to figure it out. I am Ahab, my jeans are the whale. I don't know why this is so hard! Oh wait, yes I do ... drink, drank, drunk. I give up and just fall onto the bed like a tower dropping to the ground. I'm pretty sure I pass out mid fall too. This will be a fantastic sleep, which I will enjoy, because the hangover is sure to be profound.

With not a thought in my head, I say good night to the world.

8

Mom

THE PHONE RANG LOUDLY in the middle of the night, waking me from an otherwise peaceful sleep. I always knew what was coming on the other end, but I never knew who would be calling. Throughout the years these types of calls had become more frequent. If ever there were a testament to how low we had sunk as a family, this would be what I would point to. In fact, these calls were the personification of my late-childhood strife. It was bad enough when the calls would come in, but then when it messed with my graduation from high school and everyone found out our deep, dark family secret, we were sunk. Any prestige left from the days of Dad living in the neighbourhood and Mom organizing the block BBQs was officially gone.

"Hello," I muttered, tired and half asleep.

"Is this Michael?" A voice on the other end questioned while trying miserably to not sound annoyed.

"Where is she?"

Twenty or thirty-minutes later, I would carry mom through the door of our apartment and drop her into bed. After the third time bringing my drunken mom home from a random spot in the city I started to keep a tally. This was drunken rescue number thirty-eight. Her friends, family, my friends, and even some random neighbours tried to get Mom help. There were three interventions, but on the last one only two people showed besides me. I checked her into rehab, but that lasted all of four days. Then there were all the times I would lock her in the apartment to stop her from going out. I could only do that for so long before I'd fall asleep or have to go to work.

The problem was that she technically wasn't breaking any laws. Mom never drove drunk, did anything all that stupid, or got into any altercations under the influence. She just drank until she was too drunk to stand. If she were 19 again, people would just call her *White Girl Wasted*, but my mom was 54 years-old and not exactly a cute little 19 year old that doesn't know any better. I was 20 at the time, but because of my mom, late rent, bills, and all that come with living paycheque-to-paycheque, I felt more like 50. It would seem we just switched ages.

We had to move to an apartment a couple of years after Dad left due to challenged finances. Mom gambled the money from the sale of the house away every night. The block was down the street from our old house, so she had to feel shitty every day when she'd drive past it to get where she was going. I always understood that her drinking and attitude were the result of pain, but you can only make excuses for someone for so long before you tire of their shit. At this point, I was exhausted. There was no helping her, and it had been over a year since she last expressed any interest in getting help.

I stared down at her laying in bed, not knowing

where she was. How could she? My mom was out cold, snoring like an old man. The things that would go through my head every time this happened:

a. I could just leave, but then who would take care of her?

b. There are also six pillows on her bed. She's barely living as is. If I suffocated her now, I doubt she'd even know it. *Get that thought out of your head.*

c. Perhaps I could just lock her in her room and cut a little hole in her door to serve her food. Then she could detox and all would be well in the world. Realistically though, I'd rather not go to jail for imprisoning my mom, and she would surely call the cops on me.

Nope, there truly is no good option to deal with this bullshit, so I just went to bed. In the morning I would regret not smothering her with that pillow.

"You little shit," she screamed at me from the doorway of my room.

"Keep it down. I'm trying to sleep."

"It's noon. Shouldn't you get up and do something around here?"

"I wouldn't have to sleep until noon if phone calls weren't coming in at 2am to pick your drunk ass up."

"Oh, you think that's cute? Making fun of your mom like that?"

There would be no going back to sleep. "Well it sure as shit ain't sad, mother," I say as I get out of bed and crack my back. "What is your problem today?"

"You drove the car and didn't put any gas in it. How am I supposed to get to work?"

"Well, one, going to a casino to play penny slots isn't work. Two, I had to drive my car to the bar where you passed out and drive your car home with you. There really aren't too many gas stations open at 2am between here and there. Three, it's your car. You put gas in it."

She stands there, angry and ready to throw something. I'd learned in these situations not to pay her much attention, so I just dropped to the floor and started my morning work out routine. I could feel her eyes burning a hole in the back of my head while I counted my push-ups.

"You know, one day you won't have me around. Then what?"

"Then, I guess I get some sleep?" I said without looking at her.

She stormed out as she normally would, and that would be the last time I would see or hear from her for just over a month. I didn't bother going to the cops because some of the usual haunts that she visited would let me know from time-to-time that she had been in, and frankly, it was quiet with her gone. The bartender at her favourite spot told me she had been in a few times with the same (while much younger) guy. He seemed like he was trying to take care of her, based on what the bartender said, so that satisfied me enough to just say *fuck it* and live a semi-normal life. Yes, life was peaceful until that day she came back.

I was sitting at the computer working on a project for school when she tore into the apartment like a damn hurricane, turning everything upside down looking for a ring.

I got up and went into her bedroom, where she was throwing clothes out of her closet. "Where have you been?" I questioned.

"Oh, you missed your mamma, didja?"

"Nope. Not really."

"I told you that you should have been nicer to me. You wanna know where I've been?"

I hesitated, because I knew some grand speech was coming, but I was bored, so I bit. "Sure, Mom. I'll ask again, where have you been?"

"Remember the last night I was here? The next morning I woke up and went to the corner store. Turns out I won the lottery."

"You're shitting me."

"Nope," she screams out, smiling ear-to-ear. "I won big! $8-million! How do you like dem apples?"

"Jesus Christ Mom. You won the lottery a month ago, and you're just telling me now?"

"I did. I won the lottery, and the stars—they were aligned for me. Right then and there I met Carl, and we're engaged. He's the best man I've ever known—better than your father, that's for sure. We're leaving on a cruise tonight and I need to find your grandmother's ring before I leave. I need that ring because some people actually love their parents."

"So let me get this straight. You won the lottery, and then miraculously some guy that sees you've won is your soul mate, and now you're leaving on a cruise together?"

"That's right, Michael. I won't be your problem anymore."

"When are you coming back?" I really didn't care all that much, but that's a lot of money, and I'd love to get me a piece of that. With the cash, I could afford to stay in university. The way things were going I'd have to drop out next semester. It's expensive to get an education in Canada. If there were any justice in the world, her giving me some money would just be considered a Broken Home Tax. That would be quite the law; if you suck at parenting, you at least have to provide financial stability until the child is viable in the real world.

"Never. Tomorrow. I don't know. Who cares? I'm rich and can't nobody say anything to me or make me do anything anymore."

"Like we ever could before," I mutter under my breath.

"What's that?" She gets immediately defensive. "Making more jokes at my expense?"

"Just calm down."

"You know, it's because of your wise cracks and bullshit that I didn't even want to give you any money, but Carl said I should. So here." She takes money out of her purse and throws it at me. The bills fly everywhere. "$10,000. Enjoy."

"You win $8-million dollars and give the son who has been dealing with bullshit for four years, ten-grand?"

"You're lucky you're getting that," she says as she passes by me and runs out the door.

That's the last time I saw my mom in person. As I picked up the money, I cried. When I was eight, everything was perfect. At the age of twenty, my dad didn't want to see me, my mom was gone for God knows how long, and all I was left with was this shitty apartment and $10,000. It's amazing what can happen in twelve-years. My dad went from Superman to J.D. Salinger, and mom went from June Cleaver to Eminem's mom in 8 Mile.

Life would never bounce back for me. It was just a constant stream of disappointments and breakdowns. I flunked out of school because of an inability to balance my work and my education with the haunting memories of those last few years with my mom that actually kept me up at night. The $10,000 was eaten up pretty quickly, and after that I was left with my $11.00 per hour at a duct cleaning business. The rest, you basically know now.

How I craved those Saturday mornings from back when the world made sense.

9

Kiss Away Cancer

TWO DAYS AFTER THE GRANDEST OF SHOPPING TRIPS and I can barely get out of bed. Aside from the odd piss break, and delivery man at my door, there wasn't a lot going on in my life. While I had no reason to feel guilt for cashing in some of my inheritance—so to speak—it didn't quite fulfill me the way I expected it to. What I was hoping for was a slippery slope of obscene spending. The goal was to get drunk on spending money to the point that I wouldn't stop, and then I would die knee deep in hookers and blow. The plan was ill-fated from the start. I like neither hookers, nor drugs, and when you grow up with little, all you can think of while you spend money is the zeros draining out of your account. Don't get me wrong; I enjoyed myself, but, I really wasn't satisfied with that life. Oh, and that diet I was on? Yeah, that ended pretty quick with the one healthy breakfast and one more healthy lunch.

The day after the shopping trip I Netflixed and chilled by myself. Sad, I know, but c'mon, *House of Cards* is such a badass show. Today, I know that there are decisions to make, and a resounding sense of reality hit me as I woke up. The first of the many decisions is whether I should get treatment or not. Then, if I do get treatment, what are my expectations? If I don't, how will I spend my final months?

Every time I close my eyes I pick up the story of my life as if it is playing out on a move screen. I see the pure waste of it all, and then my death; mourned by few, missed by even less. For the last two days it's been nothing but TV, reading my dad's book in bed, and munching. This dark cloud called Cancer will not go away. Closing my eyes at this point is like a game of Russian Roulette. Will my mind rest, or will it dwell on my impending doom? Sure, I have money now, but winning the lottery just before you die is kinda like finding out you would have gotten that dream job you really wanted, but your cell service was terrible that day, and they needed an answer right away. It's just too damn late.

So, money won't get me all hot and bothered. What will? I ponder this for awhile. I really, so badly want to leave a legacy behind. It makes me sad to think that there is a very real possibility that as I rot away in a casket like Dad, the world will have gone untouched. Maybe all I leave behind is a carbon foot print. I can tally my contributions in just a few seconds ... I always gave money to homeless people when I had some on me, and one time I stopped a girl from getting her purse jacked. The homeless people have no idea who I am, and the girl that almost got jacked thought for some reason that I was trying to steal from her too, so she ran away. The whole thing was very confusing. That is my legacy, and no one even knows about it so I guess it's not really a legacy at all.

There's another route to take; adventure. So many do it. They buy a BMX bike or a hiker's backpack and head out into the world. I have the money, I could do it, but that is likely to wear thin as the symptoms of this disease get worse. Last thing anyone wants is to end up in a hospital in Thailand, throwing up in a bag that's probably filled with barf from the last guy who died in the very same bed. Fuck it, the whole adventure thing is self-indulgent anyway. You're really doing it for you, and no one else.

I spend the morning racking my brain about treatment, but no answers are clear. It's scary to say that I won't go because that's accepting death right away. But with treatment, those extra months will probably be spent barely hanging on, although there is a slight chance I could get better. Jesus, now would be a really good time to get one of those signs from God that could tell me what to do. I'm sure those that joined the *Lord Have Mercy Club* get signs all the time.

Right now I'm leaning towards no treatment, and perhaps trying out skydiving. Weird choice, I know, but I have to do something with my time. First though, I should probably take a step in the direction of the living and have a shower.

The water feels great on my aching body. It's not sore from the Cancer, just from laying in bed for a couple of days. After the shower, I make some calls to skydiving places. I want to jump alone just in case I decide not to pull the chute, but that requires an eight-hour course. That just sounds exhausting. How is *put this on and pull this lever* an eight-hour course? *Oh Heavenly Father, just show me some kind of path,* I think to myself mockingly.

That's when I hear it—*knock, knock*. I sit still in that lone living room chair listening—*knock, knock*. Someone is at the door. There had been no visitors since arriving at my dad's place about a week ago. I wonder who is on the other side—*knock, knock, knock, knock, knock, knock*, in beats of two. I debate not answering, but it seems this person is not going away. With a lack of enthusiasm, I rise from the chair and head through the house. I surely can't invite anyone in with all of my dad's research strewn about. *Knock, knock, knock, knock ...*

I crack open the door to find Monica, Dr. Scorpio's receptionist standing there impatiently. She looks incredible. I've never seen her outside of work attire and I must say, all those predictions about what's under the baggy scrubs were quite true. She's rocking a tight pair of Lulus and a beige shirt that hangs off of her one shoulder, with just enough cleavage to distract a guy from even the most scintillating conversation. Until I opened that door, whoever was knocking stood to be a nuisance in my life ... except her. The one person I actually want to see is standing on my doorstep. *Praise Jesus.*

"Hey," I say, from behind the door, only revealing my eyes and nose.

"Hey yourself," she replies. "You haven't returned any of our calls to schedule a follow-up."

"Oh yeah, my phone actually died and my charger is kinda locked up in my ...," I decide not to tell her I was this enormous loser that got himself evicted. "Come to think of it, how did you find me?"

She opens her purse and pulls out the paper I slipped under my crazy former neighbour's door. I guess she knows I'm an enormous loser now. We stand there awkwardly for a moment until she breaks the silence. "So you gonna let me in?"

"Um ... I don't know if that's such a good idea right now. It's a pretty big mess in here."

"Look, either you let me in so that I can see you're

okay, or I might just go back to work and have you put on suicide watch."

"Oh, well that's not an abuse of power or anything," I say with a bit of charm behind it. "Wait, in order for you to get that paper with this address on it, you would have had to go to my old place. Did you get my address from my personal and confidential file?"

"I may have glanced at the screen."

"Oh really. So first you use my file in an unethical manner, then you're gonna use your position to get me put on suicide watch if I don't do what you say? Oh yeah, you live your life by a strict code of ethics." For the first time in quite awhile I feel like I actually have some game. I'm not sure what has come over me, but I'm full on, bold-face flirting. Maybe the moment that I was telling Derek about is right now. It's quite flattering to have someone checking up on me; and for that someone to be the picture of perfection—bonus.

I have two options: let Monica in and risk her thinking the mess of papers on the walls is my pet project, thus making her think I'm a psycho, or make her leave and lose any chance I might have. Time is of the essence after all. I take stock of my past girlfriends for a moment. There was Leanne, who left me for my friend Kevin (slut); Kaylee—who left me for God (weirdo); Amanda—who I left for sanity reasons (even bigger weirdo); Sara, who stole from me but introduced me to the perfect BJ (I kinda miss her); Bridgette—a girl who ended up being quite the whorish little lesbo (all would have been forgiven if I could have sat in). Then there was my last girlfriend Carla. We split when we finally admitted that we just really didn't like each other all that much. I always had to be the one to apologize or start up conversation after a fight with Carla. It didn't matter who was wrong, it was me that had the communication skills to make nice. Even as we talked, her apologies were hollow and sarcastic, rushed with a *fuck off* attached. It was taxing on my soul, and little did she know that every time she dismissed my apologies, she was breaking us. I wasn't perfect either, but I believe I was the one who at least tried.

These ghosts of relationships past had all the passion of an Arnold Schwarzenegger, Sarah Silverman love scene. They lacked spark that I didn't know existed until ... well, right now. There was something in the air, something so electrifying. I felt like we were having sex without touching; getting off on just the sight of each other. So basically I have no choice but to let the hot receptionist inside.

Once in my newly claimed house of horrors, I can tell she is a bit taken aback by my dad's obsession. "What is all of this?"

"It's kind of a long story, but basically my dad was a cop, this was his house, and all of this is related to his cases." With that simple explanation, all worry about whether she would understand this weird hobby of Martial's disappeared. We can psych ourselves out about the stupidest shit some times.

"Dedicated guy." She pauses for a moment, as if getting into character. In this moment she will play the heart broken, concerned stranger, just trying to make things better. "I heard you say that you lost him a week ago or so. I'm sorry, Michael. Even though I haven't lost my parents, I can just imagine the pain. I would have said something before, but the cops weren't messing around."

"Thanks, but we hardly knew each other. He kept to himself in his final years, unfortunately."

"Dad dies, and now you're sick. How are you doing

with everything? You haven't thrown anything across the room in here, have you?"

"Oh you know, pretty much trying to wish it all away," I say while slumping into the living room chair facing that huge TV.

"You do know that you can't do that right?"

"I'm kidding ... kinda. I don't really know what to do. I had this surge of energy—trying to find answers, but the last couple of days I'm just, *blah*. Everything feels heavy and dark, and no option feels right."

"That might have something to do with you living in the actual dark." She walks over to the drapes in the living room. "Open some blinds and experience this thing called the sun once and a while." As she whips them open, the sun cuts through the room like a blade. Of course, it hits me directly in the face, making me jump up out of my chair like it caught fire. It's so bright and overpowering. Just like with the dust, my body adjusts within seconds.

"You're very controlling."

"Perhaps I should lend you some of my persona then. You could afford to take some more control."

"Well it's not like I've been completely useless." Her body language says she's annoyed as she stands there, arms crossed, tapping her left foot against the floor. Perhaps she is expecting more rage out of the cage after I freaked out at the office. I do know she was losing interest with every passing second. "Okay. Look, you wanna know what I've been up to?"

She nods in approval of my offering to let her inside my world a bit. I take her hand, (getting a bit of a hard-on as soon as I do) and escort her to the make shift office area where a completely different research project is taking place, versus the one in the living room.

Strewn on the floor, hanging on walls and covering up the old desks are articles about my particular brand of Cancer.

"You've been busy," she says as she flips through some of the stacks of papers. Her interest is returning and she no longer regrets coming over; I can feel it.

"I figured it's better to be informed so I can make solid decisions about what to do with this whole diagnosis. Well that's how it started anyway. Over the last couple of days I've had a bit of a motivation problem, and my ability to make any decisions at all has vanished."

"Smart guy." She continues to rifle through the papers. "You understand this stuff?"

I nod, which she acknowledges with a smile.

"So look, the real reason why I'm here ..." She cuts herself off and walks up to me, laying the mother of all kisses on my lips. It's a damn good kiss, en Francais, starting with a simple lip lock and ending with a bit of groping. I don't even have time to think or prepare. As we part, my mind is blank. I keep my eyes closed for a little while longer, trying desperately to hold onto the feeling—it fades, but the rush of the moment lingers on.

I stammer out a sentence. "Okay, so to say I didn't expect that would be a gross understatement."

She giggles a bit before giving a completely honest answer. It's not an annoying *teehee* giggle that points to an issue with womanhood—wanting desperately to stay a little girl. No, her giggle is perfect, subtle ... warm. "Truthfully, when we met I didn't think much of you. Over the years you've gotten hotter—I'll admit that—but still, I just didn't see it. Then, of course you had girlfriends, I had boyfriends and I never gave you much thought. Then, just seeing all that rage and passion the other day, it really got me. It dawned on me that there's probably as much energy in the opposite. I also may have Googled you, and who doesn't like a man that has won seven Mario Kart championships?"

"Oh, you're going to make fun of me now. I see how it is."

She shrugs her shoulders and smiles. "Plus on top of all that, I figure if the kiss is good, you might see a reason to fight this thing and live as long as possible."

"If I knew that all I had to do was smash up your office a bit and catch a terminal disease, I would have thrown an old lady through that big window in the front of the office and downed some toxins a long time ago."

Again, a little giggle (again, perfect).

"You do know I could have a girlfriend."

"No you don't," she says with a disturbing level of certainty.

"How could you possibly know that?"

"No woman let's her man go out dressed the way I've seen you dressed, and there's no chance you have a girl that never comes with you to the doctor's office. If you do have a girlfriend, she's a terrible one, and what comes next, she deserves."

"What comes next?"

She walks past me, out of the office area and into the living room. It's a flirtatious walk, almost sexual. For the first time since I met Monica, it seems I have a real chance, but first she must do her duty and kill the mood with more talk of the disease. I can't tell if she's teasing me with the possibility of fucking, or simply a really hard read in the moment. "So tell me. What is Michael going to do about the Cancer?"

"Honestly I don't know," I reply with frustration in my voice, unsure of myself, anxious for *what's next*. "You know the chances of me beating this thing, I'm sure. There's a ninety-plus percent mortality rate. I have better odds of getting struck by lightning while winning the lottery than I do of actually surviving. From what I can tell, the drugs are pretty nasty. I might be better off just living out as many of my days as possible, drug free. I mean, that's where all the sickness and pain really comes from right—the side effects of anti-Cancer meds? I don't know if that's for me. Then there's the holistic approach, which shows promise, but isn't exactly proven."

"Some of those drugs can give you a year or more."

"A year or more for what though? That's the question weighing on my mind right now. And really, based on what I've read, even with treatment, a year or more is extremely optimistic."

"Well, let me ask you this. What's the most important thing you've done with your life?"

I think for a moment. Nothing important comes to mind. I just shrug my shoulders in a dismissive way. I really don't want to talk about this.

"The way I see it is, you should do two things."

"I'm listening."

"One, take the meds, prolong your life—go out there and do something amazing."

"And two?"

"And two—have sex with that receptionist from your doctor's office that you've been too scared to flirt with all these years."

"Seriously? Because fucking with a dying guy like this is just cruel."

She raises her left eyebrow, as if to say, you've got ten seconds Michael. Ten seconds to get with the girl you've been fantasizing about for most of your adult life, or maybe ten seconds to take advantage of this pity fuck. What man would ever question her motives? I pull her in, and pick her up. She wraps her legs around my waist; another unreal kiss. The moment has come. *Fuck you Derek* I think to myself. Okay, now he's completely removed from my mind. It's all about Monica.

"The bedroom," she whispers under her breath. The sexiness in her voice makes the hairs on my arms stand up.

As we make our way down the hallway, we clumsily pull on each other's clothes. She pushes me into walls as she undoes my belt and whips it out from the loops on my pants. Monica climbs me, I smash her into a mirror outside of the bedroom; it's passion, filled with rage, and pent up horniness after years of flirting with the idea of what is about to happen. She spins around and backs her body against mine. I grab frantically at her fantastic breasts and pull at her pants. She stops and slides them down her legs to the floor just outside of the bedroom.

I lay her down on the bed softly, which clearly annoys her a bit. Her body language is as loud as any words could be, almost as if saying *this isn't The Notebook. I want sex with the guy that got arrested, not sappy love making. Get it together stud.* I pick up the pace. As we tear away at each other's remaining clothes, her shapely body flexes with deep breaths.

We are naked and on top of each other in the bed now, flipping around frantically. There's a lot of dry humping happening until I can tell she's looking for me to man up and take the lead. That's when I kiss down her neck, in between her breasts, down her stomach and then ... go ahead, and take the lead. Most guys don't know if they're doing it right. I do. The secret to cunniligus is putting your hands on her sides. If her back arches, and you look up to only see breasts, but no head, you're doing it right. After fifteen-minutes I feel the shake of her thighs, and I can finally see her face again. *There, I put in the work. Your turn*, I think to myself.

I move back up her body, as she grabs me close. I last almost a half hour, which is shocking to me because I haven't had sex in a while, and she's intensely hot—hotter than Leanne, Kaylee, Amanda, Sara, Bridgette and Carla ... combined, with some Meghan Fox added in for good measure. After all the sweat, grinding and flipping from one position to another, it's over. Our bodies tremble and sweat now cools on our skin.

We lay there for almost ten full minutes in silence—something I'm not known for. "Man, now I know why Dr. Scorpio is so popular. It's full service over there," I say, in an effort to get some dialogue going. If I'm going to be honest, I have to admit that it took me those ten minutes to come up with that.

She slaps me on the shoulder before rolling over and placing her head on my chest, in an attempt to get comfortable, moving into three different positions before she settles on a spot between my ribs and chest. She's comfortable, as am I.

"I'm going to get a bit of sleep before I have to head to my other job at the hospital. Do you mind?"

"Nope. I'd say you deserve the nap."

"No cuddling though, kay?"

"Now that's interesting."

"I'm all for spooning while watching a movie or star gazing—stuff like that. But, when I sleep, I need my space."

"Jesus. That's fantastic."

"Just do me a favour and really think about what we talked about, whether it be tomorrow or fifty years from now, please?"

"I promise that I will try to change the world before I die," I say with a slightly condescending tone.

She says one last thing with her eyes closed before falling asleep, clearly missing my sarcasm. "Good. I look forward to seeing you make this a better place." That is the fastest I've ever seen a woman fall asleep after sex. It's lights out in the minutes.

While what she is saying might be trite, it isn't any less true. Why waste the little time I have left? I have all of this money now. Maybe I can donate it to my favourite charity or something. The only problem is, I don't have a favourite charity. I did at one point, but the information age screwed it all up. There's too much info. One site says this is good, another says that is good. It can be quite hard to keep up with the information being thrown in a person's direction. I learned the charity my parents supported growing up only gives three-cents on the dollar towards the actual cause. That's just not cool, so I stopped giving anything. I saw why their costs are so high after I stopped; the marketing materials alone to get me to donate again cost more than I would have ever given.

I'll figure it out, I think to myself.

Laying there in bed with Monica naked under the covers I realize that she just hijacked my mood. Until she knocked on my door, I had no motivation to do anything. Unknowingly, by letting her into the house my focus was taken off of death, and pushed to life. I can feel a shift in perspective, and maybe tomorrow the day will start in the light, instead of this lonely dark I've been experiencing. Tomorrow, I'll start getting treatment, because if this is what my life could be like, I have every reason to fight. The chance of being cured is slim, but I've found my reason to try.

In the meantime, I pick up Martial's book to read

all about the worst criminals in Winnipeg. That's when it hits me. There's a chance that all of this is leading somewhere. All of these seemingly random events in my life have pushed me to this point with this book and the money that is now neatly piled into stacks of ten thousand in the bedroom across the hall. Maybe the answer to doing something worthwhile is right here in this house, and maybe it's in this book, which has captured my attention. Not simply entertainment, maybe there's a way for me to catch these guys. As crazy an idea as that is, I'm starting to think not trying is even crazier. It's funny how things work out sometimes. *I'm going to use this money to catch these people*.

I won't crash tonight. Life is too good right now to sleep through it.

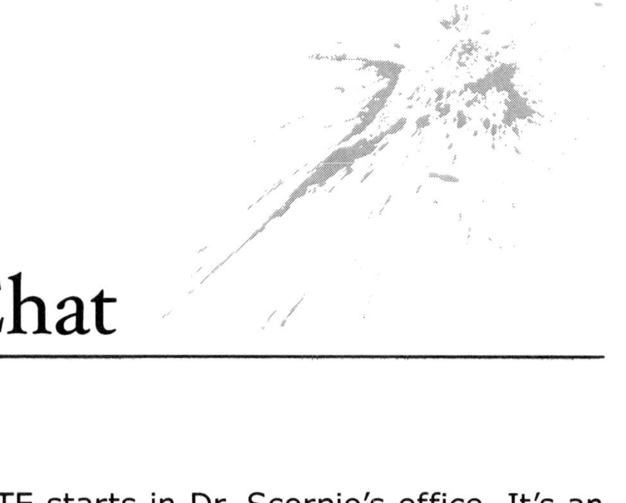

10

Chit Chat

OUR FIRST DATE starts in Dr. Scorpio's office. It's an unlikely place, but the one spot on this earth I know would make Monica happy. This time, the mood is different. We purposefully pick a day when she is off so that the three of us can sit down and talk. Hand-in-hand—a proposition that I could tell the doc is not entirely comfortable with—we listen in on his phone call with Cancer Care. Being back here is surreal. I guess doctors really do take their oath seriously. The fact that the doc is even willing to look me in the eyes again was shocking enough, but his desire to treat me is humbling. It never occurred to me that some people still believe in second chances.

"Okay. He'll be there. A week Monday at 1pm," the doc said as he finishes up the call. "I'll let him know the information ... Yes ... thank you." He hangs up the phone and once again stares at our hands clasped together between our two chairs. "Alright, you are all set."

"So this is a group session, correct?" I ask, knowing

the answer but hoping for a bit more information than I got prior to the doc getting on the phone.

"That's right, Michael. I think it's best that you start there. It's not always, and in fact it's not usually, the starting point. However, I do feel for your personality type, this is the best course of action."

"And what can I expect from this?"

Monica squeezes my hand ever so slightly. At first I think it's because she's trying to calm me, or because she thinks I'm being rude, but I realize quickly that it's simply to remind me she's there.

"You can expect to hear stories from people at all stages of their diagnoses. It won't be easy to listen to either. You're going to realize some of the signs were there all along, and then you're going to also hear about what your future is going to be like. It'll be tough to hear, but necessary. Reality is not easy in these situations, and it's my hope here you'll find acceptance of the reality in front of you.

"Okay." I say matter-of-factly before I get up out of my chair signaling the end of this joyous meeting. "A week Monday at 1pm. I'll be there."

As we drive to our next stop, Monica does everything she can to take my mind off of the meeting. After all, we are on our way to a party, and parties are supposed to be fun.

"You know, dates are supposed to be intimate and flirtatious," I say making an attempt to get my mind into party mode. "So far we've been to a fast food spot, a clinic, and now we're headed to a party. Where are the movies and make-outs?"

"Maybe I need to see how you get along with my friends before we get to movies and make-outs, as you put it."

We pull up to her friend's house just as the sun

hides behind the horizon, giving way to twilight. The house is a brownstone with a big white door, and when opened it leads to a huge foyer where three dozen pairs of shoes are strewn along the floor. Monica would mention in passing a few hours earlier that Susan's parents died when she was young. Her father was a successful car salesman, and when they passed, a fortune was dropped in her lap. The house is pleasantly low key for a rich chick, but still you can tell there's money here just based on the pool, hot tub, and huge landscaped yard. The decor and functional elements are all what you might find in the house of someone making $40,000 a year though. It's refreshing, and immediately drops my guard. Until we arrived I was slightly annoyed that our first date would be wasted on some spoiled brat's self-indulgent going away party. Now, I feel better about the whole situation. Perhaps I can engage in idle chit chat with this girl, showing Monica that I can play nice with others.

In this social setting I'll be playing the role of Monica's boyfriend, along for the ride, smiling and nodding my way through the night. We're here, in this brownstone, to give Susan a proper send-off as she moves across the world to Taiwan. There she will teach impoverished children how to speak English. It's a noble goal, but I can't help but feel that there are more pressing matters for those kids which Monica's money could solve. I keep those thoughts to myself of course. Even though I may be playing the role of boyfriend tonight, it is still too early to show her my jaded side.

The people that gather around chip bowls, bottles, and the stereo (pretending to be DJs) seem harmless enough. They're normal; jeans and skirts without elaborate details, some with glasses, some bald, some good looking ... all very normal. These people are simply background noise, which I embrace. There's nothing worse that an obscenely good looking person at a party, or some accomplished pianist who will play you something if given the chance. No one cries out for attention here ... my kind of people.

Monica introduces me to a handful of the chip eaters. Mike or Mark, or Mack, or whatever, protects the All Dressed chips like a solider watching over his post. Two of the girls are complete book worms. Every story comes back to a reference about Great Gatsby or a Kari Hunter novel. It's kind of annoying, but not so much so that you want to point out their obvious narrow interests. Mike or Mark, or Mack, or whatever really annoys me in the moment, though. I love All Dressed chips. After some clever maneuvering, and some bullshit conversation to relate to his hipster sensibilities, he lets down his guard and I successfully scoop up two-handfuls of Ruffles goodness. All in all, after Chipgate, I'd rate the conversations a six out of ten, which is about what I expected.

I take in more of the decor with a full tour of the house. Susan is the type of rich I would be if I had the time. There are subtle accents of cash throughout. Take the kitchen for example; all stainless steel appliances, the fridge has a TV and water tap built in, and the microwave has two levels for some odd reason. I'll have to remember to get her to explain that one. The entire house is much of the same until you get to the bedroom. This bitch stole Professor X's room and added a pool to it! Of course, I mean bitch affectionately. As we walk around the room, Susan and Monica talk about her trip while I take in the detail.

The room is about a thousand square feet, maybe a little less. From the doorway you walk along a ramp to a main circular area that has a bed, nightstands, a desk and chair, as well as a nice big TV. The lights in the room come from below in the water and on the ceiling with little pin lights that probably look like stars when the room is darker. Of course, she has Hue so the lights change colour to whatever she's in the mood for. The walls are different shades of blue and the water is crystal clear. It's really something else.

"This is the coolest bedroom I have ever seen," I say while I walk the ramp to the main area. "That includes every episode of Cribs ever."

Susan and Monica chuckle a bit. "He's funny, I like him," Susan says to Monica.

"I feel like I was born to live in water. I love humidity, and I can't get enough of just floating for hours and emptying out my mind." Susan says to me in the least bragging fashion she can while talking about her crazy expensive aquatic bedroom.

"You mean float like Joe Rogan talks about?"

"Yeah. This part of the pool is for floating. The part on the other side of the room is for swimming and relaxing."

"You know, it's very cool that you have your one area that's ridiculously elaborate, but the rest of the house is so understated. Most kids that inherit cash don't have that kind of class." I say to her, hoping as I finish not to offend her. "It's really refreshing."

She smiles and takes the compliment as it was intended. "A lot of my friends don't have money, and I don't want to throw it in their faces that I do."

I grab onto Monica from behind and pull her close, then whisper in her ear, "I like your friends."

After the tour of the house is done, Susan disappears to play the host, and we move on to the living room, and finally we find the drink table. It's been raided. All that is left of the twelve kinds of liquor is Eristoff, the cheapest alcohol at a liquor store. I mix Monica her drink, and hand it over as she introduces me to Margaret, a former crime reporter for the big local paper. Twenty-minutes later, we are all still talking about this and that, mostly crime. I mention that my dad was a cop, and her appreciation for our city's history is evident. Not only does she know of Martial, but she worships him.

"Oh my God, your dad is a legend at the force," she says like a fan-girl who's just met her idol. "How is he?"

"Dead." I say, drably, but matter of factly as I shove more All Dressed chips into my mouth.

"What? How?"

"Shot. I'm surprised you didn't hear. Happened about a week and a half ago." I really don't mean to be so dry about the whole thing, but I'm not one to beat around the bush.

"I've actually been on vacation for the last month since the paper cut back. Mexico. Totally unplugged," she says, hurrying to get back to the subject of Martial. "Wow. I'm so sorry for your loss."

I smile, nod and shrug, insinuating a *thank you*.

"You know, your dad was one of the guys that inspired me to take on my new project. I've been thinking about it for years, but now I have the time to actually do it."

"How so?" I ask, actually not placating. I'm interested in how Martial could inspire a woman in her thirties to take on a project. It validates that perhaps his legacy will live on through others.

"Well, when I interviewed him about six-months ago ..."

"Wait. You saw Martial six-months ago?"

"Yep. We met at Starbucks. We were mutual admirers of each other's work."

Martial couldn't be bothered to see me, but he was meeting for coffee with this chick to talk about crime? Of all the slaps in the face. I guess this proves he wasn't completely anti-social. "What was Martial like when you saw him?"

"What do you mean?"

"Well, the last time I saw him I was about sixteen, so I'm curious what he was like towards the end."

"God. I hope I didn't open up any old wounds. I'm sorry if I did."

"I've made my peace with it."

She is uncomfortable, but decides to share her experience. "He was okay, but very unkempt. Martial was still sharp as a tack though. I don't know how, but he still seemed to know everything about every criminal in Winnipeg. He really helped me shape my project."

"Well, it's good to know he still had his wits about him."

"More than that." She pauses for a moment. "Michael, don't believe a word about your dad that is anything but good. It was a dark day when he was forced out. He really did do his part to make this city a better place to live. Your dad was kick ass. He was one of the few cops that legitimately went into the areas no cop wanted to, and took down crack dens. He got more girls out of places like that than anyone. A real blue hero; no time for fuckery."

"And he's inspired you to do the same?" I say with friendly laughter, at the thought of this 100-pound, byte-sized geek of a woman breaking into crack dens.

"No no. But I'm launching a site that identifies known crack dens, the people coming in and out, details, things to watch out for. It's a huge problem in the city.

So many houses preying on young girls, getting kids and parents hooked on nasty, nasty stuff."

"I don't understand. If we know where the houses are, why don't we just follow Martial's lead, and take them down?"

"New laws. Your dad would bust down the doors with just a small amount of suspicion. Now, you really need to be sure, plus resources aren't what they used to be. By collecting intel ourselves, and posting online, we're just hoping to give the cops probable cause. It's power through information."

"That's really smart, actually."

Monica interjects. "Margaret, that sounds pretty risky. Are you sure you should be out there doing that?"

"Someone has to. I have a small team helping where they can, and Susan really helped. We can't just let these people get away with what they're doing."

From across the room, Susan yells out, "Real social justice exists in the form of that girl right there!"

Everyone laughs a bit, and even a couple of people applaud. Margaret curtsies. "Thank you, thank you. You're far too kind."

Margaret's courage is admirable. She's tiny, soft spoken, and has no background in combat of any kind, but here she is, talking about busting crack dens simply because there's no one else to do it. That's the kind of drive I need to do something great before I die. The approach seems slow, but at least she's out there doing something. Why can't I have motivation like that?

We exchange numbers, just in case I can think of a way to help her out with her cause; perhaps I have found my charity. This could be the direction I need. Maybe she could expand her mission to the criminals in Martial's book? I'm not sure of the approach to take yet, but it's obvious that if I want to do something, I should follow this girl's lead.

"Thank you for telling me about how Martial was in the months before he died. I feel like I got to be a part of his world later in his life now," I say sincerely to Margaret. I really am grateful.

"No problem, Michael. I wish you guys could have connected before he died."

I eventually break away from the conversation to go to the washroom. While I stand there staring at myself in the mirror as I piss, I see a bit of Martial in my facial features. If his whole legacy just boils down to what Margaret knows about him, then his life was worth something. I picture him busting down doors and carrying girls to safety like a hero in the movies. The thought alone makes me smile. I know this, because I'm starting at myself in the mirror. Why is there a mirror behind the toilet? Who wants to see themselves piss? Now *this* is a stupid rich thing.

I join Monica back at the drink table, where we spend the rest of the party finishing off that bottle of Eristoff—which sounds illicit, but really it's only a couple of drinks—and making up conversations we see happening across the room. She's fun, and exactly who I thought she would be. While I listen to her talk about her family, friends, and growing up in a well to-do neighbourhood, I can't help but feel a sense of pride. This amazing woman, sitting on the edge of a leather couch, looking like she jumped out of an ad for some kind of shampoo or perfume chose me. She came over to my place, and kissed me. How does this happen to a guy who, until now, was a depressed loner?

Susan is now rip-roaring drunk, as are most people in the room. The music is louder and no one would notice if we slipped away. I grab Monica by the hand

and after some convincing, I manage to get her into that pool room for a quickie. I had to have sex once in a room like that before kicking it. You would too, and you fucking know it.

We take selfies at the party, which I of course post to Instagram, and tag Derek in. *Some moments are worth waiting for. #lucky #dreamgirl #medicalbenefits.* It takes Derek all of two-minutes to reply with a comment, *Well it's about fucking time. I owe you $100 and I couldn't be happier to pay up!* I wish I could have seen that stunned look on his face as he tapped on that notif and saw me kissing Monica's cheek. I bet it was priceless. I'm not sure that my strategy of biding my time worked, but I'll go to my grave saying it did.

The party cuts in half as people leave to explore the city for another room with free alcohol. The few of us left play Cards Against Humanity. Mike or Mark, or Mack, or whatever doesn't get his way, asking at least half a dozen times for everyone to play strip poker. What a passive aggressive way of trying to get laid. After what must have been seventeen rounds of Humanity, Susan declares she wants to spend the rest of the night with her boyfriend. She leaves tomorrow for Taiwan, so tonight will be epic for this guy. Good for him.

We make our way to the car, where I pull Monica in close and kiss her ever-so-softly against the driver side door. Once again, a kiss gives me chills. Her too.

"This was one of the best nights of my life," I say as we get in the car. Now, before you judge Monica for drinking and driving, she had me pour her half-ounce glasses, and it had been more than three-hours since her last drink, and besides, I only had one drink and I'm driving, so, HA!

"Best night of your life?"

"Well, not the best night. That was when you came over the other night." She smiles shyly at my adulation. "One-of the best nights. I never had a lot of friends growing up. Getting to hang out with a bunch of awesome people with you on my arm may sound so innocuous but to me, it's really something special." I'm getting mushy in my as-old-age-as-I'm-going-to-get.

"That couldn't make me happier. You really do appreciate the small things in life, huh?"

"What you've done for me is not small. You've woken me up from a bleak death sentence. I literally thought death was my life now. I'll never forget what you've done for me, Mon."

"You better not. You're going to beat this thing and there's going to be many more nights like this in the future."

"You're fucking right I am."

"You and Margaret seemed to hit it off tonight," she says with excitement in her voice, as if forgetting that merging her two worlds (friends and me) is not possible in this particular scenario if I don't actually beat this Cancer.

"She's interesting. A social crusader. A hundred pounds of energy and total lack of fear."

"Just like your dad, it sounds like."

"Just like Martial."

"Did she give you any ideas—any brass ring, holy shit epiphanies?"

"She got me thinking. That's for sure."

"That's good."

"Well, kinda. It got me thinking about what I could do, but then again, she made me realize that I might not have enough time to do anything."

"There's always a way, Michael."

Highfalutinly, I declare, "At the very least, I'm

thinking. I shall build some sort of micro-legacy regardless of what happens."

A few minutes later we are parked outside of my house, and I coyly poke her shoulder. "Not coming in?"

"Not tonight. I have to be up in a few hours, and I need a big open bed to fall asleep tonight."

I try the sad puppy dog face, but she's not budging. "Well okay. But you owe me!"

"Mister, I don't owe you shit after that performance in Susan's bedroom."

"Touché."

"Michael, can you do me a huge favour?" She asks seriously.

"Anything for you."

"Can you start talking about the future as if it is a certainty? It's time to get positive so you can kick Cancer's ass."

"I can do that for you, no problem. You have my word that chit chat will only lead to good vibes."

She smiles, and accepts my answer. "Good. I've kinda fallen for you, and when you're positive about life, I fall for you even more."

We kiss ... for twenty-minutes, and then finally she leaves me on the curb outside of my house. *What a perfect night*, I think to myself. *What a perfect girl*.

I have far too much energy to go to sleep anytime soon. Monica has the dopamine flowing in my brain, and my adrenaline running wild! When I walk in the front door, Dad's rifle is standing up in the corner by the closet staring at me. It's time to see if I've still got it.

About fifteen minutes from the house is a field surrounded by trees, and not a home for miles. This is where Martial would take me shooting as a kid. The crickets chirp from a distance, and aside from the cracking under my feet as I walk through the long grass there are no other sounds for miles. It's a beautiful night outside with stars out as far as the eye can see. A full moon perfectly lights the exact spot we used to shoot. It seems like the world has set the stage for a nostalgic moment.

I set up a few pop bottles, do my paces, aim, breathe and fire. Seven bullets, four bottles down. It seems that shooting a gun is built into my DNA. I walk back over to pick up the bottles, and as I do, I spot an old soup can with a hole in it.

"I can't believe it," I say out loud as I pick up the can.

It's one of the cans Martial and I had shot years ago when we would come out here. I stare at that can for awhile, almost trying to connect with it on some deep level, extracting the memories from it."

"You've still got it, my boy."

I look up to find Martial standing there in his black leather jacket, blue jeans, and a black t-shirt.

"I only had one drink tonight. There's no way I'm drunk enough to be seeing things." Again, I'm talking to myself.

"You're not drunk, Michael. You're just ... open right now."

"Open?"

"Your mind. It's open to more than usual. How could it not be? Look around you. It's a perfect night. Beyond perfect. It's special. You just experienced love for probably the first time. Now you're out here reclaiming your place in the natural order of things. You've connected to me, and I to you."

"I miss you."

"I miss you too. I missed you everyday for the last decade. I just couldn't come home."

"Why?"

"You know why."

"No, I don't. We needed you."

"You may not realize it yet, but you know why I couldn't come back, you know why I had to leave, and you know what you're going to do next."

"I really don't know any of that."

"In time you'll connect with your subconscious, and that's when you'll really take this world by surprise."

"I'm dying. There's not too much time to take the world by surprise."

"There's plenty of time." He says as he looks up at the stars. "I've left you the path. All you have to do is take it. You'll figure out the roadmap on your own."

"Dad, remember Saturdays?"

"That's the first time you've called me Dad in a long time, and yes, I do."

"I want that back."

"The lessons from our time together will steer you to do the right thing."

"I hope so. I want to have a Margaret that talks about me after I die."

"Son, whatever you choose to do next, however you decide to make an impact on this world, just know I am fully aware that there are grey areas, and no matter how much you step into them, I'll always love you."

Looking at the stars, I notice the North star shining extra bright. "I love you too, Dad."

And just like that he vanishes, leaving me in a field with the universe shining down on me, a tear in my eye, and a can in my hand. Dad always knew just what to say.

11

A Time Not To Kill

A WEEK MONDAY IS NOW FOUR DAYS AWAY, and a lot has happened since we sat in Doc Scorpio's office. Monica and I have spent every waking second together when she's not working, and I have finished Dad's book. The grey area he spoke of has set me free. It's actually incredible how a moment of awakening can unlock the inner recesses of your mind, enabling you to do some pretty tremendous things. Now I know that Martial wasn't there in that field, but that moment helped heal some old wounds. It also cleared my mind.

With an incredible surge of energy, I've been able to not only finish the book, but memorize it as well. As the cloud of uncertainty lifted, I was able to learn the way I used to. My mind works like a filing room, but only if I take what's in front of me, transcribe it into my own words and digitize the data to have on me whenever I am in a position to think about it. To do that, the papers had to come down from the walls. The all encompassing feeling of having these criminals stare at me everyday may have worked for Dad, but all it did is trip me out in my sleep.

While Monica worked, I stripped the walls bare, and created a Dropbox with the diary information put into my own words. Now, if I need to know anything I just ask Siri, and the information is at my fingertips. This system is more ... me.

Of course, digital backups aren't always foolproof, and with Monica starting to make herself at home, the money needed to be hidden. I invested in a few pretty heavy duty safes, and stored them in the basement. One was for the research. The other four were for the money. I hid them away in a place where Monica would never think to look. That left only one thing left to do.

Some of the papers have been hanging on the walls for a decade or more, and the discolouring of the walls was obnoxious. In fact, the whole shack was depressing. Three days until my meeting at Cancer Care, and there Monica and I were, renovating. We painted the walls, cut the grass, bought blinds that were made in the 21st century, and threw out the old drapes. Area rugs warmed up the rooms with flooring, and we even bought a couch so the two of us could watch movies in the living room. That old grey chair, worn out at the edges was replaced with a tan coloured sectional. Yep, after the work was done, this went from Martial's house to my home.

Today is also the day that Margaret's website is set to launch. She shoots me a text to let us know that it's live. Monica has to rush off to work, so she can't check it out, but I log-on to thoroughly examine the content. I really hope it is all that she thought it would be.

On the first page, there's a map of the city with a disturbing amount of pins. You just type in your address and the map zooms in to expose the crack dens in the surrounding area. When you click on the pin there's info about the known criminals that frequent the house including surveillance photos. You also get a scale of risk and some even have live webcams. I'm not sure how that will play long-term, but they're online. It's exactly what I expected, and then some. Margaret did a great job.

Just checked it out. Very well done, I text to her.

She replies, *Thanks. Lots of traffic so far. Hoping it does some good.*

I believe it will.

The first person that springs into action because of it will make all of this worth it.

Martial would be proud.

:)

Okay, so Margaret has done her part, and now it's time to do mine. But what do I do? How do I turn this into action?

Over the next couple of hours I spend my time pairing the address with the info from Dad's diary. Fifteen match, and Dad did not have nice things to say. There are so many really scummy assholes that call these houses home, or at least party there. I covertly create a gmail and send off some of the files through a VPN to Margaret. That will give her more ammunition; dates, times, even some video of these guys with girls that she and her team can identify. It'll be the boost she needs to perhaps get the cops involved. There's too much evidence for them to ignore.

So, armed with that info, there's a good chance some action will be taken. However, fifteen houses barely breaks the mould. What can be done about the rest? The day after the party I did some digging into the process cops go through to enter a home, and Margaret is right; there is a shit ton of red tape. But it's not just the red tape stopping cops from taking action. They're busy, and when I say busy that's likely an understatement. On an average Saturday night in my city there are about 100 calls to the police. It's likely half of those are for complete bullshit, but they have to take the call no matter what.

There was an article in the paper the other day about cops taking seven hours to get to a family's home invasion complaint. Seven hours! It's not that the cops are lazily eating donuts and laughing when calls come in; they're just swamped. There's too much crime, and too few officers. They don't have time to mount cases against the people that run these houses because they have to deal with domestic violence, taggers, random fights, and all the other reports that come in as an urgent need.

Cops need to show probable cause in order to get a no-knock warrant, but to do that they need to be able to investigate and build a case. Ain't nobody got time for that. I guess that's why Martial did what he was doing; taking matters into his own hands. Those days are long behind us though. Nobody wants to risk their pension when there are camera phones and home security networks everywhere.

As I double back over my research, one aspect of the law sticks out. If a home is the scene of a crime, then the police have immediate access. So basically, if I can prove that a crime is happening, the cops can go in and bust these guys. Proving it is the tricky part. What kind of crime can I prove is happening inside the house?

I pace for almost an hour, toss a ball against one of the freshly painted walls, and walk in circles; living room, hallway, kitchen, dining room, repeat. Frustration sets in and I sit on the floor in the hallway looking into the living room. What can I do? That's when it hits me.

I don't need to prove a crime is happening inside of the house. I just need to prove that a crime is happening *to* the house, and there's only one crime that I can control from outside ... a shooting.

Of course, I'm not going to shoot someone, but in minutes I'm able to formulate a risky, insane plan to take down crack dens. It's actually not much of a plan. I just need to identify a house I want to hit that has a vacant place across the street. The rest will play out easily. It's contrived, I know. I'm just going to walk into a neighbourhood with a rifle and start shooting. I could have never predicted this would be my Friday night activity.

I get lucky when I start my surveillance. The first house I check out has an abandoned residence across the street. Okay, maybe it's not exactly luck. In this area there are quite a few boarded up houses. On that street alone, I count three. As the gangs started to move in to the neighbourhood, the good families and aging population either moved out or died off. Land value was low enough that that neighbourhood transitioned nearly overnight. It's an unfortunate trend that will work in my favour though. No one's around to catch me. Lucky me again, it looks as if there's a party at 522 Mountain Road, the house I will take down. The music is loud enough that I can make out the song from the street. These guys actually have pretty good taste in music.

I take a moment to really examine the house and formulate a plan of attack. It's a single storey with a basement. There's a large window in the front, and to the left of that is a door with more glass. Three steps get you to the door from a short sidewalk, and a small wire fence wraps around the property. From the back lane there is a garage, more fence, a small window, and the exact same door. There are no animals from what I can tell, which is good because I love animals and don't want to risk hurting a poor innocent dog or cat.

I go home and ready Dad's rifle. If the other night proved anything, it's that I can still shoot. I spent about half an hour out there popping rounds off at bottles and cans. By the last few rounds, my shots were perfect. I just had to remember the patience involved with a long-shot, and the rest is pure instinct. I pack the gun, the bullets, and secure them in the back of the truck underneath a bunch of random crap that Dad had. It doesn't take long to go through my closet and find all black clothing that I purchased that day at the mall. My uniform is complete with a black army cap that was in the back of Martial's closet. Yes, I call it a uniform. After all, tonight I will be a hero, taking down this crack den just like Dad.

I return at around 10:30pm, when it's nice and dark. I park several blocks away, and walk down back lanes to get to the abandoned house across the street. The garbage smell coming from the bins that line the lane is disgusting. It doesn't take much to break-in. I don't even have to break any glass. There's a hole where the door used to be. Clearly squatters had made this their home at least a few times. After a search of the many rooms, I see that it's empty. This is too easy.

Heading up to the third floor, I can't help but think of the history in this home. Sure, now it's an abandoned shell of its former self, but at some point a happy family lived here. Children were raised here. Love filled these rooms. It may have been years ago, but it's still sad to see that what was once a place filled with laughter and family is now my perch to snipe at this house across the street.

I setup in what looks to have been the main bedroom.

A crack in the boards over what used to be windows provides the perfect vantage point for sniping the walls of the house. The sound of rat claws against the wood floors can be heard faintly behind me. When I move to see them, they're gone. Such a creepy rodent.

My goal is to hit the front of the house, then the back, and keep them inside. The shots from my dad's M24 will be loud, but that's exactly what I want. The only aspect of this plan holding me up is a guarantee that there are drugs inside, underage girls, and at least one high-profile asshole. I watch through my binoculars, waiting to spot what I need to continue. There are clearly young girls passing by the window, and every so often I can spot the occasional bump of coke—pulled from a brick—on the table almost out of view. I really can't make out any faces though.

Then, a car pulls up and four guys get out. They're laughing as if Jerry Seinfeld himself was sitting in the car with them, and each have a bottle of some kind of liquor in hand. I can't quite make out their faces, until one of them turns and reveals himself to me. Jackpot: Jason White! As far as scumbags go, he's a golden goose, and one of the first bios that really bothered me from Dad's research. Drug dealer, pedophile, and always let out of jail due to lack of evidence or excessive force; it would be my pleasure to shoot at this piece of shit.

I abandon the binoculars and ready my rifle. The scope Dad bought is pretty sweet, and I never take my eyes off Jason as he walks up to the house. For a moment, I consider taking him out right there. The world would be a better place, but I'm no killer. My purpose here is to be a hero. Besides, the second that thought crosses my mind I break into a cold sweat and my body shakes. No, I'll stick to my plan; calling the cops.

"911, what's your emergency?"

"Hi. I'm reporting gun shots fired at 522 Mountain Road. Multiple shots."

"Are you hurt sir?"

"I'm not in the house. I'm a neighbour. Please send someone. I'm pretty sure someone has been shot!"

I hang up the phone, and smash it to pieces with my foot. Aren't burner phones from 7-11 grand? I'd actually like to know who uses them besides criminals and vigilantes. It doesn't make much sense to have them widely available for $100 because in most cases I'd imagine any criminal or vigilante could afford them. I'm not sure why we make it so easy for criminals to do what they do, but I guess they simply exploit holes. That's the art of criminality. You find that which society has setup as structure, and you exploit it to carry out your crimes. It would be exhausting to simply fill the holes in society to take down criminals, but someone has to have that job. If not, they need to start hiring ASAP.

I wait to hear sirens before I make my move. Nothing. I wait, and I wait some more. I know it's not going to take seven-hours like the home invasion since I reported someone possibly getting shot, but I have no idea how long this will actually take. While I wait, I could swear the the time on my watch is moving slower. It feels like a few seconds pass for every second I count. Eventually, I get tired of kneeling there with my rifle, so I pace and check through other windows to see if the cops are getting close. The suspense is killing me, and with no airflow except for the occasional breeze, my forehead drips with sweat. After awhile, I lay down on the dirty floor and close my eyes. That's when I hear the faint sound of sirens. I look at my watch. It took twelve-minutes ... that was only twelve minutes? I could never imagine being on a stakeout.

I ready the gun and look down the scope. As I do, my hands start to shake. I take a deep breath and try to calm myself. Up until now this all felt like a video game, even cool, but now it's real. I'm not shooting at cans or bottles. *These guys are scumbags and there are young girls in there that you're saving*, I repeat to myself over and over. The sirens are closer now, and I can see red and blue colours bouncing off of the night sky in the distance. Now is the time.

I look through the scope, take a deep breath, then fire.

BANG!

The shot is louder than I would have thought, probably amplified by fear and adrenaline. It echoes through the house, and then through the neighbourhood. That first bullet hits the stucco just below the large window. I'll call that a miss since I was going for the centre of the glass. Those in the house can't hear the shot over the music, and are unfazed by my first attempt at panicking them.

I take another deep breath, close my eyes and exhale as I take the next shot. Target hit! This time I aimed for a corner of the window since people are now standing right in front of it. The glass shatters and some shards fall, while large chunks continue to hang in the frame. People start to scream from inside the house. They're screaming are so loud that I can hear them over the music. Someone attempts to open the front door, so I shoot at that next. I see them stumble and fall back inside in a panic. Really, who heads outside towards the bullets? Criminal masterminds.

Before anyone dares try to escape out the back

door I take aim at the back yard and let off two shots. That's all the rounds from the internal magazine. I have five bullets left in the detachable and use those one after another, switching between the front of the house and the back. The last bullet, I save for Jason White's passenger side tire. If he does try to get away, he'll be slowed down at the very least.

The lights are now illuminating the trees just down the street, and the sirens are blaring. It's time to go. I stick the gun in it's case, then execute the last part of my plan. I've seen enough TV shows to know that a single hair, or some other DNA evidence can bring down even the most masterful shooter. That won't happen to me. Before leaving, I dump gasoline on the abandoned home and light a match. Whoever's ghosts haunted this house will now be free to move on. It won't take long for the entire place to go up in flames, since it's old and there's wood everywhere. This part, I actually feel bad about, so I once again hesitate, but it has to be done, and the cops are here so it's time to move down the back lane.

I run as fast as I can for two blocks in pitch black, and then walk the rest of the way to avoid suspicion. Running with the rifle proves problematic. I try to run in such a way that you can't tell I'm holding the gun, by holding it tightly at my side. My black clothes and the black cloth case camouflage well, but this will be the last time I bring such a bulky gun when I have to run away. A lot went wrong tonight: I hesitated, I'll have to fix this gun issue, and the wait time for the cops was killer, but it looks like I got away with it. There's no one around. I don't run into anyone in the back lanes. It's a ghost town. I guess nine gun shots echoing throughout a neighbourhood is enough to keep everyone indoors.

The last piece of advice that CSI shows offered me

is to keep my head down just in case there are cameras nearby. Hood up, hat on, no one will be able to identify me. The best they'll be able to come up with is a tall male, maybe caucasian dressed in all black. That could be anyone. Crime Stoppers could offer a million-dollar reward, and it wouldn't matter.

Finally, I get to my truck and jump in the driver seat. I turn it on and crank the air conditioning, then just sit there for a moment catching my breath. *I did it!* Once I cool down, I put the gun in the back by climbing over the seats (I don't want to take it back outside and risk someone seeing me), then drive off.

The adrenaline coursing through my body right now is intense. I bet my testosterone levels are through the roof. What an exhilarating feeling. I highly recommend it. No one got out of the house, and by now, I'm sure the cops are inside making arrests. I can guarantee that some of these guys go away for a long time. The fact that I could get Jason White in all of this is an added bonus. Before he died, Dad predicted Jason would get off on his latest charges, and he was right. However, Jason White never saw me coming.

I look at the city around me as I drive home. So many people are asleep right now, oblivious to the world that exists around them. Their safety is a smashed window or kicked in door away from being crushed, but not by the guys in that house tonight. No, they're not going to be victimizing anyone, anytime soon.

Tonight I saved young girls. Tonight I took down some truly sick fucks. Tonight I even took care of an abandoned eye sore of a house. I did good, even if it's not quite the way Superman would have done it.

Tonight, even though no one will ever know, I feel safe in saying, I am a hero.

12

It's My Party ...

LAST NIGHT, I WAS A BAD ASS. What else do you call it? Truly, I took matters into my own hands, formulated a plan that went off without a *major* hitch, and did real, honest good. I didn't write a letter to my city councillor, bitching endlessly like he or she would actually give a shit. I didn't protest, or march. I didn't get a petition going. I acted! Now, I wait to see the fruits of my labour. I purposely avoid looking at the paper that Dad has delivered, or the internet all day, waiting for tonight's news broadcast to get filled in on how everything went after I fled the scene.

Cops must have been everywhere, and my imagination ran wild throughout the night. My dreams really embellished the results of my work. On one hand, I dreamed about the people knowing that I took down this house of horrors crack den, and they held me up as their hero—their white knight. Then on the other hand, I had a nightmare that I killed someone accidentally. Yep, sleep was a roller coaster of emotions last night. Today, as I go about my to do list, my daydreaming is in full swing, using each moment of relaxation as another chapter in the story unfolding in my mind. The outcome is always ... I am a hero.

I make myself a honey ham sandwich with cheese mayo and mustard, grab a drink and sit on the couch in the living room, ecstatic, energized, proud. This must be how Dad felt after a big bust. The news is about to start, and I can't wait. Here we go ... *Tonight's top stories—A known drug den is busted after a mysterious shooting late last night.* Wow! Not only is it a top story, it's the top, top story. It brings me back to the time our entire family came over to see Martial on TV after a huge bust. He stood there solemn and cold, in front of a table full of money, drugs and guns. The entire family cheered at the first sight of Dad, but after a moment or two everyone became bored of watching Dad stand there, and decided to go back to idle chit chat with their drinks in hand—everyone but me of course. I stared at that TV until the last moment of the story. My dad was on TV, and that was about the coolest thing that he could have done at that stage in my life.

"Hello. I'm Peter Ramon, and here are your headlines," the proper news anchor says as the show gets underway. Have you ever wondered why the voice, the hair, the general polish of the news came about? Who talks like that? No one, except reporters and anchors. Why must they always talk like they are going into battle with the Greeks? It's weird.

"A known drug den was the scene of a mysterious shooting at approximately 2 this morning. Police received a phone call reporting shots fired. When police arrived, two missing children were found on the premises, as well as yet-unknown quantities of drugs. Also, in what the police are calling a linked incident, a house was engulfed in flames across the street. Mary Davis has more."

Peter throws to this sensational bombshell reporter, Mary. She's matter-of-factly gorgeous, which has apparently become the norm for news stations; sex sells after all. It's the one constant in the world today.

"The scene was horrific on Mountain Road this morning. As many as six shots were fired at this home in the distance behind me." Those are my shots, but the cops really need to learn how to count (pride). "Police are calling the shooting gang related, and that is about all the information they are offering."

Interestingly, blaming gangs probably leaves me completely in the clear (relief).

"What we do know from sources is that two young girls previously reported missing were found in the house, as well as what can only be described as *large* quantities of drugs."

Looks like I really did do some good here (pride again).

"Police arrested four men, and three women; all have been released on bail." Yes, 7 scumbags down (Wait ... what? All have been released on bail?).

It's been less than 24-hours and all have been released on bail. What the fuck is that? This is not the victory party I had planned. I went through all of this effort to take these guys down, and they get out on bail? Sure, the girls being saved is a fantastic win, but if these assholes keep getting let back out onto the street, then it's a short sighted victory; a loss masquerading as a victory; a broken promise to myself that I would leave a legacy. This can't be happening!

I toss my plate to the side with a half-eaten sandwich, and make haste out the door. I will make sense of this mess.

I arrive at the scene of the crime, the place where I took control, to find reporters strewn on boulevards and front lawns, neighbours watching on. Police are still going through the house, and five cop cars are parked almost drunkly in several different directions. Near the action stands Kyle—cool as a cucumber. He's near the reporters, probably hoping to be asked for a comment, or trolling for a take home chick. Either way, he looks like a douche, but a douche that will probably be able to fill me in.

"Kyle," I call out, as if we're friends of some sort.

"Michael? What are you doing here?"

"I have a friend that lives nearby, and I saw the news, so I figured I'd check it out on the way home."

"Crime scenes aren't a place to hang out."

"Yes. I know. I'm not twelve."

"So then ..." he stares at me, as if that will make me leave.

"Did they really let the people you guys arrested out on bail already?"

"Catch and release. That's the system. Hopefully, if everything is done right, we'll be able to make some of this stick, and they'll spend a whole lot of time in jail, but it's doubtful."

"I just don't understand how they can let people like that out on bail ... if they are as bad as the news is saying."

"All I know is that the house doesn't belong to any of them, so nothing can be done right away. We need to find some stuff that will stick."

"Well, they found drugs inside. That won't stick?"

"We'd have to be able to tie someone to the drugs. No one actually had any on them. It was a buffet setup. But, we shouldn't even be talking about this."

"This is fucking insane!" I say angrily. "What a bullshit system."

Kyle motions for me to come aside and away from the people. "What are you doing here, really?"

"I told you. I'm curious."

"Well, go home. This is a rough neighbourhood and you shouldn't be checking out crime scenes for fun. You also shouldn't be getting so mad at a crime scene. It makes people look at you. Keep your cool and relax. We've got this."

"Are you going to give everyone out here the same speech?"

He gives me a look of death, and then walks away. "Go home, Michael!"

Fucking law enforcement. Fucking system. Fucking lawyers and criminals—basically the same thing. After talking with Kyle I decide to drive with the windows down, and hopefully, refresh my mind. It's stupidly simple (or at least it should be) to connect the dots, and realize these people in that house are all bad people. I'm full of rage like I was in the Doc's office. The planning, the execution; all, probably for nothing. As I drive, I think of the many nights Mom and Dad would argue about his job. Martial was constantly frustrated with the force, which meant Mom had to hear about it, which meant they would get on each other's nerves, which meant awkward nights for the entire family. I get it thoroughly now, though. What a scam.

When I arrive home, I'm fuming, so I decide to take my frustrations out on the wall with two solid holes. I know women find punching a wall ridiculous, but it's such solid stress relief. Why does the world have to function like this? I decide to check out Margaret's site to see if she saw the news. Of course she did. Surely she would see where I was coming from. A blog link is listed on the front page entitled, *The Easy Way*.

Last night, someone (gang or otherwise) shot out the front windows of a known crack den in the city's core area. While I stand behind identifying and solving the issue of crack dens in the city, this is not the way police should be entering homes!! It's almost too convenient for them, having this house shot up ... almost as if they went out of their way to do it (wouldn't be the first time police have stepped outside the law to get the job done). Now there isn't too much detail being shared about the whole incident but it's clear that someone in the neighbourhood could have gotten hurt or worse as a result of this person or persons actions.

If somehow, this site's information led to the incident, I am deeply ashamed. This is not what we are here to do. We're here to make sure that crack dens are identified and dealt with legally. Vigilante justice is not what we need in this city if that is what this was. Vigilantes are just criminals like the people that keep these places up and running.

Please, if this site makes you want to take action, reach out to us for direction. Don't take matters into your own hands because then there's nothing separating us from them.

If you have any information regarding the identity of the shooter, share it. People like this need to be stopped!! I'm sorry if this was actually just gang vs gang violence but I'm frustrated at the thought of this site going up and then having this happen. We believe in following the law to the letter.

Short and bitter; just what I need to make me light up with more rage over the situation. *This bitch*, I think to myself. Not only is she a hypocrite, but she's a dangerous hypocrite. She's out there pushing a hard line on houses like the one I hit, but then she accuses the police of perhaps being behind the incident to get the people going. Turns out this girl I admired at the party is nothing more than a fake. She can keep putting dots on a map, and taking pictures; *armchair blogger bitch*.

The whole situation is frustrating and has me grumpy beyond belief. My mood is sour and Monica picks up on it immediately when she comes over. I try to perk up for her, and not let all of this get to me, but that's a harder task than I would have thought.

"Did you hear about that crack den that got busted?" Of course, she has to bring it up. It's like life is trying to make me explode, and give away that I was the one to do the deed. I had already covered up the hole in the wall with a picture, but if she pushes the issue, I won't be able to hide my anger.

"I did," I say grumpily under my breath.

She shakes off my tone and continues, "It's so interesting how some gang shoots at a house, and it saves missing girls. I guess it just proves the miracles happen, right?"

"So you support the shooter then?"

"I don't think I'd go as far as saying I support whoever did it, but they got the job done. More than the cops would have done."

"I tend to agree." Instantly, I can feel my mood lightening with the conversation. I was worried Monica would have the same viewpoints as Margaret on the subject.

"Hey, what do you think your dad would have thought of all this?"

"I don't know. I guess he would have been happy to see that someone was possibly trying to help out the cops."

"From everything I've heard, your dad despised the policy on these places."

"You know what's crazy? Margaret, who loved my dad for taking down crack dens posted a blog about how wrong this whole thing is."

"Really? Margaret? That's really odd. If anyone would be for it, you would think she would be."

"You would think."

"I was listening to the news in the car on the way over here. The girls they found are safe now, but the guys in the house got out on bail. I bet the girls will be right back out on the street looking for another house just like this one."

"Why would you say that?" I ask, annoyed.

"Well, these guys probably have them hooked on coke or something. They're probably bouncing off the walls right now. I hope their families get them some help."

"Me too. Otherwise, whoever did this didn't accomplish anything at all."

"Isn't that the way, though?" Monica questions as she enters the living room after unpacking groceries in the kitchen. "It's frustrating."

"It really is. In fact, you know what? I'm really frustrated right now with the whole thing. One might say stressed, and my first meeting is tomorrow. I can't possibly go in there stressed. Something should really be done about this," I coyly say to her while pulling her onto my lap on the couch, then getting on top of her and kissing her stomach.

After some much needed stress relief between the sheets, we lay in bed talking about subjects so far removed from the news that I feel a sense of calm come over me. We play twenty-questions with the strict rule that there be no work or illness talk. We stick to *favourite movie, dream celebrity threesome*, stuff like that—the usual, and the welcome.

The sad part about this night is that Monica is leaving for Hawaii in just a few hours. Her parents planned a family vacation months before we met, and there is no backing out now. It's Hawaii, who would? She fought to stay because of me, but ultimately it is their first family vacation in a decade, so I convinced her to go as long as we can FaceTime regularly. The really horrible news about this trip, though ... it's going to be for an entire month!

I try to hold onto this moment in my mind, and refuse to let her out of bed until I know that I absolutely have to let her go. We get dressed and head to the airport. The drive is far too short. Monica has this glow about her—probably because she's getting out of the city—that I can't resist. She's beyond cute in this moment. I pick up on everything she does, from a cute nose crinkle, to the affection in her laugh. This girl has given me hope, and treats me like I'm the only man left in this world that could possibly please her. She's stunning, and humble; fierce, and soft. She's the perfect woman.

I kiss her as we load her baggage onto a cart. I kiss her as she checks in. I kiss her as we walk towards security. I kiss her fifteen times between the car and her gate. We part and she heads for security. I get this lump in my throat, and a tear in my eye. I'm going to miss her, and I'm going to hate every second of my life while she's gone.

"I love you," I shout out of nowhere, as she is handing the security guard her passport and ticket on the way to a month in Hawaii.

She actually cries, immediately. It's like she was storing tears, just waiting for this moment. Mon runs back to me and jumps into my arms. This has to be the biggest hug ever. "I love you, too," she whispers in my ear.

It's like a scene from a movie; nighttime, the terminal is busy, but not full. People go about their lives, while we have this moment, which we own. It's all ours, as if the rest of the world stopped for us to say those words, said many times before, but as if this is the first time two people have really meant it. Sure, you could argue we have only been together but a short amount of time, or you could accept that sometimes the rules don't apply to matters of the heart.

Just before Monica disappears from my sight after going through security, she looks back at me and smiles, letting me know that even if we're 6,083 kilometers apart, we're solid. Nothing will come between us. Not some surfer with perfect teeth, not the fact that her mother has a no cell phone or computer rule on family vacations 90% of the time, nothing. It'll be the last image I have of real life Monica, and I make sure to burn it into my mind. One month apart starts now.

When I get home, I feel restless. My lingering failure from last night continues to dominate news feeds online, and I start to panic about the meeting at Cancer Care. With Monica gone—it's official—nothing is going right. How is it that even with all of these resources, I continue to fail?

Perhaps its because Monica is gone somewhere,

and I am still stuck here, that I get a little stir crazy. Perhaps it is my brain trying to keep me occupied. Regardless of the reason, I pack a bag, grab some cash and start driving. Destination, unknown.

13

A Good Death

HITTING THE HIGHWAY always helps clear my mind. There's therapy in cranking music, and giving yourself little challenges as you drive. Can I split between those two cars to burst into the lead, like I'm on a race track? If I pick this green Mustang as my pace car, will the cops stop me or him? Before I know it, I'm crossing into Saskatchewan, hours from home.

It's 1:30 in the morning, and my energy level is through the floor. I wonder if this a symptom of the Cancer, or if I am starting to lose my night owlness. I think back to when I didn't know I had Cancer. It was still in me, but I didn't recognize the symptoms on a conscious level. Just thinking that the Cancer is taking over means matter has overtaken my mind, and caused me to become symptomatic. Mastering life with this disease is going to be tricky, especially if I keep missing my meetings, which will definitely happen now. Man, Monica is going to be pissed when she finds out I missed the first one, but surely, there's no turning back now. When Doc Scorpio booked me to go to group therapy it didn't even occur to Monica or I that she would be gone.

During one of my pit stops I look in the mirror and barely recognize myself. I'm so pale and dripping in sweat. The only positive is that if this is the Cancer, these symptoms are temporary at this stage. My immune system still has some fight in it.

This pit stop is at a place that many stop at on the road; McDonalds. It's inside one of those gas station, restaurant, store combo locations. This is perfect for me. I pop some Tylenol, and down an energy shot while I wait for my salad. As I sit inside of this impeccably clean restaurant, I feel my energy starting to return. It wafts over me like a wave. I feel better, much. The salad is actually pretty delicious, and that's saying a lot consider Mc Dycs is known for it's grease. CNN is playing in the background, and of course it's more of the same—war, ragging on the President, and opinionated "reporters"—I use that term loosely.

The stop gives me the energy I need to drive another ten hours before stopping at another gas station and passing out for a few hours in the back seat. I had no intention of driving so far—I just went where the road took me. You never know where you'll end up when you really don't care about where you're going.

Waking up feeling refreshed, I decide to make the next town I see my playground for the day. That turns out to be Brooks, Alberta, population 13,676. I stop in at a diner and ask some of the locals what there is to do in their small little town; the consensus is that I should go check out Dinosaur Provincial Park. The only thing in life I loved more than superheroes as a kid, was dinosaurs, so of course, I go. I had no idea something like this existed in Canada. The geography, and history really put you in your place as a human being. You feel really small and insignificant, especially next to fossils of dinosaurs. I have always been amazed by the ability of paleontologists; putting together bones to form a creature. I bet they were all good at puzzles when they were kids. I didn't have the patience for puzzles, which is probably one of the many reasons I'm not a scientist of some sort.

I spend most of my day at the park, snapping selfies, exploring history, being a tourist; such a hidden gem. After, I end up at an all day grill. I pack in the meat until there's no more room for food. Only white meat though; gotta eat clean(ish). I debate going home, but being this stuffed and driving will not be comfortable by any means, so I decide to walk it off. The town itself is a little dull and rustic, but kinda beautiful. Tree lined streets, and the clip clop of horses in the distance give it a photoshoot feel. After about an hour, I find myself wandering through a cemetery, trying to find my way back to the grill.

What a glorious shortcut ... just what I need, more death. As I walk through the grounds, I keep my head up and ignore the hundreds of grave stones that surround me. It's not that I want to disrespect the dead, but just that I don't want to confront the subject on this peaceful day. I imagine that even those without confirmed mortality get a sense of dread for the end while being surrounded by those that have met theirs.

I hurry my pace a bit, the more the surroundings get to me. The road is just on the horizon, but as I concentrate on the finish line, I miss the rock that my right foot collides with. It's not enough to injure me, but I do tumble to the ground, face first into the grass. Luckily, no one is around ... that would have been embarrassing. After a moment of self-deprecating thoughts, I get up to a sitting position, when I notice the grave stone in front of me—*Unknown*. In fact, where I sit at this very moment is an entire row of *Unknowns*. Here, people without an identity have been laid to rest. Even if they accomplished something, they are treated like nothing. This might as well be my fate.

Nothing that I have ever done will make me known. Of course, I tried, but all I end up with is frustration. My fate, it seems, is to be an unknown with a name. Here lies *Michael Burton, Nobody Special, Unknown, Failure*. I sit there for what must have been hours, just staring into space, looking for answers to questions I can't properly formulate. Only the sun's departure from up above and directly into my eyes from the West wakes me from the death clouded haze.

I feel the need to honour these people buried here in some way. Even though it's a bit creepy, I head over to a grave site that has several bouquets of flowers, to snatch one up. I break apart the ribbon and place a flower at the base of each grave stone in that row. I've fundamentally spent time with these people now and that person with numerous bouquets—recently buried—will likely always have flowers presented in their honour. Today, so too will *the Unknowns*.

It's pitch black outside by the time I get back to the grill and into my truck, so I decide to crash at a local motel. I can't get into any of the good places without giving up my ID or credit card, which I didn't bring since I didn't know I would be traveling two Provinces. Without the necessary info, I end up in a seedy 'cash only' motel. It's hard to fall asleep in places like this. You never know what was done on the bed. I read in The Rock's autobiography that he was once so broke, he had to grab a piss and placenta stained mattress out of a dumpster. This mattress could easily be stained with piss, hooker fluid, or placenta. In fact, it's almost a certainty. I doubt the cleaning staff at a place you can stay for $29 a night pride themselves in their mastery of craft. Luckily, there's a Friends marathon on. It's enough to distract me as I fade. Of course, just as I'm about to completely crash out I hear shouting and banging from the room next to mine. It's clearly a fight between a couple. I get on my knees on top the bed and press my ear to the wall.

"You stupid bitch," the guy yells.

The woman, clearly timid, replies with reason. "Think about what you're doing, Arn. When you get like this, it's like I don't even know you."

"You make hitting women a pleasure, you fucking cunt."

"You promised me that wouldn't happen again. You swore to me up and down that you'd never hit me again. You're not a bad guy. Just calm down. If you hit me, I'm gone. You know that, so stop and think."

The room goes silent for a moment. I listen intensely; nothing. I've never actually heard of the *stop and think* argument working. Curious, I go outside and look through the window. There's a little crack in the drapes that allows me to barely see what is going on. Just as I get my eyes focused past the drape, into the room, this Arn guy picks up a phone off of the night stand and cracks the girl on the side of her head. The sheer violence of it all takes me by surprise, and I actually jump backwards like I could somehow get hit too. I'm stunned for a moment. *What do I do? Call the cops?* She could bleed out, or he could keep going. I look through the drapes once more to see him pick her up and throw her onto the bed face down. He picks up that phone again. Not liking where this is going, I decide to act.

The door is unlocked, so I burst in, and relentlessly

attack the guy. We exchange shot after shot, mine connecting more than his (thank you, Martial). As we push each other around the room, we end up breaking pretty much everything. The woman lays unconscious on the bed, but in the middle of our fighting we knock her onto the floor. At one point we trip over her, which gets her stirring. I finally get the better of him, so the coward decides to try and lock himself in the bathroom. Only problem for him, the door doesn't actually lock or hinge shut, so he's left just trying to hold the door in place between us. I'm not sure why I don't just pick her up and take her out of there, but I decide a better plan is to take a running dive—shoulder first—at the door, knocking Arn to the ground. Unluckily for me the floor is wet and I bail right into the bath tub. I try to get up as fast as I can but everything's so wet. Arn jumps on my back and covers my head with the shower curtain. I can't see much and slowly, my oxygen is cut off.

As I begin to fade, my brain kicks back in for one moment of clarity. With this fuck mounting me from behind, pulling as hard as he can, he's stretching the curtain to it's ripping point. I scratch at the curtain until a small hole pokes through, giving me air. I wonder why no one thinks of that in the movies. I gasp for every breath until my breathing is as stable as it can be.

He tries to get better footing, but slips on the wet tub and falls hard, knocking his head on the bath tap. When we lock eyes it is clear to me that he has no intention of letting me walk out of here. We're both dazed, and the fighting has exhausted us. Luckily for me a bit of oxygen deprivation is easier to recover from than a blow to the head. I'm on my feet first, and grab the plunger. With all of my weight behind it, I jam the handle straight through his left eye. He screams out in pain. It's so loud that anyone remotely close to the motel will be able to hear him. I need to shut the guy up, so I pull the handle out of his eye socket, and douse his head in the toilet. After a few seconds, he's still struggling. With one hand, I hold him down, and the other, I lay shots to the back of his head. The struggle continues, as he gasps in the water and his body flails in an effort to get me off of him. This guy will not break the hold I have. Finally, the fight is over. His limp body lies half in the tub, with his head stuck in the toilet.

I fall off of him, onto the floor panting like a dog in summer heat, and once again, there I am on my ass staring at the dead. This time though, I killed. This death is on me. Holy shit ... I just killed someone. Quickly, I rationalize; it was either him or me. I get that, and I'm not sad about the result, but I start crying none the less. I try to control my breathing, and focus on the fact that I just killed someone that in all likelihood deserved it. Still, my body shakes from the shock of it all. *Here lies Arn, a real piece of shit*.

I snap out of my focus on Arn's body after about a minute and wipe my tears. There's blood all over the bathroom, and surely the entire room is completely destroyed. As I look at the rest of the shitty little motel room from where I sit in the bathroom, I see the woman standing there in shock. She's crying; I just can't tell if it's because she's sad, or relieved. She walks over to me, staring intently at the guy's body. As I stumble to stand as she takes me by the arm, and walks me out of the bathroom without saying a word. Her hand grips the bathroom door knob softly, as she slowly closes the door. Dropping to the ground against the wall, she sobs.

I have no idea what to do, so we sit there for about ten minutes before she looks up and stammers out her name. "I'm Daisy."

"Michael."

The silence in the room is deafening. We just look through each other in the dark. There's very little light. Her recently deceased other half and I smashed them all, so the only illumination is the street light that slips through the curtain where I saw what should not have been seen. I'm looking at her to see if she's okay. She's looking at me, trying to decide whether she should hate my very existence. Moments pass before we hear a knock.

"Hello." We're frozen in place, breathing heavy, hoping for the person to go away. Of course, he doesn't. "This is the caretaker. I'm getting reports of shouting and banging in there."

We sit still. "What should we do?" she whispers.

"If you don't answer, I'm going to have to call the cops," the caretaker shouts from behind the door.

Looking around the torn up room, an idea dawns on me. "Just go with whatever happens next," I whisper back.

"Just a minute," I shout, as I strip down to my boxers.

"Take your clothes off, I tell her. Everything but your underwear. Drop your bra straps."

She's confused, and frozen still. I get really close to her and place my hands on her triceps, "If you don't want to go to jail tonight, strip!"

She quickly takes off her clothes, while I find a tie, wrap her in a blanket, cover the side of her face that's swelling from the phone hit with her hair and we answer the door together.

Standing there is an out of shape, clearly downtrodden older guy, probably in his 50's or so. His clothes are dirty, and his boot laces are untied.

The first thing the guy sees is the tie around my

wrist, and her wrapped in a blanket. "I didn't think we were that loud," I say.

"People reported shouting and banging."

"Well hunny, I think we should take that as a compliment," I say cavalierly, as I kiss Daisy on her forehead.

"You two were having sex?"

"Ahh ... yes sir. I used my safe word at least fifteen times, but there's no listening from this one, once she gets going."

She just fakes a smile and stares at the ground, while he stares at her, and I stare at him. What do you say in a moment like this?

"That's ... pretty fantastic," the caretaker says, as he cracks a smile. "Just keep it down, will ya?"

"We were actually already asleep when you knocked."

"Are you sure you're okay ma'am?" He puts the spotlight on her, and this lie is either going to work swimmingly, or we're sunk. I don't know that I have it in me to kill someone for just being nosy. I mean, try to kill your girlfriend and I'll fuck your shit up, but I'm not cold hearted enough to just start taking the life of anyone that gets in my way.

"Just tired. 3 orgasms," she says as she buries her face in my shoulder.

He tries to look into the room, but it's pitch black. "Alright kids. Have a good night."

He walks away, we shut the door, and both of us let out a sigh of relief as we fall to the bed. "What made you think of that?" she asks.

"I don't know, really. I guess I'm just good in bad situations. My mind seems to fire faster when I'm panicked."

We both lay on the bed staring at the ceiling, bewildered over our experience together. For the first time since she was hit with that phone our breathing is back to normal. The adrenaline is slowing. Aside from the dead guy drinking toilet water, there's actually some levity in the air.

"This isn't the first time you've done something like this, is it?" she asks.

"This isn't the first time he's beat you, is it?"

She sees that no answer is an answer, and takes it as is. "He's been beating me since grade eleven and I kept going back."

"You didn't tell anyone?"

"No one to tell. We're both from foster homes. Have no idea who our parents are or if they're even still alive. I mean, about a year ago I came into a bit of cash and used it for counseling. I really did believe he was done with the violence."

"That's rough."

"We were what the system calls *at risk youth*. That's what united us. What tore us apart is that he actually was, and I just played the role a couple of times. I knew being with him was the wrong way to go about things, but he kept me safe from everyone else."

"You asked me something before."

"You don't have to answer that."

"No. I want to. I should," I pause for a moment, planning out what to say next. I'm not sure why I feel the urge to tell her what I've done, but for some reason I feel safe in this room. "I recently took it upon myself to out some crack dealers by shooting up their house. That was the first time I did something like this—step in by any means necessary and help."

"So, you're what? Going around dealing with bad people in the middle of the night like that TV show, Dexter?"

"I haven't killed anyone; well, except him." I point

to the washroom door to make it very clear this is my first time. "I just find myself in a situation where the most amount of good I can do in minimal time is ridding the world of these types of guys. It's almost like my dad prepared me for it my whole life. I guess that is like Dexter. But it's not working out too well. The whole idea was to get these crack heads arrested. They got out the next day. Now they can run if they want to, hurt whoever they want to. It's pretty shitty."

"Why in a minimal amount of time? Are you dying or something?" Awkward silence just like when I cracked the tumour joke in Doc Scorpio's office. It takes her but three seconds to figure out that I'm knock, knock, knocking on Heaven's door. "Oh my God. You're dying. I'm so sorry." Another of the many awkward pauses.

"It's alright. Well, it's not, but you learn not to sweat the small stuff, as they say."

"You had a very different plan for your life, didn't you?"

"You sound like you know something about that."

"A little bit. I wasn't supposed to be this girl in this room, with that guy. I was actually supposed to be a model."

"I could see that. You've got *that look*." She really did. Tall, long hair, symmetry, drop dead gorgeous.

"I actually spent about six months really going somewhere, but that life comes with it's own set of demons. When I weighed the two lives against each other, Arnold seemed like the better choice."

"Or not."

"Or not. So that's my story. What's yours?" She has a certain level of genuine compassion that you don't find in many people. I can tell that she's definitely one of the good ones.

"My story is just as complex. My dad died, I was diagnosed with Cancer not too long ago, ended up in a relationship with the doctor's receptionist, inherited a ton of cash, and now I find myself surrounded by death and violence at every turn."

"Are you going to try doing what you did before, again?"

"Not sure. I've never been the smartest guy in the room, or the dumbest. I'm pretty average at most things. But, I'm good in combat. If my dad hadn't gone MIA, I probably would be a cop right now. I'm not sure what to do with myself. Shooting out windows won't do much if the system keeps letting them back out on the street."

"Well, Arnold isn't going to be getting back out on the street, as you say. Pretty sure you ended his tyranny. I can't say that I'm okay with the whole thing, but if you hadn't come in, I might be dead, so I owe you—at the very least—my silence."

"Thanks. You don't know much about me though, so I'm not all that worried."

"You said you have a girlfriend at home. Does she know what you do?"

"Not a clue."

"If you keep going, you're gonna have to tell her. Depending on how long you live for, you're going to need to talk to someone."

"I'm talking to you."

"Yeah, but tomorrow I'll be long gone, and you'll still need someone."

"I guess I'll cross that bridge when I come to it." I look at her, puzzled. It occurs to me that she doesn't seem too troubled by any of this. It's like I'm telling her I work in finance or something. "How are you not freaking out right now?"

"This stuff doesn't phase me. I saw a kid get killed in front of me at a foster home when I was ten. My so-called best friends did meth, lines, you name it. Arnold has put me in the hospital six times. We went to that counseling I mentioned, but clearly that didn't help. I've seen the ugly side of the world, and I get why you did what you did, both with the crack den, and here. You run the risk of your girlfriend not being able to understand, but you're going to need someone eventually."

"I have a few months left, max. I want to spend that doing some good, and not running the risk of losing her. I can last those few months."

She touches my face softly, and draws my eyes to hers. A single tear streams down her cheek. "I hope so. I can tell behind those eyes of yours, you're a good person."

Sometimes you have a moment with someone, and you know that it will stick in your mind forever. Her eyes, that tear, the softness of her hand—it will all be permanently burnt into my mind. It's clear that she's suffered in her life, but even with everything, she has grace. That's a quality you don't find in many women anymore. The things that the rest of the world have become okay with are not okay with her, but she's tough enough to handle it all. I can see those eyes changing the world one day.

"You deserve to leave it all behind," I tell her. "After tonight, just walk away from him, and never look back."

"That brings up a horrible point. You say your brain works better under pressure, so what do we do now? I mean we have this mess, and a dead body. How do I leave it all behind when it's all so messed up?"

I think for a moment, and then the obvious answer hits me. "Clean."

"Don't you watch those crime shows? No one can

ever clean good enough. They have special lights, and dogs, and forensics, and sprays."

"No one knows that there's been a crime. As far as anyone is concerned, two people had great sex in here tonight. That's it. You have a better idea?"

She simply shrugs in agreement, and then we get to work.

She takes the bedroom, I take the bathroom—for obvious reasons. The first thing I do is burn off Arnold's fingerprints with a lighter, then I rip out his teeth, and after that, I smash his face in with the shower rod. It's messy work, but it's what has to be done. I don't want the body easily recognizable if it's ever found. While I'm doing all of this I feel disgusting. I find my hands shaking at times, and at one point I cry uncontrollably again. The blood and my tears mix like a cocktail of disaster. What I'm doing is something no human should ever have to do, but tonight, it's what this human has to do.

The motel keeps garbage bags under the sink, so all it takes is a bit of duct tape—which was in my truck amongst the crap I used to hide my gun before—about eight bags, and Arnold is all wrapped up. The blood takes nearly four hours to clean. It takes so long that Daisy decides to help out. I did my best to keep her out of the bathroom, but certain women are too willful to stop from doing anything. She's now accepted the reality of her situation, and is dealing with it. Luckily, there's no carpet, so the blood from his eye is pretty easy to contain. It even wipes right off of the shower curtain. After the initial clean up, we take the body and put it in the back of my Durango, which proves difficult and tiring. If Arnold had been a fat guy I'm not even sure we would have been able to carry him at all. Dead weight is so much more complex to carry than a heavy object.

We go back into the room and take shifts switching between the main room, and bathroom, using the fresh eyes approach to find more stuff to clean. Eventually, the room is spic and span, aside from some broken mirrors, lights, and a desk. I drop $1000 on the nightstand with a note, *Sorry for the mess. We'll come back when we're trying to be romantic next time*. I feel a bit of humour will go a long way to reducing suspicion.

The first order of business, after we leave the hotel, is to dump Arnold's car off. I drive his, Daisy drives mine. It seemed like a good idea. She shouldn't be sitting in that car remembering her life with the corpse. We take his car to a wrecker, and drop the piece of shit off in the back. It'll be months before anyone notices it out there, and by then, no one will care. You can always depend on people doing as little work as possible, so I'm sure they'll chalk it up to a paperwork error.

A couple of hours later we end up in the middle of nowhere. It's still pitch black outside, and we have at least another few hours of night left. We dig, and dig, then bury, and bury. It's peaceful out here with darkness in all directions. It almost feels like another planet. On the horizon, the stars light up the sky just enough to see the faint outline of mountain. There's no music, no distractions, and something so calm about the whole situation, oddly. Daisy and I talk at length about her past, my future, and what's next for both of us.

Like a couple of thirteen year olds we try spotting the constellations while we lay on the hood of my truck. We pretend we're doing this to pass the time, but really, it's because we are exhausted, and can't bring ourselves to do much else. Our time in the middle of nowhere is flirtatious, but never steps over a line that Monica wouldn't forgive. Seeing her so carefree without the threat of Arnold, makes me feel at peace with killing him. Daisy really is a different person compared to just a few hours ago; she's happy as a result of him being out of her life, and that's all I need to make a decision in that moment—*I will kill again.*

Just getting those assholes back in Winnipeg arrested did little good. People like that, people like Arn—who create victims—need to be stopped, wiped out. The relief on Daisy's face is enough for me. If I'm going to die—a person who has never done any wrong to anybody—I'm going to take them all with me. My dad's research will read like the obits of the future. Killing Arn wasn't easy, but knowing I could potentially save more people like Daisy is enough to get me through the horror of what I'm going to do.

I don't share my revelation with her, but my mind is made up.

As the sun begins to fill the sky with colour, it's time to go. She jumps in the passenger seat of my truck and we head far away from Arnold. It takes only a few minutes before she nods off. I'm okay with driving in silence. It gives me a chance to think. I go back and forth between being resolute in killing him, and question whether he deserved to die, but as the sun continues to rise and catches her face, I know it was for the best. The bruise will heal, and she might be able to as well.

As we arrive at a bus station she tosses and turns. This is clearly a girl that likes her sleep. Even with all the noise around us and the uncomfortable car seats, she's not waking up. Leaving her in the truck, I buy Daisy a ticket for the next bus out of town.

Unfortunately, after the purchase is done it's time

to part ways, so I open up her door and nudge her awake. "Daisy, it's time to go," I whisper in her ear. It takes a bit, but she finally opens her eyes. A couple of squints to adjust her vision to the light, and a very satisfying stretch with some back cracks gets her up onto her feet.

"So this is it, huh?"

"Seems so," I reply. "Oh hey, I stopped along the way and picked you up a prepaid phone. It's loaded, and here's some money."

I hand her an envelope full of cash, she looks inside, and I can tell she doesn't want to accept the money, but has to. All that is left is a hug. For some reason, and I can't quite put my finger on it, it's the best hug I've ever experienced. I dare say it's better than any hug from Monica. A hug is usually just a hug, then there's a hug from Daisy. It sounds silly, but I guess you'd have to experience it to really get what I'm saying.

We part, and she walks towards the bus. Before boarding, she turns to me and smiles. This is the second woman that has smiled at me as she departs my life, just letting me know that everything's alright. Unlike Monica though, when that bus door shuts, Daisy will vanish, never to be seen again.

"Good luck with your new start, Daisy," I call out.

"Good luck with your ending, Michael."

14

Jason White Must Die

FRESH-BACK FROM MY DAISY EXPERIENCE, I am still convinced that my decision is the best way to go. The entire ride home, I went back and forth in my mind, weighing my options. I already have blood on my hands, the blood of a bastard. The animals like Arn would be the only blood that would stain me; criminals, victimizers, those that the law could never seem to catch up with.

I decide that I will, but that doesn't mean I can. Adrenaline and necessity allowed me to kill Arnold, but, when I shot at that crack den, even without the intent of killing someone, my hands shook. I guess that's the humanity in me. Perhaps it's my soul screaming out. I'm not sure, but what I do know is I can't kill just any criminal. Only the worst of the worst will do.

Dad's work stares me in the face. All of these criminals just keep trampling on good people, with very little repercussions. There are 27 days until Monica comes home, which means I'm on the clock. I have no intention of dying in that time, so it will be spent doing some good for the world—for my city.

Doctor Scorpio's office has called me four times today. He's no doubt mad that I missed my appointment, but there are more pressing matters to attend to.

As I search my phone for targets, I ask myself the question that has been burning in my mind since Arnold stopped breathing: how bad is bad enough to deserve to die? Surely a burglar or low-level dealer doesn't rank. There's a chance both of them could be doing what they're doing out of desperation, and maybe their families are on the line. I guess, in my mind, what constitutes a deserving death is any criminal that preys on people in a way that leaves no interpretation. That brings me to my favourite criminal so far, Jason White.

Yes, Mister White is a great benchmark. He's a pedophile, a high-level drug dealer, a victimizer, and an opportunist. He works the system in such a way that he can rub his successes in the faces of his victims. His crimes make it so a person can never be whole again.

I tried to take him down without harm, but the courts didn't do their job. That night when he was arrested after I shot up the den satisfied by hunger for justice, but his release has filled me with rage that I can't seem to shake. Now, he's probably walking around looking for his next victim. Just the sight of his picture on my phone makes my blood boil. Yes, this feels right. Jason White will be my victim. Jason White must die.

But how? What's a death befitting of such a scumbag?

I've lost neither the technical or intuitive skills to shoot, so that's probably my best bet. I can't get too close though, or be left in a position where I have to run with such a large gun again. There are logistical challenges that I have to address. But first, I need ammo and another gun. I doubt Dad will have any other weapons around here, but I have yet to go through those packed closets. This clean house is about to get cluttered again.

Turns out Martial was hiding more secrets. I find another rifle, two hand guns, and even a semi-automatic. The semi scares me a bit so there's no chance I'm using that. Not today. The hand guns even have silencers, and there's a bullet proof vest that I almost completely skip over with it hidden so well. I also find hunting gear and bullets, so I have everything I need except a plan.

Scouring Dad's work for any information that might give me an idea as to how I could execute Jason leads me to an important note written in the tiniest font outside of a margin; Jason's delivery schedule before he went to jail. Every stop along his drug dealing route was noted; 5 in total. *How did Martial follow this idiot all over the North End, and not get caught?* Dad was stealthy.

I figure the best place to strike will be outside of the area high school. The neighbourhood around the school was, at one time, prestigious. It's where all the new immigrants with money built their homes. The people were friendly, the streets were alive, and there was pride evident in the grooming of grass, and the fresh paint. Today, the area is a cesspool, mixing the poor and the depraved. It's even worse than the neighbourhood that den was in. This is why Jason White spends his time here. Dad documented Jason's patterns meticulously. He stated numerous times in his notes, "criminals are creatures of habit—can't resist their *order*"—so I don't expect that his routine has changed.

Before I leave my house to check out the school, I make myself a steak sandwich with mashed potatoes. This could be my last meal if something goes wrong, so I make it something decent. There's nothing like a barbecued steak, marinated and seasoned, with some hot sauce. Once done, I suit up and head out. Dad's bulletproof vest is heavy and uncomfortable, but necessary to ensure I'm as protected as I can be. The gun holster keeps grabbing me in between my waist and ribs. I'm unsettled, but the anticipation of my night ahead is far more prevalent in my mind. After all, there is a good chance that I'm killing a man tonight, premeditated. *Fuck, what a life this has become.*

I reach the corner of Magnus and Manitoba around 10pm, and stop my truck on an inconspicuous corner. My heart is pounding, and I need to relax, so I turn off the lights, slap in some ear buds and turn on my iPod.

10:20, 10:35, 10:50, 11 ... it seems that there is a chance Jason's routine *has* changed since dad last tracked his movements. I'm committed to this course of action, though, so I wait a bit longer. At 11:20, I decide it is time to go home; that is, until I see headlights coming up the street behind me. Could this be Jason White?

I ready my rifle and crouch down in my seat. It's pitch black in the neighbourhood, aside from one street light on the block. The car passes and I get a glimpse of the driver—it's him. My heart starts to pound harder and I can feel the light trickle of sweat beads running down my forehead. It's like in the doc's office and in the hotel room, but the adrenaline is different somehow. I'm able to control it with a few deep breaths and closing my eyes for a moment. Instead of feeling a complete lack of control, once I open my eyes, I feel steady ... almost calm.

I decide to watch what Jason does before killing him, or perhaps I hesitate. As he sits in his car alone, I get into position and settle my rifle on the hood of the truck. He's three car lengths ahead of me on the opposite side of the street. Fate has stepped in and positioned Jason perfectly for a kill from afar. As I line up my shot through the scope, I get a tightness in my chest, and lose my calm. In short, I chicken out. Dropping against the wheel of the truck, clenching my rifle, I try to psych myself up for the kill. I can't. My hesitation is a clear sign that I shouldn't be out here. Perhaps this whole thing was a mistake. *Who was I to think I could just go around the city and start killing people?* I sit for a moment longer, waiting for Jason to drive away so he won't see me, only he doesn't.

I carefully look from beyond my truck across at his car. *What is he waiting for? A customer? A friend? Maybe this isn't a drug deal at all.* There's no one around as far as I can see in both directions, and I can't hear any footprints pounding the pavement. God, I just want him to drive away.

Then, I see it—perhaps the most horrific sight of my life (and I made a bloody mess of killing Arnold, so that says something). I watch in horror as a boy—no older than fourteen—runs down a sidewalk and jumps into his car. After a few moments, I see the shadow of the kid disappear. I shudder to think what this could mean for him. A sensation of anger and pain wafts over me. I feel like crying but no tears come. I let out a silent yell while I sit there doing nothing.

I cannot let this happen in front of me. No more hesitation; I must act! If I'm going to do something about this guy, it's going to have to be up close and personal, as I have no idea if I'll hit the kid with a rifle shot. One deep breath, then I get up, pull my hand gun, and walk over to Jason's car. As I approach, he's completely unaware that I am standing there, so I decide to tap on the driver side window with my gun. He's startled and pushes the kid away.

I open the door and point the gun at Jason's forehead. "Get out of here kid," I say as I get closer to the sick fuck.

The young boy grabs a bag of drugs, gets out of the car and runs into the shadows. Jason's eyes switch between the gun and me. He's trying to figure out his next move—not easy when you are staring down the barrel of a loaded pistol. Unfortunately for me, my hands begin to shake like at the crack den. At first, I don't think he notices, but a smirk creeps onto his face.

"Put that thing away before you hurt somebody, Haus," he says to me as he gets up out of his seat and stands just outside of his car. He's dressed in a baggy grey dress shirt which is stained with sweat, black dress pants and his dick is hanging out from his fly. "Actually, give that to me. It's a really nice piece, and I could use it for my collection. It deserves to be used by a real man."

"Put that thing away," I say, pointing at his crotch with shakiness in my voice.

He puts his dick back in his pants and zips up. "So what's the play here? You gonna kill me? You got a problem with me getting my knob slobbed by a kid?"

"A little bit, yeah."

"It's not my fault his mom likes my white more than she likes her kid, is it? I'm not to blame here, so ... put ... the ... fucking gun ... DOWN!"

His face makes me ill; that cleft lip and messy hair poorly disguising a bald spot. His beady little eyes and veiny neck are exactly what you'd expect to find on someone like him. He's straight out of a wanted poster, uglier in person now that I've seen him up close with my own two eyes. If ever there was *the look* of a pedophile, this is exactly what I would imagine.

I stand fast and with resolve as he yells at me one

more time to put the gun down—he takes offense. After a moment of staring each other down, he attempts to lunge for my gun. That's when it happens—*BANG!* Without a second thought, I instinctively pull the trigger and shoot him right through the chest. The twisted metal that spins through the air and lodges inside of Jason has no regard for human life. It tears a hole through him like paper. The bullet does not respect him, nor does it know him. The bullet has one job to do: tear at his flesh and insides, causing maximum damage.

I expected the silencer to make the shot, well ... silent, however it simply diffuses the sound. I'm startled, but at least the shot sounded more like a firecracker than a bullet leaving a barrel. Jason falls back against the door of his car and slowly falls to the road. He plants himself on the ground gracefully somehow, and lets out a shaky breath. Jason tries to use his hands to cap the blood that streams from his body like water from a tap, but eventually the blood spills through his fingers. Breathing is becoming more difficult and he now begins to completely shake from head to toe—not quite as violent as a seizure, more like a person locked out of their house in winter for too long. Without notice, he craps his pants. The smell is repulsive, and I can see it in his face that he's humiliated. This isn't like in the movies. There's no quick death here.

I look around to see if anyone is coming out of their home. No one. As he begins to fade, I kneel down next to him, staring into his eyes. This man was once a child, and perhaps still someone's kid. At one point he had to have dreams beyond that which he became. Now he's just a disgusting mess, smelling like shit, dying on cold pavement. I almost feel sorry for him. No one should die this way, but I shake the remorse off. He doesn't deserve it.

Thinking of all the people he's hurt, I whisper into his ear, "I want you to know that the only reason I was able to find and stop you, is because my dad, Martin Burton—Martial—had you all figured out."

Jason fights to speak. "You think I'm going to die? Oh, I'm gonna live and come looking for you. I know your face, and a bullet can't stop me."

Maybe he's right—one bullet may not stop him. You hear it happening all the time; people surviving a single shot. I mean the guy can still taunt me for fuck sakes. His smug attitude, combined with the mental image of a boy going down on a man, which will be burnt into my mind forever, cause me to snap. I stand up, point the gun, and unload an entire clip into him. With each bullet, his body convulses against the car and pavement. Eight shots, and after the last one, Jason's body slumps to the ground while his blood pools together.

Watching blood move is strange, and for whatever reason, hypnotic. The blood from his head smacks the pavement, and causes a splash, while the blood from his chest and back pours out. The two streams join on the road. Arnold's blood was different, more what you would expect. Jason's blood is thick. It's darker than I would have imagined, too. The red—almost black—puddle that he now sits in grows methodically through cracks and distortions in the pavement.

I stand there a moment—sweating, staring at the body of a criminal, dead. I guarantee that he never saw me coming. As I kneel back down beside his body to look him dead in the eye for any final sign of life, I get, what I feel to be, a glimpse into his soul. I see a dark man, disturbed and broken, now dead, given back to his maker in pieces. In the distance I hear sirens, perhaps headed in my direction. Maybe someone saw me and has called the cops. A moment longer, I kneel over him, staring, until I hear a voice.

"You must get out of here." A woman no older than me says with a whisper and a measure of concern in her voice. I never take my eyes off of Jason. "My little boy called the cops. They'll be here any minute now. Get out of here."

I'm confused as to why this woman would help me. "I just killed a man outside of your home, and you're helping me? Why?" I still have yet to look away from my victim.

"Darling, calling him a man is an insult to all men. He was a pig; a piece of garbage. If I had the ability to, I would have killed him long ago."

"While I tend to agree, it's still fucking weird how okay you are with this."

"I am on the side of good. That man was a terrible person. I can't be bothered to defend an asshole."

It seems that this woman is my judge and jury on this night. I turn away from Jason, and look deep into the woman's eyes. It's clear she will not report me. There's pain there. Perhaps her kid was a victim of Jason at one point or another.

"What's your name?"

"Lils, now go!" She urges.

I run for my truck, turn the key, and head in a direction opposite the police sirens. A few blocks away I find myself stopped in a driveway. *How did I get here?* The drive is a blur of turns and back lanes. I can barely even remember a single feature on the woman's face as she told me to leave. My instincts got me out of there, and nothing else.

Closing my eyes and resting my head back, my

body calms again. I just killed a man. Oddly enough someone basically thanked me for doing so.

When I was a kid my dad killed a man for hurting women. Now—in this moment—I killed a man for hurting women and children. It seems that by my own definition, established as a child, tonight, I am a real hero.

15

The Grey Area

I HAVEN'T SLEPT because every time I close my eyes, I see red, then I see Jason, then ... I see the monster in me. After trying without any luck to simply drift off, I give up and attempt the Pharmaceutical approach. Dad was taking sleeping pills and had a bottle of NyQuil tucked away in the back of his fridge. Not even too much of both can shut my brain off.

When I got home last night I was still riding an extreme high after killing that waste of skin, but as the night wore on, the weight of my choice started to pull me down into an abyss. I don't actually feel bad for killing that guy, but I do feel guilt. He had to be stopped, and the world is a better place today because of what I did. No, I don't feel bad, but my nature—the basic building block of human existence—is holding on by a thread. At any moment I feel as if I'm going to tear and fall apart.

As I sit on the couch with scotch in hand watching for the sun to rise, I try to reconcile the feeling of guilt for ending a life, but not feeling bad for the specific life I took. As a kid, my mom attempted to get me to go to church. It didn't last long, but she was going through a phase, and as the dutiful son, I had to go through the phase with her. The minister spoke of God's plan, and how it is not for us to know. It's a test of our character to follow the plan and those that do are rewarded with eternal life. I'm paraphrasing, but those words stick with me in this moment, on this couch. What if, by killing Jason I'm defying God's plan? What if all those teachings in all those churches are right? I'm going straight to Hell; first in my mind, then the literal place beneath us (if you believe in that kinda shit).

Of course, if I'm going to believe any of that, I have to believe God wanted Jason to abuse children and ruin innocent lives. I'm so often confused by religion. How is it possible that God wants these children to be sexually assaulted by a pervert, then have to go through years of therapy, and possibly kill themselves? None of that makes any sense. I don't care if he's both merciful and vengeful, there's no way that's in the plan. It can't be, and if it is then I guess I don't care about messing with it.

It is more likely that the right thing to do is take these assholes out, and my guilt is the punishment for not figuring out how to solve the problem without killing. In all of history, soldiers have taken up arms to defend what is right. Caesar fought Pompey, the Allies fought the Axis Powers, and today the Coalition fight terrorist cells like ISIS. Blood has always been spilt in the name of progress, and decisively I'm spilling the blood of evil people; I'll take my haunted mind in exchange for destroying evil. It's selfish to do anything else. I wonder if this is justification or if this is just a process of understanding my own actions.

I can't close my eyes without seeing him, and in the twelfth hour since pumping Jason full of bullets, my mind has decided that when I close my eyes, I should picture myself in his place. It's a dark vision to have, and terrifies me to my core. I attempt to occupy my brain with endless distractions, but no matter what I do, I can't escape the hold he has on me. There are no visions or hallucinations, like you might expect; however, I can see him in my peripheral vision wherever I go. I almost wish Jason White could speak to me from beyond the grave. Maybe then we could have it out, and I could be rid of him. My limited imagination due to lack of sleep will not give me that reprieve, however.

I don't know what else I can do to take my mind off of this. If only Monica were here. She would think I'm just having a bad day because of the Cancer, and she would comfort me. I have a long wait until she's home.

I spend the week playing Wii, coming as close as any man before me to maxing out iTunes purchases, working out, going for long runs, drinking myself into a stupor, and I do some more renovating. This time, the upgrades are functional. The hall closet across from the living room has a lot of depth, so I take it upon myself to build a false wall. Behind it, the guns and gear are stored safely away so that Monica will never find them. I'm even bored enough to bring the safes up, and hide them permanently, too. That's not an easy task, but at least it's a workout. Even though I haven't decided if I'll continue with my journey, I might as well be prepared. Having everything in one spot will help keep me organized.

In a final attempt to escape my mental prison for awhile, I call Derek over to play some vids. It actually works in a way. Instead of thinking about the weight of my decisions, I start to think about all of this from a different angle.

"Why do you think Hollywood is always making a point of having heroes like Batman not kill anyone, but then they release characters like Deadpool that go around killing everyone?" I ask, while Derek pounds away on his controller, trying to be a virtual hero himself.

"Well, first of all, you're merging the DC and Marvel Universe, and that's just not right," he retorts.

"Okay fine. Captain America and Deadpool. They both exist, and murder is not an option for one, but a way of life for the other."

"I'd say it's because it takes all kinds to make the world a safe place."

"You think?"

He pauses the game, grabs his beer, and gets serious for a moment (because superhero talk is serious business, folks). "Look at the villains versus the heroes. You've got your Supermans and Captain Americas that don't need to kill. Then you have heroes like Iron Man who kills but it's never really an issue because he's so closely tied to the military-industrial complex. After that, you have the guys that can't kill, like Batman, because they have to hold onto their humanity. But once you clear them off the table you've got Wolverine, Deadpool, Punisher, Thor, and Black Widow. They kill because they're set in a more realistic world, I guess. They kill because that's what it takes to be a hero in the world they live in with the villains they have to fight."

"Man, you've sat up nights thinking about this, huh?"

He laughs at the idea, then shrugs his shoulders, admitting he's spent many a night geeking out alone. The viewpoint actually makes a lot of sense. At one point I knew a bodybuilder that really broke down diet to me. He said meal prep and that kind of insane dieting is meant for people like him, but all these other people have taken it too far. If you just want to be in good shape and healthier, it comes down to very basic choices: you don't get deep fried food, or extreme grease; you eat pita chips instead of potato chips; then, when you feel like you've slipped up, you go harder at the gym. With the right routine and good balance, you'll be healthy. If you think about it, you can apply that same principal to the world of heroes. There are different heroes for different worlds, and I just happen to live in one that requires more extreme action.

I mean, people can judge me, and they will. But, it's not like I'm killing randoms. Jason White had many chances before a visit from me. Criminals don't have to be criminals; it's more about their personal desire to get what they feel entitled to, and damn the people that unintentionally get in their way. In many cases, the cops could have done a better job. The judge could have seen through the bullshit. Society as a whole could hold that person accountable by not accepting a person after they've victimized. But then again, society is fucked up too. We love train wrecks, a good villain, and the rise to fall of celebrities. As a tribe, the human race craves destruction, so why can't I be the one to the destroy those looking to destroy us?

"Shit, Derek. You've made me feel much better."

"Better than what exactly? And how does talking about Marvel and DC help you?"

Sometimes you just say things you shouldn't. "I mean, c'mon. Who hasn't tried to make sense out of the superhero universes? I can finally rest easy at night."

We both laugh, and he's none the wiser. Of course, he would never imagine that I was a Punisher of sorts.

Now, you could be thinking one of two things. Either A, it's ridiculous for anyone to base their life decisions on the choices made by characters that come out of a script; or B, these guys are the biggest fucking nerds on the planet. Either way, you'd be wrong.

Real nerds live in their mom's basement, have *work*

at home jobs, collect video game consoles, and could never hold a decent conversation with anybody. To your other point ... Superman is one of the greatest characters in the history of storytelling, and that's not because he's just a one-dimensional face. Superheroes are crafted, moulded, given morals, ideals, and vision. Their virtues and imperfections are carefully considered. In many cases, the modern day superhero is an actual testament to the world we live in.

Don't believe me?

They're struggling to make Superman work amongst audiences in the 21st century because he's too good for the world we live in. Batman and other dark brooding characters own the landscape. On the flip side, we live in a much more sarcastic and emotional society so Iron Man plays well with people. Captain America is actually as good as Superman, if not more-so, but the destruction and complex character battles that are constantly happening around him make Steve Rogers popular. Think about Captain America movies for just a minute. The first movie tapped into the mindset of the world because it revolved around war, which is something that we've all been struggling to understand in recent years. The second movie featured a lot of death and darkness; the third needed a darker cast to join so people would buy in. Strip away all of that and leave Captain America to fight on his own and try to relay his values—no one would watch. Rewind a few decades when times were *softer* and communication wasn't so plentiful (negative info travels faster now), and you'll find cheesy heroes fighting for what's right ... even if it is a cat stuck in a tree. (Literally, a Superman comic once featured the Man of Steel saving a cat from a tree on the cover). Do you think they could get away with that today?

Ultimately, in an indirect way, Derek has helped me

snap out of my haze. I'll never be Superman, but I can be Wolverine (minus the claws). My mission isn't evil. It isn't without reason. It isn't wrong. Killing those that prey on society, after society has failed to deal with them is a noble mission. The only one that really gets hurt in all of this is me. Surely, all of my kills will chip away at my soul, but I can take it, because I likely don't have to take it for very long. And, if by some miracle I survive the Cancer, I'll just stop.

Derek and I crush another few hours of gaming and a full case of beer before he calls a cab and heads home. I finally feel like I can sleep. As I lay my head on the pillow, I find an envelope on the nightstand with my name written on it. That's Monica's handwriting. I hadn't seen it yet because I've been such an insomniac.

Michael,

In such a short time you've come to mean everything to me. I'm sorry I can't be there for your first meeting about treatment. The timing really sucks, but I admire you for being so strong and going regardless. You're a brave man, and brave men win their battles. I know you'll be able to take this on and win! Then, maybe you can put a ring on it at some point. Too soon? ;)

Lovingly yours,

Monica

It's a sweet letter, and reinforces why I love her. Knowing I have a woman by my side—a woman like her—is humbling. I can't possibly tell her about my mission though, if this indeed becomes my mission. This will be one aspect of my life I'll have to keep secret. Just based on the conversation about that drug den she didn't know I took down, I can tell she'd never agree with my approach. How could she? Monica is in her profession to save people, and here I am taking people out. Even though I've been able to rationalize my actions, that doesn't mean others will be able to. If it were that easy, everyone would be doing this.

How do I lie to her though? She's the one person I should tell everything, but this must be kept separate. I guess it's not like she'll ever ask if I'm the guy killing criminals, so I don't actually have to lie. No, all I have to do is not mention it. I'll be the man she loves by going to this meeting though. Tomorrow morning, I'll stop ignoring Doc Scorpio's calls, tell them I was scared, and book another meeting as soon as possible. This way Monica will come home and I can tell her all about what I learned.

It's a good plan so that the good person in my life doesn't abandon me.

16

Cancer

AS THE SLIDING DOORS OPEN to a long corridor, my heart sinks into my stomach. Somehow this disease eating me from the inside out hasn't seemed life stoppingly real, but now, reality is sinking in with crushing force. Sure, it's proving to be an annoyance now that I can recognize the symptoms, but my death was just something I thought about, not something I had to confront ... until now. I'm not sure how to explain it. It's like when you have a bunch of money in your account so you loosen the purse strings a bit; spend some dollars. You know your money dwindles with every purchase, but you don't look at your account because you feel like you'll be okay even though you know eventually if you don't get your spending under control, you'll be broke. Then, the day comes when all the money is gone, and you're just left wondering how. I'd imagine this is exactly what MJ, Pam Anderson, and Wesley Snipes went through. Now, apply the same principle to Cancer. Instead of the IRS knocking, you're standing in a corridor with a bunch of sick patients foreshadowing your demise.

My mission to do something good before I die has distracted me from the actual possibility that I may not wake up tomorrow. The nature of my type of Cancer is that you just never know what's coming next. I could very well die peacefully in my sleep, but then again, I could get violently ill and barely be able to function.

I walk up the hall of Cancer Care, passing patients sitting with family and friends. Some look good, some not. As you'd expect, there are quite a few bald heads. I've taken such pride in my hair over the years, I can't imagine being bald. It's scary to change because you have to. When you see someone with a cue ball head, you immediately wonder if they have Cancer. It's just habit to wonder. The baldness isn't the worst part, though. In these halls of Cancer Care, a whole other type of skin pigmentation can be seen. There are so many different shades of grey, like someone has a remote and is dialing down their saturation to varying degrees. Of course, it's not just the physical ailments that have changed the design of these patient's appearance; there's also the psychological effects. Some would look perfectly fine if they didn't look so stressed, or tired ... or broken.

With each step, I take in everything. They've designed the building so that there is the maximum amount of sunlight coming in to bathe the many plants. It's clean and comfortable. Whomever was the architect behind this place knew what they were doing. Unlike church, there's comfortable padding on the seats, and the paint on the walls range from different shades of blue and green to really pleasing shades of purple. This doesn't feel like a place of death, but rather a place of healing and inspiration—even though I'm sure many have been through these halls shortly before they passed.

You're often ready for adults and seniors to have

Cancer and wear the effects of treatment. It's so common place now that none of us are all that phased, unless it's a loved one. What you're never prepared for is the kid in a wheelchair, with an IV, and a bandana on his head. Dark circles around the eyes are meant to be reserved for the overworked, not a five-year old. Another mystery I'll never understand. Why give life only to have it taken away, or at the very least given major struggles right out of the gate? It's not right for a kid to be here and have to confront all that Cancer forces you to learn, see, and speak about. I've at least gotten almost thirty-years. These kids haven't even hit puberty yet.

I'm acutely aware of each step I take towards the end of the hallway. Just as I did in that abandoned house before shooting at the crack den, I psych myself up. *Do this for Monica. Do this to survive.* I repeat it to myself with every step until I reach a poster with the headline, *The Truth About Dying*. I stare at that poster, and then through it. A bald woman is staring back at me, smiling. Somehow *The Truth About Dying* is making her smile. I'm not sure the photographer thought that one through.

"Are you ready sir?" a woman's voice asks from behind me.

"Excuse me?" Seeing the words on the poster, and hearing this nurse speak brought both together in a chilling way.

"You're here for the group meeting, yes?"

"Oh, yes. Sorry. As a side note, you might want to move that poster." I say as she directs me through large heavy wood doors with tiny windows, into a room where two dozen or so people are standing around. There are chairs facing a podium, and a video screen. Of all the depressing PowerPoint presentations to make, this must be one of the worst. If the goal in this meeting is to inform, you need to go to dark places to learn about what can happen. If the goal is to comfort, you must try to get into the minds of those that are dying. Either way, not a fun job at all.

I'm not a fan of the lighting. It's dim, almost movie theatresque. Why shade corners, making them resemble a dark abyss, when so many are staring at the dark abyss of death in the face? Whoever these coordinators are, they need to think of these things. We'd all be better off with a room like the hallway. At least it inspires a healthy mindset.

Some people are filling up on donuts, while others pour themselves coffee. From everything I've read, diet is critical to successfully managing Cancer. So why then, do the people responsible for beating Cancer serve this shit? I've had a hard time staying on diet, but this is a hospital, and doctors practically live her. You'd think they'd serve up fruits, vegetables, and smoothies. Maybe they do at other meetings—I don't know—but this spread isn't all that inspired.

The rest of the people not looking for empty calories and caffeine try to awkwardly strike up conversation with each other, not really knowing what to do with themselves. A few patients are seated up front in wheelchairs, ready to learn.

From what I could gather from the doc and Monica, this meeting gives Cancer patients a safe place to talk about what they're going through, while learning about their options. I have over 700-pages at home full of options, so I'm not sure what good being here will do, but I'm willing to give it a try. If it turns into an AA environment, or a Kirby vacuum sales meeting, singing before pounding the pavement, I'm out of here.

The woman who showed me in speaks softly to all

that aren't seated, letting them know that the meeting is about to start. She doesn't need to say a word to me. I just nod when I see her coming my way and take a seat in the back row, as close as I can get to the door.

A kind looking doctor with a certain warmth to him takes to the podium. He's probably about sixty, balding, wearing a patterned brown sweater vest, beige dress pants, and a white dress shirt with a tie. His poise and calm are comforting; he's the right man for the job.

He introduces himself. "Hello, my name is Robert Juergens, and I'm a medical oncologist. I handle both patient care and research. I'm one of six doctors here who volunteer our time to have these meetings and cover important information about what the next *X* number of months will be like in your life, with or without treatment."

X number of months; that's a delicate way of putting it. I guess he's banking on the fact that no one here has weeks to live. It's a smart way of saying it, but feels cold somehow.

Dr. Juergens goes on to speak about treatment. "You're here today because you have yet to decide whether treatment is the right course of action for you. Whether it be surgery, radiation, chemotherapy, chemoradiation or targeted therapies; they all come with a degree of issue. However, they also give you a chance to beat Cancer and go on to live a normal life. Going without treatment rarely ends with the same result. Treatment can make you sick, there is no question, however, you are going to get sick without it as well. No matter what, you'll become very tired, you'll likely lose your appetite, there will be varying degrees of pain, and that's just to start. As a doctor, I have to recommend treatment, even if the odds aren't favourable. I have to, because it's the right course of action in 100% of cases."

Over the next half hour, the doctor goes on to talk about options in great detail. Several times throughout the presentation he even addresses the falsehoods on the internet. He speaks of the lack of empirical evidence to suggest that holistic Cancer treatments help, although he is very careful not to tread on anyone's beliefs. "Holistic approaches may not be backed by science, but diet is. Many holistic programs centralize around diet, so it's likely that combining them with treatment can do some good. But, before you do so, please make sure you consult with your doctor."

I find it ironic that the doctor serving donuts and coffee to Cancer patients is talking about nutrition. From what I know, MDs don't spend a lot of time in school on diet. It accounts for less than 1% of their training. The question then becomes, why would I trust Doc Scorpio—or any other doctor for that matter—with my dietary needs?

I look around the room and see so many in a similar situation as I. We all still look varying degrees of "good", but we have a disease currently trying to take us down. The whole thing makes me feel as if I'm insignificant. I'm just another guy with another form of Cancer, trying to beat the odds. How unoriginal.

Once the doctor is done, he invites those in the room to come up to the podium and share their experiences. Here we go with the AA meeting.

The first to speak is Claire, a 62 year old, three-time victor over the disease. She was a nurse, goes to church every Sunday, and believes she will win again. "I know what you're thinking, sitting there. I've been where you are three times now. The Lord challenged me far beyond that which I actually thought I could handle. But, I struck down Cancer before, and I will do it again. You see, ladies and gentlemen, Cancer is just a challenge. No matter how tired or sore you get, it's just there to challenge you to be stronger the next day, and the day after that, and so on. There's no curing it yet, but there is hope in treatment, and I thank the many doctors here for giving me an extra 10-years."

Her presence here seems odd, almost staged. This meeting (I thought) was for all of us to explore our options because we hadn't decided on treatment yet. Claire has clearly decided.

After her, comes Donald, a first-time patient. He immediately tears up. "I have a wife and kids. I have a good job. I was living my life like everyone else, just trying to enjoy it when I was diagnosed. For a few days I didn't even want to believe it. Can you believe I didn't tell my wife? I still don't know what to do. There's just so much information. I know I'm going to die because I'm in stage four. If I don't get treatment I might have more time to play ball with my boys and die with some peace. But do I rob them of their dad if I decide not to get treatment and at least try? Is that fair? I really don't know what to do."

Another three people head to the podium saying, pretty much the same shit, and at first I'm sad. Now, I'm angry. Their stories are so plain and generic. You can find them online a thousand times with one Google search. This meeting is meant to make them feel remarkable and strong, but it's so contrived.

I probably shouldn't, but I decide to go up there. My hands are clenched, which is never a good sign. As I walk to the podium, I think about what I'm going to say. On stage, I stand there with the lights on me at that mic and think. Almost a minute goes by until the doctor starts to walk back on stage. I just look at him and put my hand out to let him know I'm going to say something. Those faces in the crowd stare at me blankly, so I just open up.

"I can't be this guy," I say softly as I bow my head in shame of the tears rolling down my face. I take a moment then continue. "I get it. We're all dying in this room. I don't want to talk about that. It's the way we're dying that bothers me. It's so plain and generic. My life ... it's been plain and generic, and now my death will be the same. I'm a walking statistic, buried under a pile of stereotypes. There's nothing special about any of this."

"I'm not following," a man in the front row says, clearly resentful of what I'm saying.

"I pictured my death as something more. Now I'm just a guy in a room with 20-some odd people dying in a completely unremarkable way."

"So you're mad because your death doesn't have meaning, or?" the guy pipes up again.

"Darryl, we don't cross-talk while someone is at the podium. You know that," the doctor says.

"I'm mad because when it's all said and done—chemo, holistic, alternatives—none of this matters because I'm going to die like so many before me, from a disease that is exceptionally ordinary. What is the point of all this living when it's so boring? I am half the man that I was before all of this, and that doesn't amount to much. I'm mad because I've been robbed of the time to do something that makes a girl like the one I just found proud."

"You still have time," the doctor says, as he approaches me with a tissue.

"Fuck this disease!" I take pause, and apologize for swearing even though we're all adults. "My dad was a great man. He saved lives and protected everyone in this city. When he walked into any room you could count on at least a couple of people looking at him in awe. Still, he died while people that deserved to be buried live. I may have done very little with my life, but I know that I don't deserve to die this young. Still, I have stage four pancreatic Cancer." I look around the room to see that those who know their Cancers, know I'm done for. Those faces looked on with anger, but now with pity. "Just a couple of months ago, my biggest problem was finding a new job. Now, I have to decide whether my 5 or 10 percent chance of living is worth months of puking my guts out and feeling like death instead of being dead. It's all so boring, isn't it? Think of the number of people in rooms just like this right now, 2 hours from now, tomorrow, the next day. They'll redress this room, provide food we shouldn't even be eating in the first place, and the next pity party will start. They've cured endless diseases, but somehow, not this one. How is that possible? You read so many stories about cures and you wonder, why can't I be cured? Why can't I be given longer to live? I haven't gotten the chance to get married, have kids, find that career that makes a difference, or even think about retirement. There are kids in the hall outside that have gotten even less. How is that a thing?"

My anger builds, and finally, I explode. "I am going to die! With or without this treatment, the chances of me surviving are so slim that they might as well not exist. I will never see thirty because God or whoever it is that wrote my life script decided that I needed to go. Perhaps my aunt throws a funeral, or no one does; it really doesn't matter since there are more people here today than would be at my funeral. My own mom won't even show. So, what do I do? Get treatment, or spend my remaining months changing the world? Before I came here, I didn't know the answer. Now ... it's clear. I'm going to make so much noise before I die because I'm a good man who doesn't deserve this fate, and Cancer won't take just me. If I have to die, I will make it worth it. I'll be great like my dad. I won't sit here like all of you and do nothing. This disease is of little consequence to me. All it is ... well, it's an expiry date that I have to beat." I take one final look at everyone sitting there not knowing how to react. "Good luck with your treatment and your ordinary lives. Me? I'm going to make this all worth it."

I don't wait for any sort of reaction. I just walk off the stage, out the door, through that hallway, and straight to my truck. As I put the key in the lock, a wave of emotion comes over me. Sobbing does not begin to describe the next ten-minutes. I really break down. I hurt some feelings in that room, and that poor doctor must have a lot of damage control to do, but my presence there was not a waste. I know now that I can't stop for this disease, or I might as well have not lived at all. Treatment will stop me dead in my tracks, and if I were playing any card game at all, single digit odds do not constitute a play. You fold. I'll take the signs and proceed with raging against the machine.

Being there, in that room, has made me realize that it is time to ramp up my efforts to take down the people who rule this city with fear. Not only that, if I'm going to matter, when it's all said and done, the people need to know who is helping them.

17

Suit Up

WITH JUST TWO WEEKS until Monica returns from her vacation, I have a lot to do; surely, there will be less time to balance doing the good I'm hoping to do and the girl I said *I love you* to before she jumped on the plane. When I was a kid, I backed away from violence because Dad was shot. It's funny how life can come full circle, and now he's pulling me back in with his research. My life has been the sum of many levels of fear: screwing up, being broke, disease—you name it. Not anymore.

I am finally strong in my resolve to take the people in Dad's book with me when I die; no more indecisiveness! Whenever I have even the smallest amount of doubt in what I'm doing, I will think of Daisy and that woman who helped me after I killed Jason. They are the faces of my mission to change the world. When I'm done the people will have hope, and the criminals will be living in fear. That's the goal, now for the action. If I'm going to fully commit to taking on the lost souls of my city, perhaps I should be hiding my face.

There's no time to source out a good quality mask

for protection so I find myself wandering through a costume store trying to find a mask that will merely obstruct my identity. The store has masks and costumes hanging from the walls and even the ceiling. It's a little shit box of a store, but there's a good chance I'll find what I need here. The question is, what do I need?

There are all kinds of masks, ranging from functional to terrifying—too many options, in fact. I try on five or six, but they don't quite cut it; either they're too loose, or too bulky. Some have too many parts, and others are just plain cheap. Deep in the back, hanging on a discount rack, is a mask that closely resembles a Guy Fawkes mask, but with a few cool mods—after all, throwing on the Anonymous mask would be hella tacky. I put it on and turn to a mirror; it's perfect! All white with no distinguishable features except for a fake scar along one side. Digging through the bin, I manage to find fourteen of the same mask for just over $50. What a deal.

Once home, I spray paint them all blood red. I like the idea of these guys seeing red before they die. Giving them a different look will also bode well for me if my mask hits the news and the clerk at the store happens to be watching. Combine the change with the fact that she was both airhead and stoner, I should be okay.

I add the mask to the outfit I wore before I took down Jason. My black hoodie, black cargos, black leather gloves, Dad's bullet proof vest, as well as padding for my knees really make me appear scary. If I saw me coming down a back lane, I'd seek cover. That's all a guy trying to strike fear in the hearts of those that have done the same can ask for.

Instead of spending my days in treatment, I take the time to train. It is amazing, the information you can find online. From sites to buy tasers and bluetooth locks, to YouTube tutorials on how to make bombs, it's a virtual *how to* book for psychopaths and vengeance. For one full week I return to Jiu Jitsu everyday, just in case I end up needing to fight. Every morning around 5am I hit the field where Dad and I last *saw* each other. Practice makes perfect, and I'm not going to go into my next kills as unsure of myself as I was with Jason White. No, the next kills will be completely on my terms, with no hesitation or remorse.

The Cancer rears its ugly head a few times, through weakness and the occasional dizzy spell, while I prepare but I'm far too focused to actually care. I'm adapted to the symptoms in order to survive. There is no time for weakness when you plan on spending your time in the thick of violence. My muscle memory has returned; by the end of the week I'm back to owning the mat at the dojo, shooting targets that most wouldn't even be able to hit with a car, and my confidence is solid.

I heard from a cop one time that most officers don't have the necessary skills to actually shoot a moving target or fight, but most cops weren't Martial. He trained me well, almost preparing me for this moment. A quick fine tuning, and I'm ready.

It's time to suit up and deal with the parasites bringing my city down.

Tonight will be special, because tonight I'm diving in with both feet. Once you get over the mental roadblocks, killing can come just as easy to anyone as riding a bike. Why you kill is what's important. I'm killing because it's the language those that I want to communicate with speak in. By taking criminals lives, I'm communicating that we, the people, will not take their shit anymore. That's how all great struggles in this world have been resolved: through communication.

I've always said that I have faith that humanity will be okay until someone takes out an NFL stadium full of innocent people. At that point, a line will be crossed that humanity can't come back from. Now, I have no interest in bringing humanity down, so I'm not looking to kill 50,000 innocent people; just ten guilty assholes, starting with James Roland.

Background on Mr Roland: he started out as a nightclub promoter. When he wasn't making enough money to get by, he started dealing date rape drugs and percs to a select group of guys. But why let your customers have all the fun, right? James started using his drugs on girls that came to his events. It would be two-years before the girls would start to speak up, and he went to jail for a small stint. When he got out, jail had just provided him a place to get into shape and live without sex for far too long. He's been accused of dozens of rapes, but was only charged for two. After five-years in prison he was released again because apparently he was rehabilitated. Dad didn't agree, and based on the research, I don't either.

I arrive at his home around 9:45pm. It's a small little single storey place with light blue siding and bushes lining the yard. James lives on a street with quite a bit of traffic. The bush blocks any view of the house from the street though, giving me the perfect opportunity to get in and get out with no one noticing. There will be no gun for this one.

As I step quietly up the three-stairs to the door there is no shake in my hand like before. I'm calm and steady. Just before I make my presence known, I ready my knife with a plastic bag around my hand and forearm.

I knock politely, and wait a moment. No answer.

I knock again. No answer, although I know he's home. This loner is always home at night.

This time I ring the doorbell.

From afar in the house I hear him. "Coming. Hold on."

As I let out a deep breath to calm myself, he answers the door.

"Yeah," he says, as if he just woke up and is still half asleep.

Without hesitation I stick the blade of my knife through his neck and pull it out. The blood pours down his body to the floor quickly as he drops to the ground, so quickly he doesn't even have time to react. There is no hand over the wound to keep pressure like in the movies. His eyes instantly roll into the back of his head, and he just drops. This is a quicker kill than Jason. It takes mere seconds, and he's dead. With plastic bags over my boots, I drag the body into his house, grab his keys, lock the door, and head on my way. He did grunt a bit, but no one heard. The traffic was louder than we were.

Nope, no one is the wiser. As I walk away from the home, I throw his keys into a field. My truck is parked a couple of blocks away, and much to my surprise, I don't play the kill out in my head over-and-over as I did with Jason. I couldn't even tell you what the inside of his place looked like or any other detail, really. I was focused on doing my job.

On to the next one—that's right, I will kill again tonight. What did you think *diving in with both feet* meant?

Ten minutes down the road, Alex Rose plays basketball every Tuesday night. Not even killing people stops him from that tradition. Alex is a hit man for a local biker gang, best known for shooting people in the back. Tonight, as I walk up to the court, through the shadows where a game of 4-on-4 is taking place, I decide to give him a taste of his own medicine.

The first shot hits him square in the middle of his spine. The other players scramble for cover. The next two shots are in the kidney and the back of the head. I barely miss a step, until I hear I hear a voice behind me, "You know who you're messing with, bitch?"

Another guy on the court has decided to step up to me even though I'm holding a gun and he clearly has no weapon. He moves into the light and I immediately recognize the roid monkey, huffing and puffing—Max Graham. My dad's writings tell of a man that sells crack, and sells women on the streets—the younger the better. If they step out of line, he strangles them. No bodies have ever been found but no one gets that reputation undeservingly.

"Do you kill women, Max?" I ask as I point a gun at him.

"What? Are you some kind of feminist hitman or something?"

His ego is his achilles heal. "Do you kill women, MAX?"

He smiles, and is readying to jump me. "The things I do to my women will pale in comparison to what I'm gonna do to you."

"And how is it that you think you're going to do anything to me? I think I've proven I'm not above shooting an unarmed piece of shit."

He knows he's dead anyway, so he plays the odds and gives me a moving target. Perhaps some guys wouldn't be able to hit him, but ultimately it's a bad move. One bullet to the chest takes him down. As I stand over him, one bullet to the head finishes him off. The other players are long gone, and there's no one around. I guess they weren't very good friends to the recently and unceremoniously departed Alex and Max.

These kills are strategic. James, Alex, and Max were all connected in the neighbourhood, and with them gone there will surely be a cloud lifted. No one dared to step to these guys, but now someone has. I hope this liberates the people, and they take action. The other part of my strategy is to use another burner, and call the cops.

"9-1-1, what's your emergency?"

"Two men have been shot, and there's a guy screaming that he's going to kill more people," I say, hoping to lure the entire city police force to one end of town.

I give them the address and then disappear into the shadows that I came from. It's almost too easy to take a life at this point, which is a scary proposition. As I drive, I wonder how I'll be profiled. Surely they'll pick up on the fact that I'm only killing criminals, but I haven't used a consistent weapon, unless you count the night as a part of my arsenal. I pity that poor profiler.

From my cell phone, I listen to the police scanner in my truck. There will be plenty of cops covering the basketball court, looking for the shooter. My next targets are clear across town on purpose. It will be a busy night for the boys in blue, but at least they're not just dealing with false alarms and bum wars. Tonight, they will earn those tiny little salaries.

I arrive at the home of Ryan and Kyla Friesen about 20 minutes after the call to 9-1-1. This darling couple have done time for theft, rape, and assault. The catch is that they like to do it together. Dad wrote of their Tuesday poker and stripper nights. The rumour on the street is that they only keep the company of criminals so story time is more interesting. After all, you can't brag about rape to a room full of people who aren't *rapey*.

They might as well have just set up a shooting gallery for me. I wait for hours in the back yard, listening for the drunken conversation to become louder and more incoherent. I watch through a window as twelve people drink, do blow, trade off partners, and get trashed. This is as primal as it gets. For these kills, I will take my time, besides I need to make sure every person at the party is on my list, and the strippers need to leave. Feel as you may about strippers, but they don't deserve to be killed. Finally, I match all of the pictures in my phone with targets in the house; there is no question that everyone here deserves to die.

These deaths will weigh heavily on my mind at some point, I'm sure, as these will be the first women I kill. Dad raised me to never lay a hand on a woman. He always said that only the worst of men harm the fairer sex. Surely he wasn't speaking of Kyla and her friends though. The most respectable person in the room was named Carly Young. She had been charged for breaking into a home and kicking the woman of the house in the stomach. That doesn't sound so bad, right? Well, that woman was eight months pregnant, and Carla knew what she was doing. Not able to have children herself, she has a huge chip on her shoulder, and when she can, she has no problem making sure no other woman can have kids either. Psycho bitch.

It's one in the morning and the party is going full tilt for some, while others are passed out in the corner. Those are the lucky ones. They'll die tonight, but in their drug and alcohol induced sleep. As the final hooker gets into a waiting car and leaves, I put my mask on and enter through an unlocked back door. As I take my first few steps through the house I get excited; a new emotion on this killer ride. In any movie, this would be the scene where the guy walks in slow motion to wicked music. He draws his guns, and says something clever before opening fire. I'm not going to say anything clever, but it's a fun thought.

"The life of the party is here." Arnold Schwarzenegger accent.

"Got room for one more at this party?" Sly Stallone accent.

"It didn't look like you guys had enough shooters!" That's a classic Statham line.

Take your pick, any could apply. Now say one in your head, because shit is about to get real.

As I turn a corner from the kitchen to the living room, Kyla sees me. I'm thrown for a split second, as she is my first female victim. It's just a fraction of a moment though, and one bullet is all it takes to drop her as she attempts to run from the table she is at. I then shoot the guy closest to me, and unleash shots on the table across the room. Ryan lunges at me but he's fat and slow. I get one shot off, square in between the eyes. It's like dominos; they all fall down. The sleepy few get the bullets last. Passed out, they are of no threat to me, which is why I save them until the end. They passed out so hard that a few of them don't even stir from the sounds of the shots. Dying in their sleep is too good for them, but I guess it'll have to do. Two handguns with silencers, sixteen bullets—I use them all. But, I need one more clip.

Johnny Mendes is still passed out in the corner with a little coke under his nose, giving his mustache a salty look. He's gotta be done. I shot 16 bullets in this room and still, he snores. The skinny prick is dressed in a shiny shirt and leather pants with big glasses. All of thirty, why is he dressed like a bartender at Studio 54 in the 70's? It's sad that he'll die in that outfit. Nobody should die looking this cheesy.

I position one of my guns without a silencer next to Johnny's right ear. *BANG!* Man, does he wake up in a panic. His eyes open big as he jumps up and hits the floor. He screams out in pain as he grips his head. I can just imagine the ringing in his ears right now. Hell, even I have a bit of a ring from the sound. I kick him in the chest so that he will land on his back and look up at me, pointing a gun in his face. Fear sets into his eyes.

"Can you hear me, Jonny?" I ask as I sit in the chair he was in. "Can you?"

"Barley. Aw, you fucking asshole. God damn it. I'll never get this sound out of my head."

"Good."

He attempts to get up, and as he does he notices all of his friends dead in the room around him. "What did you do? Why would you do this?"

"Sit down." I tell him angrily. He sits on the couch across from me. We're just two guys chatting in a living room. "You mean, why would I kill all of these upstanding citizens? Why would I take such innocent lives from this world?"

"So this is a revenge kill? Who sent you?"

"His name was Martial."

"The cop?" He tries to shake off the ringing because for him, this conversation just got interesting. "You're no cop."

"How astute of you. What gave it away?"

"Cops don't wear masks."

"Cops also don't get the job done."

"So you're going to kill me now?"

"Johnny. You have neither killed or raped anyone. You don't prey on children. You don't deal hard drugs. You don't even fight. The only reason I know who you are is because Martial thought you were a piece of shit in training. Are you? Are you a piece of shit in training, Johnny?"

"Hey look man ..." He puffs his chest a bit and gives me attitude, so I put a bullet in the wall right above his head.

"Don't play tough guy, Johnny. That kinda bullshit got all your friends here killed."

"So why haven't you offed me?"

"Johnny, why you no listen? You don't deserve to die yet, so you're going to live tonight. That's the good news. Tomorrow, you're going to go pound the pavement, get a real job and take care of your son. If you keep going on the path you were, then I'll come find you again, and I will kill you."

"Holy shit man. Thank you!"

"It's not an altruistic deed. I want you to tell every other low life scumbag you've been hanging out with that I'm coming for them, and when they see red, their time is up. No criminal in this town is safe. Got it?"

He nods in agreement.

"Now on your knees, Johnny."

"What for?"

"KNEES!"

He gets down on his knees in front of the couch and shakes while he tries to stay still hoping to God I wasn't just playing with him. I wasn't. A quick pistol whip to the head knocks him out cold. He'll be alright.

As I stand in the middle of this room with rapists, killers, and psychopaths laying dead all around me, I can't help but still feel a bit conflicted. In one night, I've killed fifteen people and it was so easy. In fact it's all been too easy; a reality no one should know about. I kinda believe people think that killing and being a criminal is hard, so with that barrier to entry they just don't do it. If they only knew.

As I walk out of the house I contemplate whether killing fifteen people is a big number. When I think back to the greatest fight scenes on the silver screen, so many more die. But this is nothing like that. When a hero kills a villain there isn't usually any blood, and they fall out of frame never to be seen again. The barrels of my guns are still hot, the room is silent despite the loud music, and the carnage doesn't disappear when the camera moves. All are down and blood has abstractly painted the walls. Fifteen people! Allow that to sink in for a moment. Some of the most prolific serial killers in history didn't kill as many people as I have in just one night. The Doodler, Boston Strangler, Rifkin; I put them to shame. The whole idea of it seems inconceivable.

My one and only regret is that some of these people have families, I'm sure, but they'll get over it. In a few years time, these deaths will be seen for what they really are; karma. You can only victimize for so long until it all catches up with you ... or I guess, until *I* catch up with you.

Now, as I sit at home alone, I understand how alcoholics are born. Sometimes the mission has honour, but the visuals are too much to bear. I get dirty, stinking drunk until I black-out on that couch that was purchased by two innocent souls. When Monica gets back, there will be but one innocent soul left. I better come up with a better system to cope with the images of death in my head that seem to set-in once the adrenaline has subsided, or I'll put a bullet in my mouth before the Cancer gets me.

Thankfully, my Monica will be home soon.

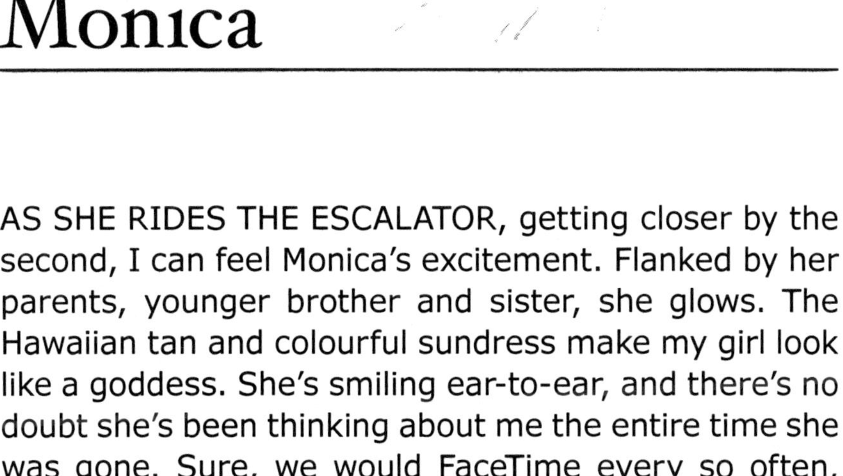

18 Monica

AS SHE RIDES THE ESCALATOR, getting closer by the second, I can feel Monica's excitement. Flanked by her parents, younger brother and sister, she glows. The Hawaiian tan and colourful sundress make my girl look like a goddess. She's smiling ear-to-ear, and there's no doubt she's been thinking about me the entire time she was gone. Sure, we would FaceTime every so often, but between being on a remote portion of the islands and her mom's insanely 1990 anti-tech rule, those moments were few and short. Here comes the real deal after a month away.

Finally, she reaches me, and grabs on tight. "I missed you," she whispers into my ear. It's a bittersweet moment, because in this month she's been gone, I've done things that have changed me, and I pray that I can join her back in the light which she introduced me to that day at the house when she took me by surprise.

I've been living a life that takes a toll. The amount of alcohol I've been drinking just to sleep is sickening, but necessary. The blood on my hands is stained, but I have to be the only one to see it. Monica works in medicine; she helps protect life, not take it. She won't understand what I'm doing, nor will she understand me not seeking treatment. In this moment though, it just feels good to have her back in my life, and I decide that I have to lie about two things to keep her; Daisy and my mission. If you were me, you'd do the same exact thing. The feeling of having her close just warms what's left of my soul.

Her family and I have yet to really connect and get to know each other. Since they had tight flight connections from Hawaii, they're all hungry, and Monica's dad treats everyone to dinner, including me. Janice, her mom, shares stories of Monica as a child, but her dad keeps mostly to himself until the end when we're all standing in the dark parking lot saying our goodbyes.

"Michael, I have to apologize." he says while in an awkward stance, while ushering me away from the family and Monica with one hand on my shoulder. "I didn't know what to talk to you about, and that's my fault."

"I'm not following, sir." I really wasn't. I've never done the whole father-boyfriend thing with any of my past girlfriends, so I'm definitely out of my comfort zone.

"Usually a father would talk to the serious boyfriend about future plans, work, and maybe politics. But, given your situation, none of that really applies, and bringing up treatment at dinner was probably not the best of ideas."

"I see what you're saying."

"I mean no offense by this. I just want you to know that we're all pulling for you. Go get that treatment and make my daughter happy. She thinks the world of you. Kick Cancer's ass, so there are more dinners like this in the future."

"Thank you sir."

I immediately feel a sense of dread. Clearly Monica has spoken at length with her parents about my situation. She's told them that I've taken steps to get treatment, and I can tell from her father that me telling her I'm not going to follow through would crush her. It's a horrible feeling to know you have to lie to the one person you love. I can't possibly tell her my plans. I can't tell her about my mission. I can't tell her how I acted at the meeting. Not only will she never forgive me, she may leave. As selfish as it sounds, she's my all right now, and I don't know if I can do this without her.

When we finally make our way home, it takes only about a minute for her to collapse onto the couch, and beg me for cuddles. She needs fifteen minutes to nap and be held before we get into any conversation—jet lag. As we lay there she fades quickly, but I'm left awake playing out my options in my mind. I have to lie to this beautiful soul because we now live in two separate worlds, but to tell the truth would tear them apart completely, leaving nothing but murder and Cancer. These are the decisions my dad was faced with, and he chose to leave. I get his choices now, but I can't afford to be alone in this house.

She's so beautiful. The lines of her face are just perfect, almost betraying the laws of nature. No matter what position she is in, her hair falls in just the right spot, and the light always accentuates her face. It's why you'll never see a bad picture of her. Monica was designed to distract, and that's just what she does for me. How did I get so lucky?

That small nap for a few minutes turns into a

nine-hour power sleep, with only the morning sun waking us. It's my first good sleep since I took to the streets and killed fifteen people. She really is my calm.

"Well, good morning," I say as she starts to stir.

She looks towards the window, and then at me. "Did we really just pass out that hard?"

"We did."

"What time is it?"

"No idea. No interest in knowing."

"I second that," she says as we reach in for a kiss that lasts for about ten-minutes. She wiggles her way out from my clasped arms, and stands for a stretch. "Before we do anything else, this girl needs a hot shower."

"Well, I should be clean too, ya know."

"If you can get off that couch, I'll be waiting," she says playfully, while taking her shirt off in that way that women know drives a man insane, and dropping it to the floor.

After a *dirty* shower, we decide to make breakfast and watch a movie. Today will be one of those days where the world doesn't exist. Monica doesn't work, I obviously don't work, and there's no need to let anything distract us. We even turn our phones off, a rarity in this day and age for any couple.

"So," Monica says coyly. I can feel the Cancer talk coming on. "How was the meeting?"

I decide to be honest with as much as I can, because a lie was coming at some point. "I actually missed the meeting we scheduled."

"Michael," she says as she puts a bowl down and stares at me.

"Don't worry," I say while cracking a smile. "I rescheduled and I went."

"And?"

"And it's a really scary place. Everyone's sick, clinging onto hope from wherever they can find it; and the stories, baby ... the stories that these people told were so hard to hear. There was a woman there on her third diagnosis in a decade. She can't escape Cancer, but she's still so positive."

"Did everyone have to speak?"

"No, not everyone."

"I guess I shouldn't even ask if you did," she says while beating eggs with a whisk.

"Actually, I did get up there and speak. I talked about Dad and how angry I was," I say while dropping bacon into a hot pan. The sizzle sound and smell take me back to Saturday mornings with Dad. "It actually helped me see things from a clearer perspective."

Technically, I still wasn't lying, but that was coming.

"I'm proud of you. That's a huge step you took."

"It really was, and I can honestly say, I feel better."

"So, when do you take the next step?"

"That's kind of what I wanted to talk to you about." As the food cooks, I take her hand and pull her close. She looks up at me with those big beautiful eyes, worried about what I'll say next. "You got me this far. I feel like that was your role in this. I really don't want you to be my nurse now, though. I want you to be my girlfriend."

"Are you saying that you want me to stay out of it?"

"Nothing that harsh. Of course, I'll come to you for advice, but I instinctively feel like this is something I need to do, and then I need to come home to a whole other reality to take my mind off of it all. Kinda like you're my safe place." The gears in her head are turning. I can tell she's not sure what to think about what I'm saying, so I hit the point home harder. "You're in medicine and deal with it all day. There's a lot of bad in that world. Now, I'm getting into a world that's just as bad. To survive it, we need to separate those worlds. When we're together, we need to be the one point in our lives where none of that matters. All that matters is how much we love each other."

"You need the separate the worlds, not me."

"Yes. You're right. I need it. You got me there. Now, I have to do this my way."

"You've thought a lot about this, haven't you?"

"Every day since the meeting, and maybe even a bit before. Of course, I'll still let you make me soup when I feel the shits or cuddle my sickness into submission."

"Okay. I can do that, but you have to say the words, *I'm going to get treatment*."

I sigh a bit, but she needs to hear the words. "I'm going to get treatment."

"Good. Then you have a deal," she says as she kisses the tip of my nose and then goes back to the food.

I almost made it through that entire conversation without lying to her, but she forced my hand. My hope was that I wouldn't have to outright lie, but only lie by omission. It feels wrong, but I need her here, and I need her happy. Like in Great Gatsby, she's my green light in the fog.

The rest of the day is spent switching between cuddling, movies, making love, and playing Nintendo. It really is the perfect day for us both. There are moments in life that you know nothing will ever feel this good again. From the moment we laid down on that couch to our final kiss goodnight, these moments will forever be with me.

Mid-way through the night I wake up in bed to Monica out cold. I decide that I want to make her last day before work something that she'll never forget.

After all, at some point this whole lie is going to come crashing down on me, and after I'm gone, I want her to have more than just shower sex and Nintendo for memories.

Sneaking away, I grab a pen and paper and start to write.

DEAR MONICA,

BEFORE A RECEPTIONIST AND STUDYING NURSE COULDN'T TAKE NO FOR AN ANSWER, I WAS JUST A BOY ON A LIFE RAFT WITH NO LAND IN SIGHT. YOU SEE, LIFE HAS NEVER TAKEN IT EASY ON ME. ON THAT RAFT THERE'S ALWAYS BEEN LIGHTNING, STORMS, AND CARNAGE. FOG FILLED THE AIR AROUND ME, AND BREATHING WAS NEVER SOMETHING I DID WITHOUT DIFFICULTY. THEN, ONE DAY, BY SHEER FORCE OF WILL, MY RAFT WAS PULLED ASHORE, AND I WAS SAVED. YOU SAVED ME, I WANT YOU TO KNOW THAT.

NO MATTER WHAT HAPPENS IN THIS LIFE, IF TOMORROW YOU'RE UNABLE TO BE WHO YOU WANT TO BE, YOU NEED TO KNOW THAT

YOU CHANGED A LIFE FOR THE BETTER, AND THAT YOU'RE MY HERO. NOT EVERYONE GETS THE CHANCE TO DO THAT. WE'RE ALL SO WRAPPED UP IN OUR TECHNOLOGY, OUR JOBS, THE DAILY SHIT THAT WE CAN FORGET WHAT IT MEANS TO REALLY CONNECT. YESTERDAY WAS MY FAVOURITE DAY, BY FAR. I HAVE FEW MEMORIES THAT EVEN COME CLOSE.

SO IF TOMORROW I DO SOMETHING THAT YOU CAN NEVER FORGIVE, OR IF A WEEK FROM NOW YOU FALL OUT OF LOVE WITH ME, OR IF MONTHS FROM NOW I SHOULD DIE ... I JUST WANTED YOU TO KNOW THAT YOU MADE THIS LIFE WORTH LIVING. A LIFETIME WITH YOU WOULD LIKELY MEAN CONCESSION TO LETTING MORE SUN IN THE ROOM, AND FLOWERS ON THE BLANKETS, BUT YOUR BEAUTY MAKES ME WEAK INSIDE, AND YOU CONNECT ME WITH A WORLD THAT I FELT NEVER ACTUALLY EXISTED.

You, Monica, are the personification of a cure to all that ails. You're the hope everyone talks about. Now get up and shower. It's time for you to have a memory that you can always hold on to.

Unmistakably Yours,

Michael

I leave the note on my pillow, set her alarm for 10am, and then send a text with instructions about where to go for noon. To plan this day, I'll need to act quickly. Another perk of the money from Dad is that you can always motivate people to move at your speed when you're waving hundreds at them.

Monica has always loved the garden in Assiniboine Park. It's truly one of the most beautiful spots in the city. As a kid, she would go there with her mom. Over the last couple of years, she couldn't get there enough because of work and other commitments. Every week Mon would talk about going, but could never find the time. Today, she has time, and I'm going to make it so if she never finds the time to come back, this memory will be enough to keep her happy.

At 10:15, she sends me a text. "OMG. So excited to see what you have planned. I'm getting up now and I'll see you soon! xox"

By 12:30, she sends me another text from the dress store I directed her to. "The dress is beautiful. Perfect for a summer day like today. Hopefully it's not the last time I'll ever wear white with you." After she's got the dress on, the manager's instructions are to give Monica a card with where to find me.

At 1:00, she arrives in the garden, looking like a princess. The sun dress I picked out was made for her (not literally). Immediately, she bursts into tears at the sight of me standing there in a suit in the middle of the garden with a minister. Security for the park keeps everyone else away, and only nature can be heard around us.

As she makes her way towards me, butterflies flutter towards the sky from the plants and flowers. I didn't plan that part, but nature is helping me along today.

"What is this, Michael?"

"I don't know what will happen in the future, but I know that today, I love you. So, I thought we'd get married unofficially in your favourite place."

"Unofficially?"

"Your dad would kill me if he couldn't walk you down the aisle. We'll save that for when we're both ready. Today, we practice."

Her smile lights up the garden, brighter than the sun. As the minister says the vows, and we repeat after him, Monica cries. I mean through the whole thing. Single tear, after single tear stream down her cheek. We exchange rings I picked up from a jeweler in the mall (on our right hands, of course) and at the end we modify the traditional vows, "I do promise and covenant, before God and this witness, to be your living and faithful partner, in plenty and want, in joy and in sorrow, in sickness and in health, as long as we both shall live."

We're even afforded the right to end with the kiss.

Sure, he couldn't pronounce us husband and wife, but with a kiss like that, it really doesn't matter.

Monica's next surprise comes in the form of a picnic in the park, and then dancing to her favourite music: Lifehouse (don't judge). We eat fancy meats and cheeses, while sipping on some really wonderful wines. The sky is blue with only the occasional cloud and the mosquitos even leave us alone, which anyone from Winnipeg will tell you is pretty miraculous. As the sun starts to set, I blindfold her and take Monica to the final surprise of the day, a hot air balloon ride. We glide through the air, with the world below for an hour before the day is over.

"Michael, this is all so amazing. I'll never forget this, like your letter said."

"I just wanted to give you a fraction of the happiness you gave me."

"You did. And then some."

"A mock wedding really tugged at your heart strings."

"It's seriously the last thing a girl would expect, and that's why it was so incredible."

We kiss until the balloon comes down, and then head back to my place. The perfect day is complete. Surely—like I said in the note—no matter what happens, she'll find it hard to top this day for as long as she lives. Now, some might say I was overcompensating for my lie, and I'd be lying again if I said that wasn't a part of it, but our life will not be easy, and I wanted to make sure we had a full 24 hours of happiness together.

Everything coming will be hell, but today we floated through heaven.

19

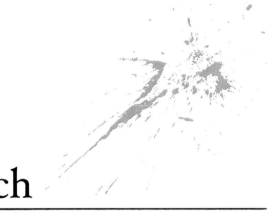

The Catch

"HELLO EVERYONE," the Chief of Police says at a press conference held outside of City Hall. He carries with him a serious tone, and a clear display of anger on his face. By his side are the Mayor, District Attorney, and several police officers. "Please be seated."

The media have caught wind of the now 16 murders throughout the city. They of course found Alex and Max's bodies the night everyone died, but it took more time to discover the rest. The party deaths were discovered two-days later by a mailman; James' body was found by his Parole Officer five-days after that. The trend has the city police worried, and this press conference is meant to be a show of strength, amid rumours floating around the media.

"As many of you now know, there have been 16 murders in our city in the last couple of weeks. What you don't know is that we now believe all of these murders to be connected. The first murder was that of Jason White in our city's North End. We believe the second pair of victims to have been killed at a basketball court located near Burrows Avenue. Another victim was found in his home just a few minutes from the basketball court. We believe that in the same night the assailant, or assailants, killed twelve people at a party in Transcona. The link between each of the victims is that they were all convicted or accused of serious criminal activity."

"Is this the work of rival gangs?" one reporter shouts out from the back row.

"Please, questions will be saved for the end of this press conference. We are unsure at this time as to whether these crimes are the result of one person, or a group. We don't suspect rival gangs, as this type of violence generally comes with a level of boasting. If gang members were involved, we'd have heard something by now. If anything, gangs aren't exactly coming out of the wood work right now, out of fear for their lives. What we do know is that with these scenes connected, then we have—and I caution that this is unconfirmed—a vigilante taking matters into his or her or their own hands. This will not be tolerated, and we will make sure to stop these people committing these murders."

The media stir in their seats. The term vigilante is usually reserved for comic books and movies. To hear the Police Chief say that there is a chance someone has stepped out of fiction to take on criminals seems mildly absurd if the news wasn't so horrible.

"We are working the crime scenes at this time, and have returned to the scene of Jason White's murder, now that we know of a definitive connection between all sixteen deaths. To provide you with more details, Ryan Brenning, a criminal profiler, will speak now."

Ryan takes the stage dressed in a blazer and jeans with a black t-shirt underneath. He has a nerdy vibe, but is clearly wicked smart. "I believe, based on the crime scenes that we are looking for one man. We cannot rule out a group, however evidence suggests we are looking for a single assailant, male. It's likely that he's suffered a loss at the hands of criminals lately, and is out for revenge. This person meant a lot to him, such as a parent or child. He does not park a vehicle nearby his targeted locations, which has ruled out using area cameras to trace him. He works at night. His victims have all been involved in or accused of some criminal activity, some high profile, and others not, suggesting he has intimate knowledge of criminal databases; however it is unlikely he is directly involved or has a job that can gain him access. He breaks away from traditional means of killing his victims. At one scene he will use a knife, and at others, different types of guns. This suggests he is highly intelligent, using weapons that best suit the individual kills, which is not unusual as true psychopaths usually have above average intelligence. It is likely that he feels that he is performing altruistic acts by killing, and that the criminal justice system has not done enough to level justice against them. He is likely anti-social, keeps to himself. Knowing this, it is highly unlikely that he has anyone close to him like a girlfriend or wife. It would be too difficult to carry out these acts without someone else noticing. So, in summary: Male. Average looks. Likely wearing a hoodie or some other form of clothing to obstruct his face. Anti-social, and works at night. We have gone public with this information because we need your help. If you see any suspicious activity in your area, please call 9-1-1 immediately. Thank you."

The Chief of Police steps back to the microphone to take questions. The media explode into a loud, raucous chorus, trying to get their couple of questions answered. This is, after all, an unprecedented story.

First, is a reporter from the largest newscast in town. "Other than the fact that each of the victims is a criminal, what leads you to believe these murders are connected?"

"We have evidence that suggests these crimes were committed by the same person or group. We can't release that evidence at this time, but it is becoming clearer to us that there is a connection." The Chief points at another reporter in the crowd. "Yes?"

"Two questions. First, is there reason to suspect this vigilante is connected to any other murders in the city? Second, do you feel that civilians without criminal history have reason to be worried?"

"I caution using the word vigilante. It's a working theory, but no, we don't suspect him of any other murders in the city. While we do not suspect that those without a criminal record have any reason to be fearful, we strongly caution against approaching anyone you believe may be committing these crimes. John, from the Free Press?"

"Am I correct in that you said this guy killed fifteen people in one night?"

"The assailant or assailants did kill fifteen people in one night, yes."

"And not one civilian was harmed?"

"Not that we know of currently."

"What kind of crimes are we talking about here? The people that were killed."

"The crimes range from theft and sexual assault to drug distribution and murder."

"So whoever is doing this, is doing us a favour?"

The Chief stammers, not expecting a reporter to say such a thing. "John, this may seem like a good natured thing that someone is doing; killing criminals. But vigilantism is a slippery slope. We can't just go around killing people. Whoever this assailant is, he's becoming a criminal to beat criminals. This makes him no better or worse than anyone he's murdering in cold blood."

"Yes, but Jason White was in and out of the system for years. He has continually escaped prosecution. In fact, I would argue that he was one of the city's most prolific criminals. Shouldn't we have expected this kind of escalation at some point with the constant catch-and-release?"

"Look, guys, I caution you to be careful about how you distribute this information. You're the media, which means people will be out there talking about what you tell them. They'll be sharing your clippings and broadcasts on social media. Making this assailant out to be anything but a murderer will not benefit anyone. There's order to society, and the person or persons responsible is breaking that order." The Chief's tone is stern and angry. He's insulted at the direction this press conference has gone. "Now I'll take a couple more questions, but make them sensical, please. Laurel, from the Metro."

"With a serial killer on the loose, is there any plan for a curfew?"

"We're examining all options."

"What does that mean?"

"It means we are examining all options. Just as a I said. It's on the table."

"Carl." The Police Chief points at another reporter.

"What are the chances that this guy is a cop? I know in the profile, Mr. Brenning said it's unlikely the killer is from inside of the system, but from the sounds of it, he knows who to go after and how to kill. I mean, in your release here, you say that he shot twelve people in a single room. That requires training, skill."

"We don't believe that this assailant has any formal ties to the police. Thank you everybody."

"What are you calling him?" a female reporter shouts out.

The Chief stops and turns back to the podium. "Excuse me?"

"Well, calling him 'the assailant' all the time doesn't make much sense. There's really no way to report about him without some sort of nickname."

"No, we don't have a pet name for him. Are you serious?" The Chief has officially lost his cool. "Guys, that's all for now. We have a lot of work to do. Thank you."

One reporter shouts out, "Well he's killing ex-convicts, so how about The Con Killer?" There seems to be a unified agreement in the room that the press will run with that nickname.

The Con Killer. Will He Strike Again? That's the headline the city wakes up to the next morning. Social media is abuzz. By noon, #theconkiller is trending on Facebook, Twitter, and Instagram. The debate as to whether what this vigilante is doing can be classified as good or bad has started. Angry citizens and trolls do battle online, while reporters clamour to crime scenes to report on the story. In under 24 hours, national media pick up on the hottest news story in Winnipeg. This is sure to make it harder to kill.

Everyone will be looking for me now. Targets will have to be carefully selected and monitored, although the press conference did reveal holes in their theory that allow me to take advantage of the situation. Just like a criminal, The Con Killer will see these holes, and exploit them.

As I sit on my couch watching the press conference, I can't help but feel a bit of pride. My mission has been recognized, and I am making my stamp on this world. Now, perhaps it's not the stamp that anyone might consider to be positive, but if I play this right I will make my city safer, while challenging traditional ideals regarding justice. It's just a matter of time until I become urban legend and the criminals are running scared. I think it's safe to say that I now deserve the title of Martial's son.

20

The Bell Tolls for Martial

AFTER DROPPING MONICA OFF AT WORK, I take Dad's truck for a clean. I need time to think anyway. The last couple of days with her have been amazing, but I have two conflicting realities to juggle at once. Chilling and playing marriage is exactly what I need, but now my lie about treatment, and withholding the truth about being The Con Killer is weighing heavily on my mind. It's almost depressing. There's no possibility to reconcile my worlds so I need to somehow make peace with these decisions I've made. Somehow lying to the woman I love is harder to come to grips with than killing people. How fucked up is that?

While I wait in the lobby for the truck to be cleaned, I notice a patch on the bag of the guy sitting on the couch opposite me. He's a military man; a hardcore looking one at that. You know the type.

Bald head. Check.

Beard. Check.

Massive. Double check.

Tattoos. Of course.

I notice something else about this solider. He has a look in his eyes that I see every time I look in the mirror. It's a look that is just kinda missing something. I don't know how to explain it, and I don't even think some regular guy off the street would see it. There's just a certain emptiness. When an employee of the car wash comes up and asks him a question he attempts to smile, and to her it likely seems fine. But I know better. He's smiling through something. It's fake, even if it's sincere.

"You tour?" I ask him nonchalantly.

"Yep. You?" he asks politely.

"No. I'm not a military man. I probably should have been, but this and that happened, and I never enlisted. Life, ya know?"

"Oh, I know."

"My dad was a military man. He did two tours; Vietnam."

"Brutal fight those guys had. How's he doing now that he's a bit older?"

"He actually died not too long ago. After the war, he signed up to be a cop."

"That's a strong man. Most of us coming back from the wars now want nothing to do with anything remotely close to what we experienced over there."

He seems nice enough. His burliness and deep gravely voice would deter many, but honestly, he's more cordial than most people I've met. "Can I ask you a question, related to your service?"

He nods in tentative agreement.

"There's obviously some shit you had to do over there that you'll never talk about. I mean, it's war. It's dark. But, you have a ring on, which means that you either have to talk to her, or you have to keep secrets."

"Is there a question in there somewhere?"

"How do you do it? If you keep the secrets, how?"

"I'm not sure that's something I want to answer," he says, as he gets up and attempts to leave the seated area. No one else is around except for a couple of staff, so he's not embarrassed. This kind of stuff must be nearly impossible to talk about, especially with a stranger.

"Please," I beg of him. "It's important."

He turns back and faces me. "Why? Why is it important?"

"Because I'm The Con Killer, and I need to figure out how to do that while being in a relationship." I probably can't say that, so I fib a bit. "My mom is having a hard time with things she's learning about my dad. I have no idea how to help her."

He sits back down, and really lays his cards on the table. "You see these people," he says while pointing at the staff and the people outside. "They go to work. They go to movies. They have kids. They do whatever it is they do without a second thought as to why they are able to do it. When you're fighting evil like the type of people military boys face, you are the one taking on the burden for their daily lives. You have no idea what you'll wake up to next when you're in the middle of a war, but you know it's either you that's going to die, or some other guy. It's inevitable. Put that into perspective. You sign up to do something that you know will come down to you or someone else dying. I don't tell my wife about what happened over there because she couldn't handle it. You have to be a certain kind of person to go into battle. I keep the secrets because I love my Debbie with all my heart and soul. I went to war so she'd never need to know what it's all about ... what it takes to keep her and my child safe. If you're a real man, you carry that burden for them, not in spite of them."

That's more of an answer than I was expecting. If this guy's wife went on tour with him, chances are she wouldn't be with him right now after she watched some of the things he had to do to get out alive. The same goes for Monica.

"So what's the difference between a military man taking out the trash, as apposed to, let's say this Con Killer they're talking about so much today?"

Without hesitation he says, "Absolutely nothing. This guy is doing what we did over there. He's taking out the trash, like you said. As long as he sticks to killing hardcore criminals, I'll sit back and watch him clean up the mess. He kills enough guys and chances are, some of the bad guys will move on. It takes one innocent casualty to turn him into the villain, though. He hurts someone I love, and he'll know pain."

"Sir, your car is ready," an employee says to him.

"Thanks man." I shake his hand, and he's gone.

It's interesting to hear the perspectives of many on The Con Killer. Social media has blown up with varying opinions, and this military guy is actually in favour of what I'm doing. I hoped, but never expected the outpouring of support that I've received. About ten-minutes go by before my truck is done. I use that time to read the comments online about *me*. The even split I was expecting just doesn't exist. There are more supporters than detractors, that is for sure. Another prime example of why superhero movies need to be dark.

As I get in the truck after a fresh clean inside and out, I see two pieces of paper folded over sitting on the centre console, along with about thirty-five cents.

I guess they found this stuff under the seats. Good to know they are honest.

I open up the papers to find Martial's handwriting. It's a diary entry, but unlikely anything else I had read from him before.

This city is broken. It's a cesspool, rotting at it's core. FUCKED! As obliterated as I am at the current moment the truth shall set me free. I have spent years in the shadows, and all I have to show for it is a house that looks like a scrapbook, and a mission that will probably never be realized. What a piece of shit life. My family—gone. My job—gone. My sanity—questionable. Soon, my life—gone. There is no question in my mind that I am about to die. The only question is, will I die a heroes death?

I spent my whole life being that guy. You want someone to kick ass? Call Martial. You want someone to talk a person off the ledge? Call Martial. You want to know the real deal?

Call Martial. Then, somewhere down the line, it all unraveled. I can blame so many others for where I am right now, but truthfully, a man can only blame himself. I could have made different choices. Let's see:

- I shouldn't have beaten up that guy on my first bust.

- I definitely shouldn't have tried to take on the guy that shot me.

- I should have given my wife and son the attention they deserved.

- I probably could have gone without the money in the basement. Now I'm a thief.

- I should have never even joined the military. That's where the darkness started.

- But since I did, I should have killed everyone I knew was guilty by now. What have I been waiting for?

These fucking assholes are going to be the end of me, and they don't even deserve to breathe. That's where it all goes wrong; society, life, humanity. There's a standard that one must set for himself and everyone around him. As soon as you put yourself before someone, knowing you're going to hurt them, BANG BANG! I guess that's why they executed prisoners all those years ago. But now, we're more civilized. Oooooh, look at us ... we don't kill the guilty anymore, we let them kill us.

Well, enough is enough. Tonight, I'm the executioner. Then, hopefully if I get through this, I can hand over enough evidence in the next couple of years for the biggest bust ever.

Years ago, when my boy Michael was young, he called me a hero for killing someone in the line of duty. Well, Michael, dad is going to make you proud tonight! What is duty? It's not a uniform, but dedication of one's self to a cause. An unwavering disregard for self in the name of doing what it is you feel is right. It is my duty to kill these people that have hung on my walls for years.

Now, if I do die, and someone finds this, before you call me uncivilized, I would like you to take the following into account. First, I haven't killed outside of the line of duty before, even the dirtbags I know deserved it. They have gone on to kill, rape, deal drugs, destroy families, victimize. How can a man rationally be considered civilized when he has the chance to stop all of that pain but does nothing?

Second ... well actually, there is no second. That's it. That's what it all comes down to. Some cops never see any real action. They direct some traffic, attend some domestics, and learn how to clean their gun for no particular reason—they'll never shoot it. Many days I have wished I was that cop. But

I'm not, and I can't pretend to be. I've seen too much. Top five worst moments of my life have nothing to do with me.

I got a call on some woman shouting at her crying baby. I get there, door open, baby in the bath tub face down. I hear a noise. Baby mom's in the bedroom banging her boyfriend. There's no psychosis there, just a sick bitch that killed her baby and then got laid.

Shooting outside of a nightclub. One bullet to the chest. Guy bleeds out and dies out front. As I'm asking questions I get to a guy who's really rattled. Turns out he's the owner of the club. He tried to keep the guy alive, but nothing worked. No CPR training can prepare you for death in front of your eyes. Here's a guy that built a business to make people happy, and now he's rattled to his core, questioning everything. His eyes; the saddest eyes I've ever seen.

I'm a dog man. I love dogs. One of my first calls out was to a barn in a back yard filled with dogs left to fend for themselves. I can't even think about it without tearing up.

I won't go into any detail on this one, but I can only say, you never want to hear a sound from behind a dumpster, only to find out it's a woman barely moving, just trying to make noise so someone will help her, underwear torn, eye swollen shut. I couldn't sleep for a week after that one.

Two kids get in a fight at school. One walks away without a scratch. The other has had his pride and sense of self beat out of him. He decides to get revenge by burning down the other guy's house. Turns out his family was inside. This kid comes home to a whole new life, and now both of the kids are about as broken as anyone you'll ever see.

Some of these people authentically deserved to die, and I let them go, and they're not even the worst of it. No more. I've spent so much time crafting this research. It's finally almost done. But it's time to act on a few of these guys. What they're about to do will open the flood gates of crime here.

They leave me no choice. Tonight, Zero will be no more.

I sit in the truck, dazed from the words of my dad. I've basically picked up where he left off, and he's left me a clue as to who killed him. The anger in me boils over, and I punch the steering wheel, while yelling out. I'm red in the face—no mask needed, and shaking. This note doesn't sound like the Martial I knew, but then again if I were to write my emotions right now, who knows what I would say. In fact, the tone and the way he writes, Dad almost sounds like ... me. I have to remind myself to unclench my jaw, or my teeth will be scraped to nubs. I take a minute to get composed as I get out of the truck and pace. *Breathe in, breathe out ... nice long breaths. You need to calm down and take action.*

Searching through the database on my phone, I refresh regarding Zero. It's a collective group of assholes that pretend they are civilized criminals. You know, the difference between street thugs and

Al Capone. None of them are in the same league as Capone, though. They're still street thugs, but in suits, with a club house.

Dad wrote this note the day he died, I can feel it in my bones. Stashing it in his truck was smart, considering he knew I'd be the next person to sit in it, or perhaps it is here by mistake. Either way, these mother fuckers need to die. They killed my father! You've heard the phrase, *my blood boiled*? That doesn't begin to do my rage justice. The only way I'll ever have any peace is if they all burn in hell together.

Over the next three days, I spend my time watching the targets from afar, and plotting the worst death I can think of. Monica has been picking up extra shifts at work because of the extended vacation, which is perfect. That gives me the time to balance my life between her and this.

Their meeting place has obvious security shortcomings, but these guys are cocky enough to believe no one will come after them, so they ignore lethal flaws in the design and architecture. My planning would involve a cash deal for two junk cars left parked a few blocks away, a stop at Home Depot for heavy duty chains, rubber tubing to wrap them in, and a serious padlock. They'll be talking about The Con Killer a lot after this one.

The sun seems stronger today as I drive in the Durango. It's really hot, mind numbingly so. On a day like this I would usually be holed up in an air conditioned room, but I'm often cold now, so there's another gift from Cancer—the ability to function in temperatures that usually hold me down.

Today's goal is particularly lofty. One, because these kills will be in broad daylight. Two, because I'm not going after one or a few men. This time, I'm cutting off an entire arm of crime in the city. When the profiler talked about me he let me know that they would only be really searching for me at night. That makes this crime a little easier to accomplish.

Dad didn't actually explain why these guys called themselves Zero, but I found out from a low level guy I shared a joint with while casing the clubhouse. Their name came about as a result of the police never being able to peg how many members were a part of their organization. The name mocks police, as well as their attempts to put them away. These thugs have torn apart families, killed good men, turned innocent girls into prostitutes, and the list goes on. Most importantly, I'm sure they killed Martial. There's simply no bad deed that would keep these guys up at night.

I stop by a coffee shop before parking myself outside of 21 Adelaide. I'm a few blocks away watching, one-by-one, as these criminals enter the building. It starts with Malcolm Every opening up the shop for the day, just like Dad described. Then the lower level guys show. After that, it's the bosses. The only way this kill will work is if every one of the faces exiting cars, and entering the building can be identified by Dad's research. If one innocent civilian walks in, the plan will be abandoned. Dad said no one's allowed in except for Zero members, so that shouldn't be too much of an issue. An hour goes by as I take pictures and scan the database to see if there is any reason to not go through with my plan—no reason exists. There are no innocents inside, and the gang's all here.

The neighbourhood surrounding the building is less than stellar. Despite that, there are no cameras for quite a few blocks; meaning no way to confirm who is behind what is about to happen. I did thorough research; the only cameras to and from their clubhouse are at a busy intersection about five busy intersections deep. They have no way of knowing who performed the kill, and even if they did, it's unlikely they'll look. After all, my profile says I don't park near the scene. This kill will be loud, and make a statement. It will not be easy to carry on after this goes down, at night or in daylight.

All the heads of Zero are now inside, tucked away in the middle room, which is a safe distance from the outer rooms where armed guards stand at attention. It's a waste of resources, though. I won't be coming from the sides; I'll be coming from the top. The days spent watching and planning come to ahead with one violent act in broad daylight.

The stage is set, the streets are clear, and it is time to act. I use the padlock and chains to secure door number one. The rubber around the chain makes threading it through the metal handles nearly silent. Doors number two and three presented a problem when I was planning—neither have handles on the outside; that's where the junk cars come in. Quietly, I park them so that the fender just touches the doors. No one will be running out these exits unless they can move an entire car in park.

With Zero stuck inside, I climb the ladder on the side of the building next door. That gets me to the first level roof. The second level to the roof is a little more challenging. I put my back against a duct shaft and push my feet against the wall. Slowly, I creep up until a dicey spin gets me up top. Quietly again, I step from one roof to the other, until five ducts stare back at me. The openings are too small for a human to fit down, but not too small for what I have planned.

As I hold C4 in my hands, I feel a rush of power come over me. I can picture it in my head, these guys burning to death. A lot of people are going to die today. Correction, a lot of bad people are going to die today. It's amazing how one word like bad can change a negative into a positive.

I carefully drop the explosives down each shaft on a string, making very little noise. I had no choice but to do this while Zero was in their meeting. The last thing I need is for a bomb to go off early because I set it up and left margin for error, then accidentally kill someone innocent. In under fifteen-minutes, all of the bombs are rigged.

As I climb down the building and make my way to my truck I have yet another feeling of accomplishment. Guys like this don't suspect anyone would have the balls to take them down. History would teach them so, and now they're complacent. I'm really using my brain and instincts here. Dad taught me well. Their egos, their meeting spot, their planned sense of safety; I exploited it all.

The piece de resistance though, comes in the form of a letter. I dropped a simple one-page warning in their mailbox earlier. "Boom! - Sincerely, Martial" It was risky because they could have opened it before everything was in place, but it's a risk that was necessary. These guys need to know that Martial is the one killing them. Just think about the looks on their faces. A ghost comes back from the grave to end them. It's mother fucking poetry.

I sit in my truck, and crack a cold Coke. It's delicious on a day like today. The action may be a bit of a wait, so I pop on my favourite podcast and kick the seat back. Some might have just blown the building right away. Not me. I wait until that front entrance begins to shake. Then I know the note has been seen and the men behind the doors know they're trapped like the rats they are.

About an hour goes by, and finally, I hear the door slam into position as the chains tighten. The doors open just a crack. It's enough for the men to see out, but not actually get out. That's my cue to get out of the truck and walk over to the chained doors. I look silently at the men through my mask, while they scream and yell at me. As they do, I spray paint a message on the street, "One Man. One Mission. Kill these Cons."

Surely there are some other men trying the 2 exits blocked by cars, and the fear of what to come is setting in. I want this. They need to feel fear like so many have at their hands. Finally, realizing that the chains aren't coming off, the men stop trying to get through and I suspect are inside trying to find a place to hide. I press my ear to the door, and I can't hear anything. No more screams, no more shouting, no more attitude. Calm; that's when you know the desperation has really set in.

It's time to rid the city of Zero.

A simple call to the phone in the middle vent attached to the C4 is all it takes. I made it so the detonator on each device is extremely vulnerable to the first explosion, thus setting off a chain reaction.

The explosion is far more spectacular than I could have imagined. That front door was open just a crack, and within seconds, flames shoot out. These men were surely burning now. The windows on the top floor blow out across the street, and the rumble shakes everything nearby. Car alarms are going off, flames try to reach the sky through vents, and I guess the old building wasn't equipped for an explosion because the roof caves in, bringing down the North wall. Zero's world is on fire, and Dad's killers are dead. What a sight.

I drive away with a burning building in my rear view mirror. There is zero chance (pardon the celebratory pun) that anyone survived such a brutal attack, and I'm perfectly okay with that. Martial can now rest in peace.

21

The Superstar

"HE'S NOTHIN'. I'm ready for him, and he can't possibly be ready for me. It's no secret where I spend my time, Con Killer. You want some, come get some."

The words of Julian Munroe over YouTube. Julian is about as bad as they come. He started his career in crime at the age of nineteen as an enforcer for a small biker gang. Word got around quickly that not only was he big and mean, he had the skills to actually back up any threats he puts out into the world. As far as criminals go, he's one of the worst; no conscience, no family to hold him back, no one willing to go toe-to-toe with him. There are few guys that actually scared Martial, but based on his notes, he was none too excited for the day he'd have to confront Julian.

I find the entire threat absurd. Julian is sitting on camera admitting to being a criminal, and admitting to being ready to kill me. I guess the cops can't do anything about that, so he's free to post whatever he wants.

"This killer that you're all admiring so much doesn't stand a chance. When I see him, I'll snap him like a twig and continue on with my day as if he never existed in the first place."

That's how he ends his deranged video, and he's probably right. I'm in pretty good shape, and by no means small, but next to him I am a twig.

It really doesn't matter whether he wants me to come after him or not. Today, The Con Killer is stuck at home, feeling the shits. Monica got her shifts covered to take care of me. A high fever, chills, pain, and a cough have me feeling about as weak as I ever have.

"Your immune system is compromised baby," Monica says. "The only thing that will help right now are some meds and bed rest."

I don't argue. It's like someone flipped a switch and turned my system off. My body is under attack, but luckily, it's only temporary. The thing about Cancer is that the actual disease is less problematic than the viruses you catch from your defenses being down. It really is a bitch being sick when you have a guy like Julian calling out your manhood. Monica's bed side manner is impeccable though. Without any choice, my diet is now completely changed to fight the Cancer and any viruses that might come about (like this one). I've never felt so cold and so hot at the same time. One second I need a heating pack, and the next I'm asking for a cold cloth.

There's this meme floating around the internet; I can't remember exactly how it goes, but it's something to the effect of, "They say men don't know pain like child birth. That's not true. Ask them how they feel when they have a fever." Basically, we'll open the jars, we'll pound in the nails, and pick a woman off of her feet on the way to the bedroom, but if we get sick ... watch out, baby on board.

For the next three days I'm laid up trying to get

myself better. This gives me plenty of time to read up on what the world thinks of my mission—you know, when I'm not puking or shaking uncontrollably. You might have missed the subtlety of what I just said, so let me repeat. I take the time to read what world thinks of my mission. The world!

After I blew up Zero's building, The Con Killer became international news. The argument over whether I'm right or wrong has polarized groups of people that are now protesting in the streets of my city. On one side, there are protests demanding the cops do more to catch me. On the other side, there are protests against the cops doing anything. I could never have predicted the kind of a reaction I'm seeing in my feed. One Facebook Live video shows a protest at City Hall, and the energy is electrifying. The city police have gone on record saying that as long as the protests remain peaceful, there will be no curfew, but in light of my recent actions, if violence escalates, they'll have no choice. The one point I find most interesting in the news articles being shared is that people feel safer as a result of what I'm doing. That was the ultimate goal.

In one article, a reporter interviewed twenty-five major crimes felons who had served their time and were free. Fourteen of them said they were packing their bags. Eleven were staying put. It's probably safe to say the criminals staying put are now on their best behaviour. The ones packing their bags haven't given up their old ways; that obvious sign of illegal activity was not missed by the cops either. Two of those guys were picked up for dealing, one for violating probation by being at a school, and another was arrested for trying to kidnap a kid. Their comments led to the cops setting up tails, the tails caught these guys breaking the law, and now we have four criminals behind bars that may have not been there if it weren't for my mission.

In another article, a man was interviewed who had come to the city to be a part of the movement supporting my actions. When asked if he was scared, he said, "Why would I be scared? He's not looking for me. This is probably the safest city in the world right now. Over thirty of your worst criminals are gone."

After day three, I'm going absolutely stir crazy. It's been nice having Monica around, but I told her I don't want her to be my nurse and I mean it. The second I'm self-reliant, I have to give her back her freedom. Luckily, the fever has broken and I have only a minor cough. I look like shit, but that's okay. There's no need to look good when your face is behind a mask. I just need to get Monica to agree to leave so that I can go after the guy who's been tweeting about me daily.

Another day and The Con Killer hasn't
come knocking. #scaredlittleman
Hey CK I'm right here. Where are you?
Has anyone seen CK? He's MIA.
Better than being DOA I guess.

Oh, and my personal favourite that actually made me laugh:

CK it's okay to be scared. All little girls get
scared of monsters at some point.

"Honestly, I feel much better. I may still look like a bag of crap, but I promise you, the worst is over for now." I try to make Monica see that I'm okay, and that it's perfectly understandable for her to leave and go back to work. "You took an entire month off. Now three days. You're losing your mind just sitting here. I'm boring and coughing all over the place. Go home, take a shower, go out with a friend for wine, and get some rest. You absolutely deserve it. Then you can put in a full day at the clinic and come right back here."

"You sure you're not just trying to be a nice guy?"

"You think I want you to go anywhere? I want you to stay, but life has to go on, and you have an important job. There's more than one patient in this city."

"You're right, you're right," she says begrudgingly. "It's hard getting used to someone telling you what to do."

"Oh, I know. You've been the boss for three days now, and I was terrified."

She packs up and heads out. We can't kiss because I'm still sick which is utterly painful, but at least we're both on course to what we need to do. When she drives out of sight, I get to work on my computer. I study up on Julian beyond Dad's notes. This kill will be different. Everyone I've faced off with has been on my terms. Julian called me out, which means he's going to be guarded and ready for anything. Shooting him is probably out of the question, he won't open himself up like that. There's no chance I can stab him like James, he's too big. He'd take the knife and keep on coming. My Jiu Jitsu doesn't mean shit, because again, he's just so damn big. My hitting him would be like throwing a feather at a brick wall.

Perhaps you're thinking I could just break-in to his house and wait in his basement until he gets home, or something like that. When I know he's there, I make a noise that draws him in, saying hello a hundred times in the dark, hoping someone will answer. Then when he's coming down the stairs I can shoot him nine times. It doesn't actually work that way. Only people in movies are stupid enough to make their way towards a noise when they know something could be fundamentally wrong with the situation.

When he said I'd know where to find him, he wasn't kidding. His routine is strict. Criminal charges mean he can't travel. The money he made over the years means he has protection. His life is as regimented as a clock's. He gets up, goes to a private gym that I won't be able to get into, then he heads to a building he owns which is protected by cameras and guards, so there's no chance of repeating my Zero plan. Then he goes out with his girlfriend, but is always covered by security. His car windows are bullet proof, and since calling me out, he's started wearing kevlar—the stuff Batman's suit is made out of.

Dad tracked his movements for over a year, and they haven't changed. It sounds boring, but his girlfriend is hot as hell, and I can just imagine the toys he has to play with at his place. Julian is known for buying everything that's had a Kickstarter campaign. To top things off, he tweeted about the cops having a tail on him, which he called a violation of his rights. His lawyer filed an injunction, and now they have to stay away unless they can show probable cause. Right after he won, Julian tweeted that he didn't want me to have any excuse not to come try and kill him. The man's an animal.

So, how do you get to a man who has a forcefield around him, and even if you can, how do you do it without hurting someone that doesn't deserve it? Then I see it. The flaw in his world; Shane Wylde.

Mr. Wylde is one of Julian's bodyguards, and he has a secret that he's keeping from everyone, including Julian. Dad marked Shane down as one of the good guys caught in a bad world, for all the right reasons. I can use this.

You know in movies and TV shows when someone comes home to find a gunman sitting there in a comfy chair, pointing a gun at them as they walk into the room? Well, I figured I'd try that out on Shane. Turns out, it isn't quite as epic as the Bond movies or Get Shorty might have you believe. I get to Shane's house at about 10pm, right around the time he's finishing up guarding our big scary friend. Shane decided to go grocery shopping and stop at a bar to watch the end of a hockey game before getting home, though. I sit there for two-hours in that chair, gun pointed, waiting. I end up getting so bored that I eat some honey ham in his fridge and snoop a bit. Lurking in the shadows is really not at all what I thought it would be like. I just spin around in that chair, and wait.

Finally, he walks in the door, and drops his groceries when he sees me. He even reaches for his gun.

"Uh uh. You stay there or I'm putting a bullet between your legs," I say from behind my mask. He throws his hands up in the air, probably out of instinct. "Do I look like a cop to you?" I say as I stand up, gun pointing, and walk into the light.

"I'm no criminal man. I'm just a security guy, and Mr. Munroe pays extremely well."

"You do know he's a criminal, right? Like the worst of the worst."

"Yeah. Of course I do. But I really need the money."

"I know. And that's why I'm here. What if you didn't need the money?"

I make a slight miscalculation and get too close to him. It gives him the opportunity to swiftly knock the gun out of my hand and behind the entertainment unit. It's on; Jiu Jitsu vs boxing. He took me by surprise, and gets a few more shots in—one to my face, two to my body—before I can get myself away from him. I fall back into the chair which gives me the space I need to get the upper-hand.

Rolling out of the chair and across the room, I'm able to get into a fighter stance. Now, we're on even footing. We trade shots, but most of them don't break through either of our defenses. If one of us doesn't trip up soon, this could be a very long fight. Feeling sick and shitty does not help my chances. I decide there is only one way to beat him. I need to get Shane on the ground. I come at him hard, intending for his defense to go up. I punch and kick at him, just trying to back him up into the coffee table behind him. Finally, when I'm feeling pretty tired, I muster up as much energy as I can to give him a solid kick to the thigh; he trips backwards over the table. As he attempts to get his balance he makes the mistake I was looking for. I'm able to take his back and choke him out.

It takes awhile for him to wake up. By then, I have him tied to a kitchen chair with zip ties ... his zip ties. Talk about added insult to actual injury. He opens his eyes to see the gun pointed square at his face.

"Now about that question I asked earlier," I say in the most politely condescending way possible.

We chat about options. Shane's actually a pretty good guy; not good enough to put my gun away, but agreeable, which makes my life somewhat less problematic.

When I was trying to think of how I could get to Julian and kill him, I was discounting one very simple idea: I don't actually have to get anywhere near to kill him. Shane and I both agree that Julian needs to go. The only reason he is working for Julian is because he needs the money to fight his girlfriend for custody of his daughter, and because Julian threatens that very daughter's life if Shane doesn't do his bidding.

He was literally in the wrong place at the wrong time, and now he's basically held hostage by Julian. What I come to learn when talking to Shane is that he's not the only one. Not just that, but leaving Julian's organization is as good as a death sentence, so really, there was no motivation for Shane to not accept my offer of $500,000 cash.

The plan is quite simple. Earlier in the day, Shane disconnected the air conditioning on Julian's car, ensuring that whenever they stop, Julian will stand outside. It's 40 degrees today, and no one wants to sit in a hot car on a day like this—not even a man as regimented as him. Every day, Julian stops at the same 7-11 for a Slurpee, and today is no different. Of course, he can't get it for himself. He needs Shane to do that while he and another body guard post up near the trunk of the car. Julian has already decided that I am too scared to come after him anyway, so his guard is down after over a week of waiting.

Shane hands Julian his Slurpee and I appear across the parking lot when the timing is right, in broad daylight. Now, you might ask why I would do that. Well, Julian is a statement kill. If I can actually take out one of the scariest guys in the city—a guy who called me out—I will be a legend.

It takes a moment, but Julian spots me. "Is that you Con Killer?" he yells it out for all to hear.

There are about a dozen people around, and they all stop what they're doing, some to take video, and some just wait and see what happens. One thing they all have in common is they take cover behind whatever they can.

"I'm going to enjoy ending you," Julian says as he starts to approach me with his guards.

I just stand there, motionless, not saying a word.

"Cat got your tongue, boy?" He takes off his button up shirt to reveal just how big he is. In nothing but a muscle shirt and shorts, Julian flexes as he walks slowly towards me. Jesus Christ, this guy is scary. "Oh, you're small. I really can just snap you like a twig."

Still, I stand there without saying a word, waiting. Not going to lie, I'm nervous. He's basically a ninja turtle with his traps looking like the shell connecting with his ears. What a genetic freak. This plan better work, because if he gets hold of me, I'm fucking done.

Finally, and luckily, about ten feet away from me, without having to move a muscle, Julian stops and winces. His eyes are big as saucers. This is my ultimate power moment. I put both of my arms out in the air, and tilt my head slightly. I drop my arms as he falls face first to the concrete. All those watching on are in awe. I bet every one of them thinks I have some sort of powers. I mean, I'd imagine it looked like I took him out without touching him through Necrokinesis or something.

Really, I just made a deal with Shane to add Phenol into Julian's Slurpee. The tiniest amount ingested kills almost instantly. It was used by the Nazis, which is sick, but really the best way I knew of to kill him. It's not exactly readily available, unless of course you have three-days of bed rest and know how to access the deep web. What a sick and twisted place that is.

Unfortunately, I won't get out of here without creating some chaos, so I pull my gun and shoot into the air. Everyone scrambles and I run down a back lane, out of sight. Under a dock, I have a change of clothes waiting. I get into my other outfit, and then walk out into broad daylight with no one suspecting a thing.

Shane would pay the other bodyguard $200,000 to

look the other way (he was also under Julian's thumb), and my risky plan in the middle of the day goes off without a hitch. Ten more feet though, and Cancer would have been the least of my worries. Call it luck, fate, or destiny ... whatever you want. I'm standing and Julian is not.

The media will have a field day with this one. There is no question. As if shooting, blowing up, and stabbing people wasn't enough. Now I'm killing them without so much as a touch. Shane texts me on a burner to let me know that the cops talked to the two guards at the scene. They both played off like they had no idea what happened, and that they would miss their boss so very much. I'm a little uneasy that this is the first kill I've executed where I've had to enlist some help, but Shane has no idea who I am under the mask so I'm alright with a bit of help.

As I arrive back at home, I feel nothing about the fact that I just killed Julian. I could have just as easily ran over a squirrel. The effects of Jason White on my mind are no longer a factor. It seems that I am now completely used to killing. It's a scary but necessary transition for me. Jason, James, Alex, Max, the 12 at the party, Zero, and now Julian—they've all fallen so easily at my hand.

Little did I know, everything was about to change. I guess you can't tempt fate forever.

22

Now You See Me

SINCE KILLING JULIAN THE CON KILLER URBAN LEGENDS HAVE STARTED. It's been pretty cool to see all the speculation about me out there in the media; everyone's talking about my alter ego. But, you can't ride a high forever, and today is just not my day.

I learned earlier in the morning that the other bodyguard Shane paid off killed himself over what he had done, Monica and I got in a fight about The Con Killer of all things on text, and now ... this. As my body tries to self-cauterize the wound to the back of my head, I can't help but feel a little less than accomplished in my goals on this sunny day in Hell. Now, tied to a chair in my living room, I must face the fact that I may not die of Cancer. Instead, this guy with bad breath and a tattoo of a pink fish on his forearm might be the end of me.

"Ya know, for a guy that's been taking everyone out, you make some pretty common mistakes," he says to me while sharpening his knife on my metal TV stand.

"We all make mistakes," I retort.

"The problem for you is that your mistakes just

might get you killed. I mean, what were you thinking? You come straight home from killing someone? What, you're too good to be followed?"

"I had a date. Time was tight."

"Look at you with the jokes. Well I hope she was good man, because you're gonna die for pussy; and you're not the first. I've killed a few guys because of the women they chose to go after. Your case is a little different though, and maybe I'll thank her in person one day for making you sloppy."

Clearly I misjudged some things. Perhaps not blending into a crowd before coming home was something I did out of ego, or maybe ignorance. I'm not sure anymore. Maybe I thought that changing under the dock was more than enough, but in broad daylight, it's just easier to be followed. The fact that I'm here just a short time after killing Dad's murderers, and taking out one of the baddest men in the city is probably a sign that I should stop this madness. "Man, whatever you're going to do, just get it over with."

"You don't make the rules. Not right now." He holds up today's paper. The cover features the faces of all those I've killed with a question mark over a blacked out icon of a man in the middle. The headline: *THE MANY FACES OF THE CON KILLER. Death is Now a Way of Life*.

"So, you're going to what—stare me to death?" His gaze is so intense. If I didn't know any better, I'd swear he wants to jump my bones.

"More jokes. You think us criminal types are dumb, *don'tcha*? Well, this criminal standing in front of you is named Matthew, and I'm a curious type as well, with an IQ damn near genius. I like to know things, and right now, what I want to know is why?"

"Why do I do it?"

"That's right," he says as he rests his back on the TV stand and gets comfortable. The blinds are drawn, so only small blades of light shine through. It doesn't feel like daytime at all.

"It's pretty simple really. My dad was a cop. He put guys like you away. The problem with that is, guys like you get out, and the wheels on the bus go round and round. My way, you don't get to keep preying on people."

"So to get criminals you need to be a criminal? That's some fucked up logic, man."

"Look, I'm not trying to take a run at Sainthood here. I'm just a guy at the end of his road trying to do something for this world before I leave it. I'm following the natural path my life led me down. Training as a kid to fight and shoot, finding stacks of money and the tools to do what I gotta do, and then a road map to find fuckers like you, or at least, that's what I thought."

"I sense some unsureness in your voice, boy."

"Let's just say that I don't really know what's right or wrong anymore. Everyone can be either, and every situation can be either. A man killed himself last night because he helped me. Who knows what adverse effects I'm having on the world?"

"Oh, so you mean that you're just discovering now that the world isn't so black and white?"

"No, you aren't hearing me. The world is still black and white. There's you, and there's me. I'm a good guy doing bad things to put bad guys doing bad things down. That's black and white. Figuring out who the bad guys are is the issue. Is it a criminal stealing to feed his family? A cop on the take because we pay hockey players millions, and our EMS crews may never save to see six-figures? Who's good doing bad, and bad doing bad? That's the real question. I've seen a lot of shit since I started this, and one thing I know is that no book can be judged by it's cover. Morality is subjective, and that's why these protests that the city has decided to engage in won't matter in the end. What's wrong to some, is right to others. I'm wrong, and I know it. My reasons are right, I am wrong. Society doesn't think like that, and it's fucking crazy. The guy that killed himself was Julian's bodyguard; was he wrong to protect Julian? Probably. Was his suicide all about nature correcting course after I didn't kill him? I guess it's possible. I had no idea whether he was good or bad, and so I didn't factor him into the equation."

"Sounds like a crisis of faith. Me? I know what I want, and I take it." He says this as I attempt to maneuver my hands free of the ropes. I can't though. They're too tight, and every movement tears away at my skin. It's so itchy. There's no getting out of this. "Problem is a guy like you comes along and kills my boss, and now I'm out major money. You don't think of the consequences. I'm not the only one that's going to suffer as a result. A lot of people were connected to Zero. You cost a lot of people money."

"Well that's an over-simplification. You kill and victimize people, so you guys get what you get."

"Says you. But just as you said a minute ago, maybe we're good people doing bad." He says this with a crooked smile, as if to say he knows he's not one of the good guys.

"Let me ask you something. For real, completely serious. What got you started down this path?" It's almost as if we've settled into polite debate. If I wasn't tied to a chair with the threat of being killed, I would say the mood would be lighter than one would expect.

"My story is pretty typical. Bad parents, bad way, bad choices."

"So if you know they're bad choices, why keep making them?"

"Because eventually you get good at something, and it becomes all you know. I'm good at applying pressure. In the corporate world, I would be a savage. Short of trying out for UFC, I'm a savage everywhere, except in my world. There's plenty of people like me with step-dads that beat them, police that showed their ugly side. Eventually you just become a criminal, like someone becomes a banker. It's just reality one day, and humans love to settle into habit."

"So your argument is that you have no will power then?"

"Boy. You just accused me of not listening ... It's not for lack of will power." He gets up and starts pacing the room. I've agitated him. Probably not the best idea. "There's something inside of me that only finds satisfaction when someone is bowing down to me. Put your foot on a man's throat and you'll find out what he's made of. Most men run around pretending to be tough guys. I come knocking and they're ready to give me their wife to stay alive. Now who's in the wrong? Me? I'm just upholding an order of things. This guy, with a boot on him is ready to give up his woman like she's property. One guy, I had no intention of killing, but he offered his mom as a sacrifice. Bitch was hot, but you never give up your mom. Killed that prick right then and there."

"Well aren't you sweet."

Some of what this guy is saying makes sense. Who's in the wrong? I guess you never put a guy in the situation to sacrifice his mom or wife, and he won't, but that's boiling under the surface somewhere, and it's good to know who a man truly is. I feel like most of us have no idea who we really are because we're rarely tested. The unnatural way we live pushes us in an untested direction. When man had to fight for his every meal, display cunning in order to survive; that's when we knew. Now, a guy could be at work in front of a computer for eight hours a day, and his aggression will explode if he's fired. There's no release anymore. The wimps are hiding in plain sight, as are the animals.

"I get it," I say as I try to get my hands free again. Now I'm bleeding from the rope burn. Fantastic. "But, I guess the question you have to ask yourself is, would the world be a better place without you and Zero in it?"

"Well now you're just arguing semantics."

"I really hate when people say that. Semantics are the building blocks of debate. You can't actually have a conversation without semantics. It's theory."

He takes a moment to think. Clearly this guy wasn't ready for a sensible conversation. I think his intent versus what it is that he has encountered are two very different things.

"No."

"No? You don't think it would be a better world without you?"

"I don't. I think that it would be a different world, but who's to say it would be better? There's no measure of good when there is no bad."

"Maybe so, but you kill for money. We're not talking about a kid that steals a GI Joe from Walmart."

"But we're out numbered. So it all balances out, I think."

"If you only knew what I do," I say in an effort to keep him talking. This conversation is buying me time. Time for what, I don't know, but time nonetheless.

"What is it that you know? You act like you know my world better than I do."

"I don't. But my dad sure as shit did."

"Enlighten me, young Jedi."

"To do that, you have to let me out of this chair."

"Yeah, that's going to happen. Do you think I'm fucking retarded?" He holds the knife to my neck and pokes just enough to break skin.

"Look, I'm not going anywhere. I'm woozy as fuck right now. You got me good when I was walking out of the house. Add Cancer to that, and I wouldn't make it thirty feet before you'd catch up to me. Oh, and don't use retarded. You say you're educated, and that's just not cool, man." He's contemplating letting me free from the chair. "Hey, if I'm going to do die tonight, I at least want to go down with some sorta knowledge that I did at least a bit to make you consider your course."

"You have Cancer?"

"I do. I've been given my death sentence already. You killing me tonight just speeds up the inevitable. The way I've been feeling, I'm going to say I probably have a month tops. I just want to show you what I know to be true. That's it. You can stab me after I'm done."

It's a stand off. His mind, weighing the pros and cons. Mine, hoping against hope that the intellectual that clearly exists inside of this guy is curious enough to let me loose.

And so he does, but holds two knives close. I stumble a bit with my first few steps. I won't go down without at least making a point. The binders full of criminals are in the locked closet next to the living room. I carefully open the door, and then move the wall separating the main closet and my treasures. He keeps a close eye on me as I open the safes.

"You aren't as out numbered as you think," I say as I throw the binders at his feet. One hits the floor, and the pages spill out.

"What is all of this?"

"It's you, your boss, your friends, everyone like you in this city." I toss all the binders at his feet. "Thirteen fucking binders full of those who victimize people just going about their days, trying not to run into you. There aren't any fucking weed dealers in amongst those faces either. That's all murderers, pedophiles, rapists—you name it. I'd say that's roughly a few thousand, give or take. When you use brute force the way you do, it might as well be a million, because most people don't know how to deal with aggressors like you."

"But you're not most people."

"That's right," I say as I put The Con Killer mask on.

We just stand there for a moment, realizing that neither of us have really won our debate, and in this world, when no one wins the war of words, it's time to fight. We both know it, but neither of us wants to make the first move. It's a stand-off in my dad's living room; he with knives, and me, with an arsenal in the closet that I can't even use. I don't dare pull a gun—neighbours would surely hear the shot.

Moments pass that feel like a lifetime, until he makes the first move, dropping his knives.

"If we're going to do this, it will be the right way," he says as he puts his fists up into a South Paw stance.

My first fight in years was with Shane, and it was fairly harmless. I didn't even end up with any bruises, and when he hit me in the face, the mask absorbed most of the blow. This would not be that easy.

We lunge at each other, with him connecting first. Getting punched in the face is very sobering. He even cracks my mask. The staticky feeling that runs under your skin is about as undesirable a sensation as one can experience. We go back and forth, trading blows, throwing objects from around the room. Matthew decides to give in to his underhanded ways, and grabs one of his knives. He slashes at the air around me, as I try not to become a piece of meat on the end of his blade. I get the upper-hand as he tires a bit, kicking him hard and fast in the sternum. It gives me the opening I need to get to the closet, and grab the knife that I used on James. Before I can though, he grabs me from behind and pulls as I hold onto a shelf for dear life. My death grip on the shelf doesn't give way, but the shelf does. As he pulls me out of the closet, all of The Con Killer's identity comes spilling out—a pile of cash, guns, the outfit ... it's all there laying on the floor.

He gets me into a choke hold, as I'm down on hands and knees. His grip is firm and tight, and I can feel the oxygen leaving my body. The room begins to spin uncontrollably. As I reach out for anything I can grab onto, there's nothing.

I feel an uncomfortable pain in my groin. This stupid bastard didn't check my pockets before he tied me up. Some intellectual he is. I quickly make a move, grab my small pocket knife out of my pants, and stab him square in the left eye. He falls back, and screams out in pain. With no time to lose, I kick him in the head, pushing the knife further into his eye. Something about me fighting and stabbing guys in the eyes: it's rough, but as good a go to move as any, I guess. He drops onto his back, giving me the opening I need to jump on him and lay hard shots to his face. With each blow, I can feel his skull turning to mush. In the end, like so many nights recently, it was him or me ... tonight I got extremely lucky. His curiosity killed him, and nothing else.

I drop to the floor face first beside his still body, breathing heavily. I'm not used to this close combat style of killing. His blood begins to pool on the floor, catching the cracks, just like Jason White's. This man, who lay dead in my living room, could have probably been someone had he just gone another route with his life. Now, he's dead by my hand.

As I rise up from the floor with half the mask on my face, my hazy vision becomes a bit clearer ... clear enough to see Monica. She's standing in the living room entrance, with the closet behind her, holding one of the other Con Killer masks. Tears stream down her face. She knows.

"Mon ..." I let out only that before she runs out of my home. I do my best to chase after her, but I've got blood in my eyes, and I stumble—probably due to a concussion. "Where are you going?" I call out as I get outside and see her across the street. She's run clear past her car, frantic, as am I.

I can't let her run to the police. I have to explain; make her understand. My worst nightmare is coming true. Fuck.

I run after her, but my pursuit is short lived. I take two steps into the street before a cab clips me on my left side. I sail into the air, landing on and smashing the windshield. As I roll over the roof and trunk, I feel my arm snap, and that's just the precursor to the hard hit my head takes on the pavement. The car comes screeching to a halt, and in the distance I see that Monica has stopped. As my eyes close, I feel someone's touch on my shoulder. "Are you okay?" Those are the last words I hear before passing out. I can't possibly speak, but as I fade I think to myself, "I'll never be okay again."

23

Doors Open, Doors Close

IT'S TWO DAYS AFTER THE CAB hit me, and I finally wake up. There's a haze over my mind and eyes. I feel as if someone tore memories out of my brain, leaving blank space. With each passing moment though, the memories rebuild. Matthew tying me up, our debate, the fight, Monica. The healer finally met the killer, and I guess my world that existed before the accident no longer exists today.

To my surprise, there she is, sleeping in a chair next to my bed. She might understand, but it's more likely that she wants to be here when I wake up so she can confront me. I'm not handcuffed to the bed, and I don't see any cops around, so clearly she hasn't told anyone yet. Maybe she won't. Regardless, this is probably the last time I'll get a chance to watch her sleep, so that's what I do. Almost three months into our relationship and I still can't get over how beautiful she is when she sleeps.

I don't wake her. No, I savour every moment until

she opens her eyes. As she wakes, she can see that I'm awake as well, and for a moment I can see concern on her face. It's short lived, however. Monica knows, and I won't insult her by denying it.

"I want to hear you say it," she says, while fighting back tears. No, *Hey, are you okay?* She's got a stony look in her eyes now, and all she wants is the truth.

I nod to let her know that it's all true.

"No. You will say the words."

I haven't admitted who I am to anyone that matters to me yet, and admitting it to Monica is one of the hardest things I've ever had to do. I hesitate, and then just man up like I had to do when she came over that first time. "Okay. I'm The Con Killer."

In this life, there have been many doors closed in my face, but none is harsher than that of a good woman dumping you. As Monica and I sit in my adopted hospital room, there are few words. She doesn't want to hear much from me, and I don't want to hear her say that she's leaving. We just sit there for almost an hour in silence.

"I locked up your vigilante gear in the closet, and locked the house too," she finally says in a condescending tone.

"Thank you."

"I don't know why I did that, but I did. When I realized you were going to be fine, I left you with the driver of the car, and tried to revive the guy in your living room, but he was dead."

"I'm sorry you had to ..."

"Dead Michael! Along with God knows how many others you've killed."

"Keep your voice down please."

"Why? Maybe I think you deserve to get caught."

"If you did, you wouldn't have locked down the house." More silence. "Do you want to know why?"

"I'm smart enough to know why. Your dad started something with those papers that used to hang on the walls, then I told you to go make a difference, and this is what you came up with. But Michael, this is not what I meant. Do you think you're a hero? Do you?"

"I don't have flight, or claws, or the ability to run at the speed of sound. So no, I'm not a hero ... not like that. But people will look back at what I've done as a stand against those that want to victimize us. I'm doing this because this is where my skill set took me. I was given the ability to shoot, to fight, and the intelligence to not get caught. Then I was given very little time. So sure, it may seem wrong in the moment, but there are children, women, and families safer today than they were yesterday because of what I've done." I hope my impassioned speech gives her some pause.

Nope. "You just can't kill people whenever you feel like it, no matter how bad they are."

"I know your view points. You've made them abundantly clear before. What I need to know is what you're going to do next."

"You selfish bastard. All you care about is that you don't get caught."

"That's not true. You know I care about you. Just because I'm the guy they call CK, doesn't mean that I'm not also the guy you call *baby*."

She collects her jacket and purse. "I guarantee you don't love me enough to stop." As she grasps the handle of the door to my room, I'm fiercely aware that this is the last time I'll see her. "You know, Michael, this isn't dealing; with the Cancer, your dad's death, your void in this world—none of it. It's not going to make anything better, but I'm not about to put myself and my family through what will come next if I turn you in. The media are like rabid dogs and they'll never leave us alone. My family has secrets that I don't want out there, so your secret is safe." She pauses for a moment, and the tear from before re-emerges. "Fuck you. Fuck you for forcing me to make this choice."

With such clarity in her final words, I don't begin to dilute myself that I can make amends. It's not like I can get out of bed anyway. She disappears in to the busy hallway and suddenly the dream is gone along with her. Through all of this, I had some sort of hope that Monica would cure the Cancer. You see it all the time in movies; sheer will and hope work miracles. Sometimes it comes in the form of a speech to the people, and sometimes just in the form of a person who gives so much love that it actually conquers all. But, much like most of the shit you see in movies and on TV, that's not the way this world works. There is now no question in my mind that my time is up.

Moments later, my doctor makes an appearance. I'm pretty banged up, but ultimately, I'll be okay. My left arm will be in a brace for some time, but everything else will heal just fine. My concussion turns out to be the worst of it. The doctor warns of me of permanent damage if I were to hit my head again. He also informs me that in the two days I was out cold, they ran additional Cancer tests, and surely enough the disease is progressing rapidly.

This guy ... a guy I barely know, just delivered the news that I likely won't see the end of the month. Another bi-stander in my life offering a practiced sense of compassion—just what I need. He tries to get me to seek treatment, but of course, that's not happening. Seeing that he's hit a brick wall, he leaves my room.

As I lay there in silence, I take stock.

With weeks left to live, do I continue my mission, or enjoy the money? The problem for me has become that continuing my mission *is* enjoyment to me. Killing Julian was a rush. As scary a thought as it is, I've become comfortable with murder, like any other job. I think back to my part-time gig at Wendy's when I was younger. There were so many instructions and things that could go wrong. The first few days were overwhelming, but after awhile I didn't even have to think about what I was doing. I had as much fun with the job as I could, and now I'm having the same reaction to murdering scumbags.

Surely, I would not feel the same if I killed someone innocent. At least, I hope not. *Fuck, I hope not.* I brush that thought to the side since there's no chance of it happening. Hell, I could die healing from my injuries before I even get the chance to go out there again. This is likely the end of the road for my mission, and to finish it off taking out Julian is good enough for me.

I decide to distract myself by flipping through Facebook. A distraction, it is not. Most of my feed is about me, well ... The Con Killer. No one's checking up on me in the hospital; no one cares. But, everyone's wondering where CK (as they're now calling me because of Julian's tweets) has gone. Many worry that I have left or died, others consider it a blessing. The way Julian died with so many witnesses has left the public to wonder if I'm some sort of meta-human. Memes have even surfaced.

Dirty door knob? Uses mind to open door.
Not sure if CK kills with his mind or our
Slurpees contain killer GMOs.

And as with everything in life, there's a
Kermit meme: CK can kill with his mind.
But that ain't none of my business.

The city is as polarized as it was before the accident, but the debate has certainly heated up. Am I in right? How did I kill Julian? Will I kill again, and if so, who will be next?

A street artist has been creating "We Support CK" artwork and posting it throughout the city. Church groups, and those who believe The Con Killer to be wrong try their best to remove the art whenever they can. The Internet is a boom, and the story has brought reporters from all over the world to our small little city. Oddly enough, my mission has made Winnipeg a tourist attraction. Fanatics have come to cheer me on. Private investigators have come to try and be the one who catches me. Dog, The Bounty Hunter is even weighing in on TV. It's remarkable to see, but I'm not sure it's a good trend until an interview with a former Zero member is shown. His face is blurred out, and voice disguised.

"You were a member of Zero?" the well-groomed reporter asks. Were male reporters this pretty before Anderson Cooper hit the airwaves?

"I was. Nothing too crazy, but I was heavily involved in their day-to-day trafficking operations."

"And why did you leave?"

"I was sent up for a few years. When I got out, they didn't have a place for me anymore, and I didn't really want to come back. Once you're out of that life, you start to realize how broken you were."

"What are you hearing from Zero members and other criminals on the street? What do they think of The Con Killer?"

"There is no more Zero. When the office was bombed, all the top guys were taken out. It went from one of the strongest criminal organizations in the country to nothing overnight. Not only did this guy take out the people that made Zero function, all of the information, all of the projects—it was all wiped out. Zero literally burnt to the ground."

"So what happens to the lower level members of Zero?"

"No one's doing anything. I know guys that have just taken off. It's not worth it. What he's out there doing was never even a possibility in anyone's minds because we were the alpha dogs of the city. We were the lions. Now, we're the antelopes."

"So, as a man who has served his time and now lives on the straight and narrow, what are your thoughts? Is The Con Killer cleaning up the city?"

"Yeah. I would say so. That is until he's gone and infrastructure rebuilds. Over the next couple of years there will be far less drugs, murders, people disappearing. Just think of the kids that won't have to submit to that Jason White freak ever again. Just that one kill was enough to make a difference. The police weren't getting it done."

"So, you blame the police?"

"The police. The politicians. They're all acting outraged that this guy is out there killing criminals, but secretly, I know they're fine with it. He's doing their job for them. It was bound to happen sooner or later."

"You mean someone killing criminals?"

"Well, yeah. What do these leaders of our city think is going to happen? Julian Munroe was able to taunt this guy through the internet, and wore his criminal activity like a badge. He mocked the cops, as so many criminals do. If anything, this has just revealed how out numbered the police are. There are more people willing to do bad things in this world than there are people willing to stop them. When a guy like this comes along, he balances out the system."

"What about collateral damage? Escalation? Some are worried that the criminals are going to get more brazen now."

"More brazen? You really have no idea what's going on out there. Consider who's already been killed. A pedophile, hit men, crime bosses, and that's just the one's we know about. These guys were preying on people for years. It can't get much worse. You think all those missing persons cases are people just hanging out with Tupac as a prank to their families? No. They're dead. They're dead because no one's been out there willing to take the fight to the people killing them. That is, until now. It's already brazen. It's been brazen for far too long."

"As a former criminal who now has a family and is contributing positively to society, do you support The Con Killer?"

"As long as he's not taking anyone out that doesn't deserve it, and he sticks to the proven worst-of-the-worst, then yeah."

"Okay, one last question before we cut to commercial: what do you think of the people's reaction to this vigilante?"

"I think CK is awakening the people. As long as they stay in line and support him without getting violent, we'll be okay."

The reporter turns to the camera. "And there you have it. We'll be right back."

As a commercial for laundry detergent comes on, I dig deep to figure out how I feel. My actions are controlled, but the people are an unpredictable factor.

If this gets out of control, and the city turns violent in my name, that surely won't bode well for my legacy. This whole mission is meant to get people to act, react, be proactive, punish those who victimize. My goal is to have more Con Killers on the streets, not just protestors.

You know in the movies when a person makes a speech to a group of people about to turn violent, and it settles everything? I wish that actually worked, but the LA riots, Donald Trump in the primary, and Vancouver after the Stanley Cup prove otherwise. For now, we're okay. There's only been a few minor incidents, but who knows what the future may bring?

I spend the next few days in rehab and bed, healing until it's time to go home. Hospitals really are turnkey operations. Get in, get on your feet, and get out.

No one's there to take me home, so I hail a cab, and make my way alone. Considering that I was in a fight and then hit by a car, I'm in pretty decent shape. My head hurts, my vision is a bit off, and my arm will be in a sling for another few days, and a brace for longer. Otherwise, I'm lucky.

I miss Monica, but I won't contact her. There's no point rocking the boat. I just have to trust that my secret is safe, and there will be no cops knocking on my door anytime soon. I know she genuinely loves me, despite her pain, and I think she can reconcile the good with the bad, so there's no reason to doubt her. Fingers crossed that she did her damage by dumping my ass, and that she knows it can't get much worse for me.

I arrive home just as the sun is making it's final appearance for the day, a common theme in my life. I put my key into the lock, but to my surprise, it's already open. Monica did say she locked up, so I cautiously enter the house, and grab a gun that I have stashed in the front hall vase. The living room is perfectly clean. No dead body or smashed belongings. In fact, my place looks cleaner than it did before Matthew broke in. Mon never mentioned that she cleaned up. I'm surprised that she would. There was quite a bit of blood, and while she is a nurse, I just didn't see her doing this for me. The entire mess from that day is gone, like nothing ever happened.

Slowly, I make my way through the dining room to the kitchen, where I can hear some noise.

Something's off.

I can smell spaghetti sauce.

Someone's cooking!

Perhaps Monica had a change of heart? I round the final corner cautiously with my gun pointed straight ahead in case this is some sort of trap. I see a figure standing at the stove, silhouetted by light coming through the window. The figure turns to reveal herself; it's Daisy.

She cracks a smile. "It's about time you got back home," she says, not missing a beat.

"Daisy? What are you doing here?" I ask, puzzled by her presence in my home, and my life.

"I let myself in. Hope you don't mind." I practically trip trying to get to her at the stove, and hug her tightly, erasing any doubt that I would mind. As I go to kiss her on the forehead, she turns and makes sure that kiss lands perfectly on her lips. "You look beautiful darling," she says.

"That's great, because I feel like a bag of shit ... Daisy, how are you here?"

"I've been following the story of CK online, and then

I saw in a small little blurb that you were hit by a cab, so I decided it's probably time to come by and help you out."

"How could you have possibly known I was The Con Killer?"

"I just put two-and-two together. Instinct maybe? I knew you were from here, and I knew you wanted to take on the underworld. I also obviously knew you could handle yourself. It just made sense."

People can't figure out Superman is Clark Kent in the comics because of his glasses, but Daisy can piece together small scraps of info to figure out my identity? That glasses storyline has always bothered me. It's like the producers of Superman just don't want to deal with the elephant in the room. The disguise is stupid, unless you make the glass, some sort of Kryptonian crystal that somehow obstructs a person's perception of Clark ... there you go Hollywood, I've explained the biggest plot hole in history. Run with it.

"Well aren't you just the craftiest," I say, as I sit down at the table to a plate of spaghetti.

"I'm here to help you like you helped me."

"I could use it."

"Oh, I know. Monica left you a note. Looks like you're single now. Sorry to hear that. I also took the opportunity to clean up the mess you left in the living room."

"That was you?"

"Yeah, and I think we're even now. You helped me take care of my dead body, and now I've helped you take care of yours. It was disgusting, and probably the worst experience of my life, but you need a sidekick right now."

"Sounds pretty even to me. God, I'm happy to see you."

She sits down in the chair next to mine with her plate of spaghetti, and smiles once again. "The feeling is very mutual ... and don't worry about keeping secrets from me the way you did with Monica. I'm not here for a free place to stay. I'm here to help you finish what you started."

"I'm not understanding."

"Well then, let me be clear. Your arm is busted, you're in rough shape, you have Cancer, and you just got dumped. You need someone to help, and that's what I'm going to do."

"Seriously? Why?"

"Because Michael, you helped me when I needed it, and I love you."

"You love me?"

"I've never grown up in a world of fairy tales and romance, but I do know love when I feel it. We're kindred spirits, and while you may not be around for me when I'm old, that doesn't mean we shouldn't be here for each other now. It's not love like you had with Monica. I love your spirit and your beautiful mind."

"Jesus, I never would have guessed that this was the next chapter in this story."

"Well, now it is. I am your Robin. But, the first order of business is to get you into bed, and rest up. You need to heal before we can finish what you started."

I can't help but feel euphoric. Just an hour ago I was alone, ready to go to bed and die. Now I have this amazing girl declaring that she loves me (not as a lover, but as a human being), and, it seems, a partner in crime. As we sit and eat her spaghetti, we catch up on everything that has happened. After she got on the bus, she couldn't get me out of her head. She wanted to find me before, but knew it wasn't her place. So, she travelled a bit, treated herself, and at one point had a job as a bottle server at a club in BC. She came back out of instinct, knowing that I would need someone, and that based on our conversation before, Monica could not be that person.

"At a different time, without the Cancer and your job, you and Monica may have worked. But, she's not what you need now. That's me, and that's why I'm here," she proclaims as we continue to chow. "Oh, and by the way, I read the books, and I have a name to add."

"You mean, wait ..." I laugh awkwardly. "You have someone you want killed?"

"His name is Draisen Michaels, and he's next on The Con Killer's list."

She's probably right. Michael, pre-Martial dying, would probably have lived happily ever after with Monica. We would have had children, and spent evenings making fun of each other, protected from the world by our blind love. But, clearly there was an off ramp with that relationship, and I've taken it. Daisy has seen the people for who they really are, and she can separate my mission from a common criminal in her mind. Monica was my former self's soulmate.

I can't believe I'm thinking this, but it looks like I've found a sidekick.

24

Draisen

IT'S NOW FIVE DAYS SINCE DAISY ARRIVED, and I feel much better. She really pushes me to keep up my physio, take my meds, and rest. We spent almost a week in bed watching movies and just being together. There's nothing sexual here, despite her attractiveness. Every night, Daisy and I fall asleep in each other's arms, but it's more about security and safety than it is about primal urges. The topic of sex doesn't come up once, and it's actually refreshing. There's no pretense with us. It's just two people that get each other, being together, and sharing in an experience.

Today is a very good day. The sling is finally gone, I have energy, and for the first time in a couple of weeks I don't need to take pain meds to get over a pounding headache. Today, I am back to myself. It only seems right that after all Daisy has done, I take a look at the profile on Draisen.

Dad had a bit of research on this guy. He was nothing special; a bully who dealt drugs and acted like nothing could touch him. He hung out with Julian a bit, but they were never truly tight. He was just a low level asshole, trying to be a big man. That's where Dad's bio ended. Barely a mention.

The real harsh stuff happened not too long ago. He paid some guy named Trent to kill his girlfriend, Kary Elysiuk. The story goes that Draisen and Kary fought over his bad boy persona being more than just an act. Newscasts and friends would point to Kary's unearthing of some disgusting details about Draisen's past as the catalyst for a huge argument. She wanted him to quit the questionable shit that he did, and join her on the lighter side. He took exception to this, and laid into her a bit. Scared that she would press charges after not answering his many phone calls, Draisen hired Trent to kill her as she tried to get in her car on a beautiful Monday morning. Trent did this for $200! Not that any amount of money would be excusable, but c'mon ... $200? You can make more as a squeegee kid. But, I guess Draisen is a bad mother fucker to the guys lower than him, and Trent knew it, so he couldn't turn him down.

Enter *the system,* and Daisy's research. Turns out Draisen was released on house arrest last week. Rumour has it that despite text messages, witnesses, and a money trail, he has agreed to a deal. Draisen will testify against Trent and in exchange, he'll be on probation, house arrest, and he'll have to take the jobs he's given by the courts. Even though all legal experts say there is more than enough evidence to convict Trent, in the eyes of the law, I guess it's better to build an air tight case and get the actual killer, instead of the conspirator. In my eyes though—and Daisy's—it's better to get both.

This particular kill is tricky, like Julian's but for different reasons. The judge is worried that someone might come after Draisen (rightfully so) and as such has a protective detail on his house. That's right, this guy orders someone else to kill his girlfriend, and now we're paying for his protection. *If ever there were a prime example of a broken system, this is it.*

So, Draisen can't leave his house, there are two cops parked out front 24-hours a day, one cop sitting by the back door, and to make matters worse, he lives in an end of town known for camera coverage—it seems like every home has a camera pointed somewhere. Years ago, there was a lot of theft, and the residents decided to put up cameras and catch the sons of bitches. It worked, but will put me at a disadvantage.

Recon is necessary, as I don't have Martial's notes to fall back on. I pose as a jogger in full hood. I even go out and buy a completely different outfit from anything else I own to cover my tracks better. I pass by Draisen's house cavalierly. Out front, there is absolutely no way to get in. The two cops parked out front are alert. So much so, that when I stop to "tie my shoe" they tell me to move along. I'll have to come at him from the back.

As I make my way down the back lane, I see two cops, not just one. To my surprise, the second cop is Kyle. I also notice that Draisen is sitting in front of a TV in his basement. I get out of there quickly. The last thing I need is Kyle spotting me. I'd be sunk for sure when Draisen dies. He'd be able to connect me to this and the shooting at that crack den. The dominos would fall from there.

This is a tricky kill, but not an impossible one. My vehicle can't be anywhere in the area, so a bus ride is necessary. It'll have to be at night, since I'll have to snipe Draisen from a garage roof top. That cop in the back isn't going to let me get close, and I can't risk him seeing me before I take the shot. I'll have to be unbelievably quiet.

That's not even the hard part. Somehow I have to draw the officer's attention to the front of the house. That takes some thought, but eventually Daisy comes up with the answer. We'll lure him away by setting up speakers in a field across the street from Draisen's house. With one call to a burner phone, the most loud and obnoxious ring tone will blare throughout the neighbourhood. They're cops, but they're humans. Curiosity will get the best of them. At least, that's my hope.

Instead of conversations about nothing, Daisy and I spend the evening talking about the plan, and going over the fine details. She's right into it, and helps a lot. While she won't be coming with me, she's as good as there, given that she came up with half the plan. We fall asleep trying to one up each other with different tortures we would do if we could get Draisen alone in a room. Oh, pillow talk.

Today's the day. Draisen will die.

As I get ready to leave, Daisy sees me off like a good housewife in a 1950's sitcom, just saying bye to her man before he heads off to a desk job. "Go get 'em tiger." Yep, she even said that. We part with a hug and a kiss.

I head out to the field across from Draisen's house at around six in the evening. From a side that the cops can't see, I set the speakers up behind some bushes, and power everything with a car battery. From there, I take a jog to another nearby park where I've left my gun bag buried under a sandbox. Before you judge, there was no risk of a kid finding my bag, so calm down. I sit in that park and read some magazines while

I wait for the sun to go down. Four hours there and not a soul comes by.

With darkness, lights go on throughout the neighbourhood, and so I make my way to the garage in the back lane I'll be perched on top of. I picked carefully, making sure there were no motion detection lights. It takes me almost an hour to get on top of the roof; I'm trying to be quiet. Finally, I set up my concealable Remington Defense rifle (another item purchased on the deep web), and peer through the scope. No, I wasn't about to take the chance with Dad's rifle again. This one compacts down into a back pack.

Oddly enough, the officer at the back of the house isn't there. I look for deep undercovers; random bums sleeping, neighbours tending to their yard, joggers—it's a ghost town. I get the small basement window into my sights, to find Draisen asleep in a chair, fully exposed. The fat fuck is passed out in basketball shorts (and not much else) with a bowl of chips and a beer within his grasp, cradled like his babies.

Laying on my stomach, I line up the shot. It's just too easy—scarily so. Where is that cop? My silencer will kill most of the sound, but I still need the alarm from those speakers to drown out the noise. Turns out, as the alarm starts to play it's much louder than I thought it would be. I close my eyes for a moment and take a deep breath, trying to absorb the lasting pain in my arm. As I let go of the breath, I pull the trigger.

Draisen wakes just as the first bullet cuts through the glass and hits him in the knee cap. I was aiming for his chest, but the glass threw the bullet off course. He writhes in pain, screaming out. The joy of seeing him squirm is something I could watch forever, but I need to be quick. He looks up, and I think he sees me. The next two bullets hit their mark, leaving Draisen dead in his chair. Poor guy, dropped his bottle. I take just a split second to really take in this death, then jump up and dash for the street. As I make my way down the sidewalk from the garage, past the house, the owner comes out and sees me.

"Holy shit. It's you." The guy says as he stands there in shock.

I motion for him to be quiet. He's clearly a fan, so he runs back in the house, leaving me alone. God, that was lucky. A few seconds later he reappears ... with a gun! Okay, so maybe he's not a fan. Of course, I'm pretty tired of being injured, so I bolt as fast as I can. He takes a shot, and misses. As I run down the street, he takes a few more shots at me. Luckily, the bullets don't hit me or anyone else. Just based on the way he holds the gun and deals with the recoil those are some of the first shots he's ever taken.

Between the Cancer and my injuries, I'm wiped after a couple of blocks. I just collapse into a heap in that park amongst some trees. As I lay there, I see a car drive by, and a flash light move around the park. It's the guy who is clearly not my fan! He's really determined to get me, but doesn't think to look down. It's only a matter of time until he goes and gets the cops from out front of Draisen's house. I have to go.

Cutting through a mini-urban forest at night is a good way to go so that I'm not seen but it's rough on my skin. Damn branches cut me up pretty good. I bury my gun and my mask in that forest, along with my shirt and hat. I still have a muscle shirt on, and pants, but I look like a completely different person. Without my CK persona in full effect, I walk out onto a street, and catch a bus.

It takes me longer than it should have to get home. I don't know the bus routes in the city, and since I jumped on the first bus I saw, I'm way out on the other side of town. I'm not sure when they'll find the body, but I'm sure it won't take very long. From the headlines, I know Draisen was released into his father's custody. I feel bad for the guy. He's going to come home to find his son, dead. But he'll get over it. Somewhere deep in his mind, he knows his son is a real piece of shit. Maybe the guy that was searching for me has already alerted the cops. I can't be mad at him though. He was just doing what he felt was right, like me.

As I arrive home, Daisy wants to hear all about it. I talk about the events that took place, as if I am speaking about a flow chart I made for a big meeting. I discuss everything from the setup to the kill, as if I were preparing a PowerPoint presentation. Then, I fill her in on almost getting shot myself ... similar to how someone would describe firing an employee.

This is my job, and I'm proud of my work. Now, Kary's family will have peace, and Draisen can rest in pieces. All in all, I'd call this a pretty successful chapter to my mission.

"I want to come for one," Daisy says.

"No you don't."

"I actually do."

"Look, I am so thankful you're here, but not even *I* want to be out there."

"I don't want to be there to help you kill someone. I want to be there to help you in case you get in trouble again."

"Oh, that won't happen again. I'll be more careful."

"You said it yourself. You're getting weaker, and the accident didn't help. Like it or not, I'm your sidekick and I'm going help you take care of these assholes. This isn't a request."

"You are one tough nut, you know that, Daisy?"

"I just don't want to see you get hurt. We both know what's coming, and I might as well make myself useful."

There's a realness to her—a rationale— that you'd never expect just seeing Daisy walk down the street. She's actually the total package; beauty, brains, she has common sense, she's Teflon tough, and there's no stopping her when she's determined. A formidable opponent. I'm just happy we're on the same side.

25

Dinner for 3

AFTER A SUCCESSFUL KILL, Daisy wants to celebrate with a 5-course meal that she cooks herself. I take a shower and get dressed in my finest sweats for the feast. When I get downstairs to the dining room, I find a place set for three people. She's gone all out with trimmings I haven't seen since Mom would set up for big meals. I'm not even sure where she found all of this stuff. There are even a couple of different forks on the table, and napkins. Shit, there's even candles. You'd swear we're entertaining the queen.

"Daisy, why is there room for 3 at the table?"

She comes out of the kitchen, and gives me a look as if she might be in trouble. You know the one. It's half a cringe with an awkward smile, and it usually involves some crazy dance with the eyebrows. "Do you trust me?"

"You know I do, but I don't see ..."

"Let me put it this way. When you see who's coming for dinner, initially you're going to be pretty pissed. BUT, but, I promise you that it will all work out." She cringes again. "Don't hate me."

"I know like, four people. I don't see who you could have possibly invited to dinner that would make me mad." Just then the door bell rings. I sigh, then head to the door to find out who the mystery guest is.

I actually close my eyes as I open the door—half out of worry, half wanting to delay the inevitable revelation.

"Hello, Michael."

I know that voice, and open my eyes. Speechless, we stand there for a moment just looking at each other. "Mom?"

It's her. The woman who raised me like June Cleaver until she became an alcoholic and left me to fend for myself. Here she is, the drunk I used to pickup at 2am, who screamed at me for doing it, and who would ultimately just go back to the bar the next night. For some reason, she's standing at my door, but she doesn't look the same. Age has set in, yet somehow she looks better than she used to. Judging by the outfit, and the fact that she's not face down in a ditch somewhere, my best guess is that she's cleaned herself up a bit.

"May I come in, son?"

Just as when Monica surprised me, I play out the various scenarios in my head. Inevitably, I'm sure she'll tell tales of world travel, getting sober, and how she regrets leaving. Perhaps she'll have some sort of big family reveal, or she could just be here to talk about Dad. Either way, I'm curious, so I let her in.

She looks around the room for awhile. "The place is much nicer than when your dad was living here," she says, matter-of-factly. "It was covered in papers last time I was here, and there was only a chair in the middle of the room." Spotting Daisy near the dining room table, she quickly turns her attention to the co-conspirator in this whole drama. "You must be Daisy. Thank you for reaching ..."

"Mom. What are you doing here?"

Daisy interjects. "Given the way things are going, I figured I'd look your mom up, and see if her coming for dinner was something that I could make happen."

I pull Daisy aside and quietly oppose. "Why would you do this? Last time I saw her, she was walking out the door and she never came back."

Daisy gets close, puts her hands on my chest, and whispers, "But she's here now, and I promise you that based on what I know from her Facebook, you'll be happy she is. Please Michael, just trust me."

"Perhaps I should just go," mom says. "This probably wasn't the best idea."

As she heads for the door, Daisy gives me puppy dog eyes. I need to let this play out, for her. "Mom. Wait."

With that, the three of us are sitting down for dinner at Dad's dining room table.

"So when did you two start dating?" mom asks.

"Oh. We're not a couple. Just very good friends," Daisy responds.

"Really? You two look so good together."

"It's not about that for us, Mom," I say, killing that piece of conversation.

As we pass the food around the table, it's silent and awkward. I really have no idea what to say to this woman. Finally, it's my mom who breaks the silence. "I was sorry to hear about your father."

"Is that true?"

"Of course. We may have had our differences, but I still loved that man dearly."

"Look, I'm not a kid anymore. I get that you guys drifted apart and that's why you split. I can accept that, even sympathize. Those demons were set aside long ago. What I do want to hear is your excuse for leaving me, and never really getting back in touch."

"Michael, I was in a very bad place for many years. If it hadn't been for a friend I met along the way I wouldn't have made it. The money would be gone, and I'd probably be dead. Honest. By the time I got sober we were so far apart, and I didn't see it benefiting you to have your mom reach out."

"All those nights. All those brutal nights."

"I know. It was completely unfair for me to put you in the position I did. You were still a boy, and I forced you to become a man too soon. Worse that that—a babysitter. I just ... I couldn't handle the pain of the split with your dad, and I didn't know what to do. The only reprieve from it all was at the bottom of a bottle. You have to understand, we went from a near perfect life to a complete disaster, almost overnight."

"I was there for the fighting, I know. But a mother—a real mother—doesn't abandon her kid."

"I am sorry, Michael. I am. There aren't enough words to express how disappointed in myself I am. I think back to those days and it's like I was someone else."

"You said earlier that you had been in here before. When?" I can feel my anger subsiding towards her, almost like I have no choice.

"I came here one night in a drunken rage. Your dad wasn't going to hear me out or let me in, so I even threw a bottle of vodka at his door. Not wanting to embarrass himself in front of the neighbours, he eventually let me in. We fought forever that night, until I passed out in that very living room. I woke up the next morning to find that your dad had wrapped a blanket around me, and laid me in his chair to sleep it off. I read the papers on his walls and knew nothing had changed so I left, and never looked back."

"That's the last time you saw him?"

"It was. Even in his darker days, he was still a gentleman under it all."

"Man!" I say as I get up from the table. The pacing starts. "You two have no idea how you messed up my head. I mean, about women, about money, about everything. Having a father who locked himself away, and a mother who abandoned me made it very hard to get a grip on life. It hurt. You two hurt me more than anyone every has, or ever will."

She simply closes her eyes, and shakes her head. "From the bottom of my heart, I'm sorry," she says as a tear rolls down her cheek.

Silence fills the room once more. In this situation, I have a choice to make. Either I hold on to my pain, or I let it all go. It's clear to me that she regrets her choices, and has gotten it together. She is not absolved of her past, but I'm dying, and this is the my chance to spend time with my mother.

I place my hand on her shoulder. "Well, you're here now, so we might as well eat."

From that point on, the meal is a polite trip down memory lane. We skip the dark days and stick with the good memories—when we were all together. Daisy learns a great deal about me, and what my life was once like.

"Your childhood sounds so unbelievable inspiring," she says to me with a huge smile on her face. She's loving being a part of a family.

"I just wish you could have had the memories that I do, Daisy."

"Me too, but I can live vicariously through you though."

"Your parents weren't around, Daisy?"

"I was orphaned young. Unlike you, my mom didn't have any good days before taking off. I'll never really know who my parents were. I was just dropped off at CFS and left to fend for myself."

"That's horrible."

"Our experiences made us who we are today, so it's not all bad news," I say, trying to add some positivity to the conversation.

"Very true. I want you to know that your son saved me. Literally and figuratively. He is my hero."

"Tell me again why you're not a couple?"

Since I saw Mom at my doorstep, I wondered if I would tell her about that Cancer. I decide it is best to do so. "Well, there wouldn't be much of a point."

"Oh, and why is that?"

"Because in all likelihood, I'll be dead before the snow falls." Silence again. "I have pancreatic Cancer, and I've decided to forego treatment. It's stage four, and I'm into the home stretch."

"Oh, Michael," Mom says as the tears start again. This time Daisy joins in, and I shed a few as well. "I'm not going to sit here and lecture you on treatment, because I know I've lost that right. I just hope you've made the decision from an educated viewpoint, and not out of fear."

"I chose to forego treatment because it's the rational thing to do, and now I have Daisy here to help me make the most of my final days."

"His symptoms come up here and there, but he's doing pretty good. I'd say he's doing much better than if he were getting shot with radiation," Daisy says, to further give my mom some reassurance that my decision is right.

"I'm so thankful to you, Daisy. Thank you for taking care of my boy."

For the first time in years, my mom hugs me. We both stand instinctively and grab onto each other. I can't help but feel good knowing I have my mom back. It's too bad it's so late in the game, but the important thing is that it's happened.

We spend the rest of the night playing board games, and talking about what's next for Mom. Turns out, she works for a charity that looks after mistreated animals. Mom really did get herself together. She shows us pictures of the animals she's personally helped save. The before and after photos are unbelievable. To think that people actually treat animals so cruelly; if I had more time, perhaps I'd have a new list courtesy of my other parent.

By the time my mom is ready to leave, we've come full circle. I never would have imagined seeing her before I die, let alone spending quality time together. The final hug of the night is a tight one. She holds on for a long time, because we both know it's the last hug we'll ever have. She's due for her flight in just a few hours, and she offered to stay, but I told her to go. Why ruin this great night by letting reality sink in the next time we see each other? As I close the door, she looks back and smiles at me. I return the gesture, and with that we find peace.

I pull Daisy in close as we walk up the steps to the bedroom. "You are something else, ya know that?"

"You're okay with the way it went?"

"You took a risk, and you were right." We stop on the stairs and kiss like a couple. It's not because we're trying to get anywhere with each other, the kiss is admiration and respect packed into a gesture. It's a great kiss; respectful, beautiful, and it lasts for a good couple of minutes.

As we part, we stand there foreheads and noses touching. "I'm just happy it turned out. No one wants to piss off The Con Killer," she says playfully as she runs up the stairs. I follow behind in hot pursuit.

Somehow, we've settled into a life here. She takes care of me, I provide, and together we have both accepted that death is a part of our lives. No longer is my mission a dirty secret like it was with Monica. My life is an open book, and the peace she's helped me find makes my final time on this earth that much better. When I go, she'll get everything, because someone needs to treat Daisy like she's deserved to be treated her whole life.

Dinner for three ends with Daisy and I cuddling in bed, watching Batman v Superman, and there's no place I'd rather be.

26

Trigger Finger

IT IS SAID THAT the average police officer's IQ is 104. The average IQ of a serial killer sits somewhere around 94. That puts criminals and cops in the same average IQ range. When you think about what it is that both do, essentially they're solving a problem. Criminals are confronted with an inability to perform in some way so they commit a crime. When a crime is committed, cops must catch that criminal. And we wonder why we have so many unsolved crimes? It's the blind leading the blind, and today is no different.

As it sit perched on the top of a parking garage, I see Shane Wylde being escorted out of the police station. Just 24 hours ago he was arrested for shooting Martial. I know what you're thinking: Shane Wylde was that nice guy just trying to have a fighting chance with his daughter. He even had a bit of a hard time killing Julian. Well, my IQ may be higher than your average criminal or cop, but even I can get it all wrong. I did say that Shane was Julian's errands boy, I just didn't know how far he went to please him.

Kyle called me last night to tell me that they believe

Shane was the guy who shot my dad. New evidence popped up that suggests Zero ordered the hit, and Julian was supposed to do it, but instead he he had Shane take care of things. However, due to lack of evidence and an alibi that checks out, they would have to free him in the morning. When I asked him how sure he was that Shane was the guy, he responded without hesitation, "One hundred percent".

The last couple of days haven't been so good for me. Daisy was on double duty taking care of things as I coughed up blood and phlegm. Nothing could get me out of bed except for that phone call. Kyle got my blood pumping and my adrenaline surging.

"So when are you going to do it?" Daisy asks, while barely looking over the side of the garage. Apparently, my fearless side kick has a slight case of Kryptonite—heights.

"Not now. Not in daylight."

"Tonight?"

"Only if I can do it right."

"I have no idea what that means, Michael."

"It means I'm going to bring the pain."

My eyes are fixated on Shane as he walks away from the sight of officers, and meets up with some guy at a Chevy Tahoe. They both look so happy to be alive. My only goal now is to make him incredibly sad.

"Are you sure you can do this? Just yesterday you were too weak to get out of bed."

I jump off the side of the parkade and embrace Daisy. "I can do this, and probably only this," I say, as I stare deep into her eyes, letting her know that I am serious.

"Okay. Well, I'm here to help. What do you need?"

"I need my sidekick with me on this one, through

the whole thing. Can you stomach that? You said you could, but are you sure you want to do this?"

"I told you when we met that I am probably more prepared than you were when you killed Arn. I've been through enough in my life to know that if someone deserves it, they should get what's coming to them. I've got your back."

As I prepare to confront Shane back at the house, Daisy gets ready too. She doesn't tell me, but I know she's been in the washroom for over half an hour psyching herself up to see another murder unfold. I'm pretty sure I heard her throw up, but I won't mention it. She's a tough girl, with a tough past, but killing is not something someone just does without some form of guilt. I have complete faith she'll be able to make this happen with me.

I stuff my bag with several weapons of choice. I'm not sure what I'll use, but I know that I don't want Shane to die quickly. This is the first of my victims I don't want to die as quickly as possible, actually. It's not clear—even in my mind—if I've just gotten too comfortable with the idea of killing, or if I need to savour the moment when I kill the man who pulled the trigger and took my dad down. Zero is gone, but they only ordered the hit. It's time to take out the last criminal on my list. When I go to lift the bag, it feels heavier than it should be. I get dizzy and fall to one knee.

Daisy rounds the corner from the washroom. "Michael, are you okay?"

"I'll be fine. I tripped."

She's no more convinced than I am, but she's not

going to stand in the way of getting Shane, so we both play off like my excuse was an actual thing. I take her up on her offer to drive, though. This way, I can lie and get away with it, while she maintains some sort of control over the situation. Don't ever let anyone tell you that a relationship isn't simply a game of chess. As we drive, we hold hands. It's to keep each other calm. Her nerves are shot over what might come of this night, and mine are rattled because I know that I'm probably too sick to do this.

Daisy and I arrive outside of Shane's house at around 10pm, just like last time, except there will be no waiting for him as he's already inside. That's not where I need him though. Situations like this are why heroes have sidekicks.

She gets out pretending that she's having issues with the truck. No way does a guy who lives alone on a power trip resist a hot chick outside trying to figure out what's wrong with her vehicle. In fact, it doesn't even take him a full minute to come out and offer some help. Why wouldn't he? Shane's convinced that The Con Killer thinks he's a good guy. There's nothing for him to fear.

"Hey there beautiful, car trouble?" he asks as he approaches Daisy, who's looking under the hood of the truck.

"Yeah. It just died and I know nothing about cars. Do you?"

"I spent some time around a shop when I was a bit younger. I might be able to figure it out."

"That would be amazing. I seriously have had the craziest day, and all I want to do is get home, put on something comfy, and crawl into bed." A little subtle flirting always gets a guy. *God, we are stupid.*

"Oh yeah? Well, with a such a tough day, maybe you

should have dinner first," he hints while looking under the hood, close to Daisy. "I know a great place."

"How do you know I haven't eaten already?"

"Well, I guess I don't, but I'm hoping if you have, you'll just replace dinner with whatever it is that you do want to do."

"What are you doing under there?"

"Honestly, I have no clue," he slyly says, trying to be playful. "You know, maybe you just overheated. Have you tried the key since you stalled?"

"I actually haven't. That's a good call."

The big man needs to show he's got it under control. "Here, let me try."

He walks around the front of the truck and leans over the driver side seat to start it, but it's a push start so he'll have to sit in the seat. As he does, and as Daisy waves at him and gives that playful smile of hers to distract him, I rise from the back seat and cover his head with a plastic bag filled with rags, soaked in ether. Shane puts up a bit of a fight, but fades within just a few seconds, and is out in under a minute.

Daisy shuts the hood as I pull Shane into the back seat. We quickly take off, and no one is the wiser that there was just a kidnapping in their neighbourhood. Hell, this is typical suburbia; land of the closet drunks that drink themselves to sleep after work, or parents that are too busy chasing after their kids to even notice. Either way, everyone's likely in bed. Shane should have known something was up when Daisy stopped outside his house, but I can't stress the point enough, as to how stupid us men are when a sexy female is near.

It takes us almost an hour to get where we're going. Midway through the ride, he even starts to stir, so I dose him again, just hoping he doesn't die before I get my time to deal with him. Finally, we arrive.

"Why here?" Daisy asks as she stops the truck.

"Because this is the last place I saw Martial."

We're stopped in that same field that Martial and I would come shooting when I was a kid; that same field where I would see him and make peace with the memory of my father. Who knows, maybe even Shane might see Dad out here. Regardless though, no one will hear him scream. Without much consideration for him, Daisy and I punt his limp body out of the truck and onto the ground. Then we drag him to a nearby tree.

Daisy goes back to the truck and drives away as I tie Shane securely to the tree. This won't be like in the movies, where the person tied up gets out and creates a fuss. No, this won't be like the movies at all. The air is thick tonight after a quick rain earlier. Humidity makes everything sweaty, and the tall grass that we now find ourselves amongst still have beads of water that soak my pants as I pass though them. The moon is full, and sheds enough light down on the field that I am able to make out the can I found last time I was here. A light wind pushes leaves around, making a sound ... a sound that can only be described as the innocence of nature. It's peaceful here in this field, but it won't be for long. I do hope that nature doesn't have a memory, because if it does, it's about to be haunted by tonight forever.

"Wake up!" I scream at Shane as I dump a bottle of water on his head. "WAKE UP!" It takes awhile, but her starts to stir.

Dazed and confused, and without clear vision, he speaks. "Where am I?"

I kneel down close to Shane, and wait until his vision is clear, so he can see it's me—no, not The Con Killer in mask, but me, Michael Burton. He tries to get out of the ropes, but they don't budge. He realizes very quickly that he's stuck.

"Who are you? What are you doing?"

I stand up with a sledge hammer in my hand, and just laugh. That's all there is to do.

"What the fuck?" he says as he sees the hammer. "You ... you know who I am?"

"Oh, I know who you are, Shane. You're the innocent security guard who might lose his daughter. You're just a guy who's fallen on tough times."

It takes a second—remember the average IQ of a criminal is barely average. "You're him. You're CK."

"I am. And you have the honour of being the first and last piece of shit to see me without my mask."

"Look, like you said, I'm just a security guard. Man, please don't do this," he pleads while starting to tear up. "I didn't tell anyone about Julian, I swear!"

"I don't know. I'm not sure you are just a security guard, because security guards don't kill cops, and first time killers rarely take someone out with one bullet then dump the body outside of a police station."

"Man, I have no idea ..."

"DON'T LIE TO ME!"

We stare at each other, waiting for the other break. He doesn't last. The fake tears, the fake remorse, the fake unsure persona all evaporate in front of my eyes. All that is left is a crooked smile, sadistic eyes, and a criminal.

"I had you going. You have to admit that. Even you believed that I was just some guy caught in a bad situation."

"You did, but luckily for me, life is full of second chances to make up for past mistakes."

"You thought that whole time that I was doing you a solid by killing Julian. I needed him dead, but had no idea how to go about it without someone knowing. Then you gave me the means to do it and, you dumb fuck, you paid me to do what I would have done for free."

"Why did you need Julian dead?"

"Really? You can't figure that out for yourself?"

"You wanted out from under his iron fist, or you're a walking talking, killer stereotype—it was in some way all about money."

"You're damn right, on both accounts! I was his best guy and never got the high paying jobs. With him gone, I would be the top dog since I was the only one that knew his entire operation, where he kept his client book, and had access to his phones. With Julian gone, the city would fear me."

"Impressive plan, and you almost pulled it off."

"Yeah. Until you came around. You've fucked up everything for us. No more Zero, no more high level crime, the cops are mobilized ... even you won't be able to escape the wrath that's coming. This mayor isn't going to stand for this in his city. There's going to be hell to pay for me, you, all of us."

"Well, that's where there's some good news for you and me, Shane." I lean back down close to him. "There's absolutely no chance that you or I will be around to see that happen."

I stand up again and give him just a moment. I wait for him to realize that he's going to die, then I swing. My first shot with the hammer crushes his knee cap. He screams out in agony, until there is no more sound coming out of his body. His fake tears have turned real. The second shot gets him square in the right rib cage, crushing at least two (but probably more) ribs. He screams out again but the blood rushes up his throat and out of his mouth. His screams turn to gargling, and then coughing.

While he writhes in pain, I taunt him. "You know

Shane, I was actually really scared to kill guys like you in the beginning. When I killed Jason, I hesitated, and my hands shook. But then, everyone just kept thanking me for killing him: Max, Zero, all of you. Everywhere I went people were talking about how grateful they were that The Con Killer was here to save their city! It was glorious, so eventually the feeling of remorse subsided, and I was left with a cold, calculated mission."

He starts to pass out, so I hit him again, this time breaking his foot in half. He can't scream, the blood is stopping him from doing that, but the adrenaline will keep him awake for a bit longer.

"Shane. With most guys, this was just a job. But then, you went and killed my dad." He looks up at me. The clear understanding of how badly he fucked up becomes clear in his eyes. "You took a great man from this world, and inadvertently gave birth to The Con Killer. You ... the wolf in sheep's clothing, made me what I am today by killing Martial. So, it's only fitting that before I die, which will be soon by the way ... you are my last kill."

With that final hit I stumble. My vision blurs slightly and pain in my back shoots up my spine. It's nothing close to what Shane's going through right now, but I really don't feel so hot. I can't tell if the lack of food over the last week has me feeling like shit now that I'm actually exerting myself, or if it's something more. Not willing to take the risk that I drop dead right here before finishing the job, I take one final swing and stick the sledge in Shane's head. I hit him with such force there is little left of his face.

My vision blurs completely, and I hit the grassy field with force. Something is very wrong. I reach for my phone and by feeling around on the keypad, I'm able to dial Daisy, just as I start coughing uncontrollably.

The taste of blood fills my mouth. *His or mine? Oh God no, it's mine.*

The last thing I remember before I pass out is Daisy and another person picking me up and putting me in the back seat of my truck. I can see slightly for just a moment before completely passing out. I must be seeing things; it's Kyle.

27

Bed Rest

AS MY EYES OPEN, I see the ceiling I have become so accustomed to studying. It's the same ceiling my dad probably analyzed a thousand times in his head. The more you look, the more you see, because our brains are programmed to recognize, and even chase patterns. Today, I see dots—random, without reason, dots.

"How are you feeling?" Daisy asks as she sits next to me in bed.

"Not sure. Really groggy," I respond with a great deal of difficulty. "How long have a I been out for?"

"How long do you think?"

"A while for sure. My body aches from being in one place for too long, my lips are dry, and I smell terrible."

"You've still got it," she says as she stands up and goes to open the door. "Kyle wants to see you."

Kyle; the man who ruined my family somehow ended up in that field, and for some reason, even though I bashed a guy's brains in with a sledgehammer, brought me here instead of jail. He enters the room without that air of confidence that I'm used to.

"Hello, Michael."

"Kyle." I give a simple head nod, and even that doesn't feel all too wonderful. Man, I'm hurting.

"I think there are somethings you need to know, and since you can't get up, I guess you'll finally have to listen to me."

Something in this moment tells me to let this guy talk.

"I didn't get your dad fired. Well, not like you're thinking. It was a part of a plan that he and I set into motion."

"You expect me to believe that you and my dad were working together when he was fired?" I can barely get the words out. Coughing can be so exhausting.

"Yes, and it was all for the same reason that you decided to become The Con Killer."

"You know. So why am I still here?"

"Maybe it's time you just listen. Let me get through this, and then you can ask all the questions you want."

I nod with approval through a deep breath that shakes my body.

"Your dad had been on the force for quite a few years before I got there. We were both military men, and we were both tired with the way things were going. I don't know if your dad ever told you, but he killed a lot of people in the name of peace. So did I. After that, our country left us in the wind ... so naturally, with a particular set of skills, we became cops. Martial knew it wasn't enough though, and one night we hatched a plan—a complicated plan. I would be the reason he was let go from the force so no one would ever suspect we were communicating. That was key, because if I was going to give him continual access to everything we had, there needed to be plausible deniability on my end. Why would they ever look at the guy that Martial hated more than anyone, right?"

"I have to ask. Why feed him the info?"

"Because Martial knew that it took more than the justice system to get things done. We both did. I feed him the info, he isn't bound by the same rules to gather evidence, and then we would give the system one more chance to finally deal with these criminals that preyed on so many. If that didn't work ... well, let's just say you carried out your dad's legacy just as he would have wanted."

"So the note I found. He wasn't just venting. Dad was planning on killing them all."

"But his time ran out before he could. Martial had a hard time gathering anything on Julian, so he leaned on Shane, not knowing Shane was just as bad. Shane tells Julian, who gets the go ahead from Zero to kill your pop. Julian has Shane do it, and the rest is a story for the ages, as they say."

"My dad and you, huh?" I can't doubt his story. if any of it wasn't true, I'd be in cuffs right now. I'm smart enough to put together the pieces.

"You figured it out yourself. You figured it all out. To say I had doubts that you could continue our plan is an understatement, but Martial was always confident that you would see reason."

"So Dad, he what, planned for me to go out and kill?"

"He planned for you to take over, and do what needed to be done ... whatever that meant to you. He had me keep very close tabs on you, and what we learned led him to believe that you would take up the mission. I don't know that he knew you would do all of this, but he knew that you'd make something happen."

This all seems too surreal; Dad and Kyle working

together to take down as many as they could. "So why tell me now?"

"That's how he wanted it. Martial didn't want you doing anything with any kind of persuasion. You had to arrive at your choices on your own. I didn't expect you to kill this many of them ... or any at all. That's the missing piece for me. Sure, you had some training courtesy of your dad, but no field experience. How did you make up your mind to kill them?"

Daisy, seated across the room, listening to every word chimes in. "That would be my doing ... well, sorta." She tells Kyle the story of that fateful night when Arn tried to kill her. No detail is left out.

"So that's when it happened. That's when you got the hunger."

"I don't know if I'd describe killing as a hunger for me, but yes, that's when it all started."

"Michael, killing is an acquired taste, like sugar. Some people will get some in their system and hate it instantly. Those are the hardcore vegans. Some will like it, but it's not really a factor in their life. Then, there are those of us who get a taste and need more. It doesn't matter where it comes from, but sugar becomes fuel. It's instant, and we never expect it. Then we look back one day and realize we've consumed more sugar than anyone could possibly imagine; it's disgusting for the others, but for you, it's exactly what you need. The military quickly reveals who's addicted to sugar, and the life of a damsel in distress revealed your addiction, too."

"And I ended up with an amazing woman to call my best friend out of it."

"Yeah, she even came along to deal with Shane, just as a I did."

"What do you mean?" Daisy asks.

"I've been there the whole time. When Michael was

arrested at the clinic, I got him out. I encouraged Monica to come over here when I found out you were sick. That night at Draisen's house, I called off the guy on the backdoor. I arrested Shane and let him go so you would know who shot Martial without intervening. I didn't want him rotting in a cell. Meals, bed, basketball, and conjugal visits were too good for that punk. You don't even know this, but at the house party, you were caught on camera. I destroyed the footage. I've been helping you whenever I could figure out your next move."

It's a lot to take in: Dad's enemy was actually his friend; my mission broken down to a simple hunger; and the help I never knew I was getting. "I have a question for you then. When I was arrested for what I pulled at Doc Scorpio's office, you were going to tell me something. I felt it was important, but didn't want to hear it. What were you going to say?"

"I was going to tell you that I'm not perfect. Your dad was, I'm not. You stopped me, and it's a good thing you did." He puts his left hand on my shoulder, and gets sincere for a moment. "Michael, your dad would be incredibly proud of you. Somehow the very people that would put us away from what we've done, ended up leading us all down this path. They made me and your dad killers out of the necessity of war. They forced you to want to fight against injustice. It's a twisted reality we all have going here, but it works."

I slowly and steadily reach my hand out as a sign of respect to Kyle. We shake on it. "Thank you."

"No, thank you. While you were out there doing what needed to be done, I was able to look for Marital's killer. We were a team, even if you didn't know it. Oh, and by the way, I am not the one that decided on those shorts."

We both let out a laugh—mine is more of a lough though, riddled with coughing. "I hated those fucking shorts."

"I know, me too. Fucking traditions!" We're laughing so hard, we're both crying.

"Look, Michael, I have something for you."

He gets up and exits the room, leaving Daisy and I to just smile at each other. She comes over and kisses me ever so softly on the forehead. "I love you, you beautiful killer you," she whispers as Kyle comes back in the room.

He hands me a book. "This was Martial's. You read his research, now you can read how he felt about it. I'm pretty sure some of the stuff in here dates back to when he was still at home with you guys. I never opened it because it wasn't my place, but it was on him when he died, and I suspect you found the missing page from the back based on what you said earlier."

I stare at that book in my hands. This is who Martial was on the inside, deep down. Tonight, I will learn what drove my dad to do what he did.

"I'm going to go now, Michael, but I'll be back tomorrow to check up on you and Daisy," he says. "Oh, and Michael. Your dad leaving you and your mom was the hardest thing that he ever had to do, but he had to. He knew this whole journey was bigger than himself and his happiness. He wanted to legitimately save this city."

As Kyle leaves, Daisy cuddles up next to me in bed. I open the book, but my eyes just don't want to focus on the words. So, for two days and nights, Daisy reads my dad's words to me. As the light of day enters the room and leaves, she continues on. We only take breaks for food and sleep. We laugh and cry, and even cringe at Dad's words.

I can feel my body getting weaker, and for the most part Daisy is reading to me as my eyes are closed. I picture the man who raised me until he couldn't. Martial, my dad, had an unbelievable story of pain and remorse, but there's beauty in his words.

The way he described my mom when he first saw her:

> "I knew I was in for a great deal of trouble that day. When someone can stop you in your tracks while in formation, your life is altered. That woman, she truly taught me how to be a man."

The way he described our Saturday mornings:

> "My son always needed and wanted to be a hero. He has the determination that convinces you he will one day fly. I admire my son, and hope he has the time to be greater than me. Every Saturday morning is my new favourite day."

The way he described his mission:

> "Most will never understand what we're doing here, but that's alright. The people don't have

> to understand or even believe in what you do for it to be right. I wish I didn't have to do all of this, but the way we, as a people, have gotten so soft, someone has to."

And finally, the way he described the perfect world:

> "A world without crime isn't perfect. Crime is often passion, and passion is so vital to our existence. The perfect world is one that can teach criminals to re-focus that passion into great things. In this world we jail weed dealers and petty thieves. We discount the horrible history of so many men. We break the souls of soldiers for selfish wars. We can be so much better, but instead we breed lawless animals that have to be put down. I know I'll never see such a time, but I can always dream."

"Your dad was hopeful, even in his darkness, Michael. Hold onto that." Daisy says.

On this—our final night together—we finish Dad's journal and can't help but to hold on to that very same hope. While I'm not sure anything I have done will contribute to a more beautiful world, I hang onto the thought that I at least gave it a fighting chance.

Kyle stops by everyday to show me news clippings about The Con Killer. He even prints out an editorial piece from Margaret's website:

> The criminals outnumber the cops, but regular citizens outnumber the criminals, and if The Con Killer has taught us anything, it's that we have the control. While you may not agree with his methods, the man who's name we may never know has started something. People are taking back their neighbourhoods. I may have judged CK harshly in the beginning, and still stand against taking a life, but there are less dots on my map because people are awake now. We're seeing stories of criminality in our city being foiled: crack houses are being dismantled, there's been an increase in citizens arrests, and groups are taking back their neighbourhood watch programs. Cops are spending time in neighbourhoods talking to the people again too. CK has made a difference, and for that (and that only) I thank him.

It's not a glowing recommendation of my work, but it's better than it was. In fact, that's the general tone of all the articles that Kyle reads out to me. As a man behind a mask I was able to wake the people from their slumber. Now, as a city, the criminals are learning they don't have a home here. Turns out some have even taken up as surrogates of CK. Thousands march through neighbourhoods with my mask on. Perhaps the concept will spread. I don't know the future, but I do know that I have an honest to God legacy that I'm leaving behind. It's a legacy intertwined with amazing people and my dad. It's a legacy not everyone can be proud of, but I absolutely am.

"What are you guys going to do with yourselves?" I ask while the three of us share stories about our pasts, chowing down on cheeseburgers. Don't judge; I'm on my way out and no salad is going to save me now. I might as well enjoy myself.

Daisy and Kyle pause, but ever stoic, she replies simply, "I'm going to leave this city and go find my parents. For good or for bad, I want to know where I come from, because if this has taught me anything, it's that we need to know our past to truly have an appreciation for where our futures will take us."

Kyle picks up a CK mask, and looks at me through it. His answer is clear. With no one left, he will ensure the mission continues, and continue the legend that will likely guide so many more to stand up. He won't kill. He can't, he's a cop and that's why he and Martial came up with this plan in the first place, but the powers that be will have no choice but to pay attention to the research now. Kyle will make sure CK's mission is not forgotten.

"I'm going to let the two of you have some alone time," he says as he packs the mask in his bag and heads out. "Oh, Michael ... when you see him, say hi to Martial for me."

More tears, but tears of joy at the thought of seeing Martial again. "Will do, Kyle."

Daisy and I share in a kiss before she rests her head next to mine on the pillow. I share with her my final wishes as I slip away. I know she'll look after me, my memory, and my legacy. In these final moments, I've found my perfect equal, and the right woman is by my side. She falls asleep before me, as I hoped she would. Can you blame her? She's been up for days. With my last few breaths, I muster up my departing words, and whisper in her ear, "Good luck with your new, new beginning, Daisy."

As I lay my head back on that soft pillow and close my eyes, with the perfect woman by my side, a legacy to leave behind, lives made better, and peace with my family, I can't help but feel ... I'm not afraid of dying. Not tonight.

28

Last Wishes

BEFORE HE DIED, Michael asked me to fulfill four last wishes that he had.

Of course, as his closest friend, I do just as he asked. The first task is to post a video on YouTube that we had made together a few days before his death. Michael's instructions are very specific. I wait until the day after his death and then post the five minute and thirty-three second video through a VPN from a lap top that I purchase at a small computer store, on a public wifi signal. After the video is published, I post it to the city's Facebook page through a fake profile. I then tag the Mayor, and various other city officials. Once that is done, I smash the computer, and toss it in the garbage.

Task two: restore Martial's home exactly as it was. I hang the papers and string again (as best I can) right after I wake up and realize Michael had died. Well, maybe not right after. I spent about an hour crying in bed with him. After everything's back to normal, I write a note for the cops and leave Michael's phone in the living room in front of the TV, charged with no passcode.

Task three: reward those that helped. The woman in the street after Jason White was killed, the solider at the car wash that allowed Michael to come to grips with what he was doing, the old lady battling Cancer for a third time, and of course, one more person. The solider took some time to find, and so did the old lady, but using Kyle's means we found the solider through his plate, and the old lady, Mrs Williamson, through questioning the doctor who spoke at the meeting. Michael wanted each of them to have $100,000 cash with the same note:

> YOU DON'T KNOW IT, BUT YOU HELPED ME WHEN YOU DIDN'T HAVE TO. YOU GAVE ME PURPOSE AND ALLOWED ME TO CONTINUE, AND FOR THAT I'LL BE FOREVER GRATEFUL. I HOPE THIS MONEY CAN BE PUT TO GOOD USE, AND HELPS YOU ACCOMPLISH YOUR GOALS AS I DID MINE.

Each person I give the money to has the same reaction—hesitation. It was actually rather hard to give the money away. I decide that if they take the money, they need to know where it came from. I tell each that *my boss* regularly rewards people anonymously that helped him in some way, then I drop the bag at their feet and walk away. They all took it, of course. Anyone would. It's just a little white lie to make sure these people take what Michael felt they are owed.

My last stop is to see the final person on the list—Monica. It's about 7pm and she's leaving Doctor Scorpio's clinic for the night. She is as beautiful as Michael said, and this will be our first encounter.

"Hello Monica," I say as I walk up to her with a bigger bag than I had to give the others.

"Do I know you?"

"No. But we have a mutual friend. Michael."

"I want nothing to do with him." She starts to walk away in a hurry.

"Or should I say, The Con Killer?"

She stops and turns. "You know?"

"I do."

"Are you some sorta cop or something?"

"I don't think I look or sound like a cop. As I said, he's a friend, or was."

The colour instantly drains from her face. "He's gone?"

"About twelve hours ago."

"And what do you want from me?"

"I want you to know that Michael loved you, and maybe without the road his dad sent him on, without the Cancer, and without him meeting me, you two could have been perfect together. At least, that's how he felt."

"How would meeting you impact our relationship?"

"Because Michael probably wouldn't have killed had he not met me. You see Monica, he wasn't a monster. The thought of taking a life never seriously entered his mind until he had to kill my boyfriend who was trying to kill me.

He saw that bastard take a phone to my face, and stepped in for a complete stranger. While you were in Hawaii, he was saving me."

I can see from her reaction that I'm breaking through the *I hate Michael* wall she put up. "And you were what, his new girlfriend?"

"We were close, but nothing like that. In the end, he had no one, and after my boyfriend died, I didn't have anyone either. When you left, I stepped in to take care of him. He was never going to be with anyone but you in the end. He loved you."

"And you're here to make sure that I don't hate him?"

"No, you can hate him all you want, because like I said, if none of this had happened, you would have been the perfect girl for him. But it did. So I was the perfect girl, and we saved each other. But, he has me running around the city giving people that helped him rewards. You're different though. You get more." I say as I throw the bag at her feet. "The others helped him, but you were burdened."

"If this is his blood money, I don't want it."

Okay, now I'm annoyed. I get right up in the ungrateful little snob's face. "It was his inheritance from his father. Take it, burn it, spend it, give it away. Just don't disrespect his memory by leaving it here. You know, he told me all about you. This attitude of yours isn't because you're tough. It's because you're weak."

"How would you even know? You don't know me."

"Because I'm tough, and tough recognizes weak. I've known a ton of girls like you. I don't really get what Michael saw in you, but I'll take his word that you are as amazing a person as he said. Just drop the attitude. Michael believed you were better than that."

I walk away from her, angry that the one person Michael loved would never understand him.

"Did he die peacefully?" she asks shyly.

I turn and look her squarely in the eyes. "He died in his bed, with me at his side, after finding peace. Peace with what he had to do, peace with Martial, peace with his mom. Real peace."

"He was happy?"

"I don't know if you can say he was ever happy doing what he did. The journey he was on, that was out of necessity. He would have been truly happy if he never had to do it in the first place, and had died old and grey next to you."

Her defenses are down, and finally, I can tell she's regretting her decision to leave.

"Monica, you had to leave. You're not from the world he had to enter. You did the right thing. But just know that a man loved you with all his heart and soul. You're lucky. Some girls never get to know what that's like." I almost want to leave her worried about the video she has yet to see, but I don't. "Oh and just so you know, your name will never come up in the investigation once everyone knows he was The Con Killer. He made sure of that."

I get in the truck and drive away, hoping that Monica knows what she meant to Michael. On the ride to the airport, I blast some Coldplay and ball like a baby just one more time for my friend. He left the rest of the money for me, and begged me to use it to get out of here, find my parents and then do whatever I wanted. His gentle suggestion was to find a beach, a nice guy, and a job I love, then live.

I can't stop thinking about Michael as I sit in the airport waiting for my boarding call. I guess I now have to find my legacy with this money that oddly enough was never really explained to either of us. Where Martial got it, we'll never know.

Just to see his face, I check in on that YouTube video. It's only been a few hours and already there are 688,000 views. I watch it again with tears in my eyes.

Michael's wrapped in a blanket and pale, but still a beautiful man. His eyes; they'll get you every time. They are a direct window to his soul. Seeing him so sick, but still so strong, gives me strength to keep going.

Hello everyone. My name is Michael Burton, but none of you know me by that name. You all know me as The Con Killer. Whether you agree with my my actions over the past few months or not, what you must understand is that I had no choice but to become CK.

In a matter of days, I'll be dead. Cancer. I was diagnosed the day after my father, a great cop by name of Martin "Martial" Burton was buried.

What I did was a continuation of his work. What I did was all that could be done, because criminals ran this town. They preyed on our sense of morality. They knew we were too weak to stop them. They stepped all over us, victimizing children, women, all of us. The law wasn't stopping them. In fact, the law was designed not to. This wasn't intentional, but somewhere along the way the lawyers got really good at finding loopholes, the criminals started learning, and the very laws designed to protect us were red tape stopping cops from doing their jobs.

When Shane Wylde gunned my dad down, he had to pay. So did Jason White, Alex, Max, Zero, and the many others that I took from this earth. Your family is safe from them now, that's all I care about. Now, together we're beating them. I've seen it every day. The people of this city just needed a push, and criminals are on the run. Don't stop taking back your neighbourhoods. Those that set out to create victims don't deserve to call you neighbour. No, don't stop fighting, but please stop fighting amongst yourselves. No more protests, or picketing. No more death.

What you have to understand most succinctly is that I am not a man who believes in God. I don't have the luxury of faith (never have), even when I tried to find it. That is why I don't believe what I have done is wrong. Even God Himself, if indeed real, murdered those with his wrath when he felt justified. Today, our leaders blow up entire countries for no clear reasons. Essentially, they are taking out the bad guys. But God, me, you; no one should have to kill. It's a dark and thankless deed. Please make sure the death ends with mine.

By now the cops are probably raiding my father's home, and they are finding evidence that can convict hundreds of criminals. That's the next step in this. I created order, now the cops can maintain it. But the last step is up to all of you. Fighting this battle will surely mean casualties, but as a city, if we stand up and don't turn a blind eye, we will win this. I took the power from the courts and placed it in my disease. I used my imminent death to formulate a plan. I was going to die soon anyway, sowhy not do something that no one with a future would be foolish enough to take on?

Some will demonize me. Some will use my mission as strength. At the end of the day, all I wanted to do was some good—and I believe I have. I know it. Just after I killed Jason White, I saw the hope in a woman's eyes. The kids in her neighbourhood were safe. I am not, nor will I ever be sorry for what I did. These people deserved to die. They were pedophiles, rapists, serious drug pushers. They victimized and walked on the backs of the people, making sure to break them along the way. Yes, of course some had families, and are described as quiet and generally good, but at the end of the day everyone knew what they did, and just failed to act.

Don't let it ever get that bad again. Don't cut deals, don't give light sentences, and close the loopholes that get these victimizers off with a slap on the wrist. People, there is strength in numbers. Hundreds of people against the criminals will win every time. You do that, and you'll never have to deal with another Con Killer again. I can promise you that. Let the criminals win, and your streets will again be stained with blood.

I'm weak, and I'm about to die, but my message is this. If you're looking to create a victim, just know the people won't stand for it anymore. The second you try, you lose your right to being a member of humanity. Your ability to break us is gone now. So run and hide, because the sun is out and in the light you are exposed. We, the people, are done playing nice. We, the people, are victims no more.

No one will ever know Michael as I did. It's just not possible. For years, people will dissect his motives, and debate his logic. They will do so from the outside. I was inside. I know what made the man tick, and I know that he and his dad sacrificed their souls for a better world, all the way to the end. Before I left, as I packed up the money, I felt the urge to say goodbye to him in a way that may last generations (or at least until the house is demolished by someone). Next to the bed where he lay at peace I etched a parting message to my best friend:

Good Luck with
Your Ending
Michael.

CPSIA information can be obtained
at www.ICGtesting.com
Printed in the USA
LVOW12s0358110118
562631LV00001B/33/P

9 781532 035609